# Praise for Ellen Hart and her Jane Lawless series

*Hallowed Murder*

"Hart's crisp, elegant writing and atmosphere [are] reminiscent of the British detective style, but she has a nicer sense of character, confrontation, and sparsely utilized violence. . . . *Hallowed Murder* is as valuable for its mainstream influences as for its sexual politics."

—*Mystery Scene*

*Vital Lies*

"This compelling whodunit has the psychological maze of a Barbara Vine mystery and the feel of Agatha Christie. . . . Hart keeps even the most seasoned mystery buff baffled until the end."

—*Publishers Weekly*

*Stage Fright*

"Hart deftly turns the spotlight on the dusty secrets and shadowy souls of a prominent theatre family. The resulting mystery is worthy of a standing ovation."

—*Alfred Hitchcock Mystery Magazine*

By Ellen Hart
*Published by Ballantine Books:*

**Jane Lawless mysteries:**
HALLOWED MURDER
VITAL LIES
STAGE FRIGHT
A KILLING CURE

**Sophie Greenway mysteries:**
THIS LITTLE PIGGY WENT TO MURDER
FOR EVERY EVIL

# FOR EVERY EVIL

## Ellen Hart

To Suzanne —
Thanks for coming!
Hope you like Sophie &
Bram! All Best Wishes,
Ellen Hart

BALLANTINE BOOKS • NEW YORK

Published in the United States by Ballantine Books, a division of Random House, Inc., New York, and simultaneously in Canada by Random House of Canada Limited, Toronto.

Library of Congress Catalog Card Number: 95-94041

ISBN 0-345-38190-4

Manufactured in the United States of America

First Edition: August 1995

10 9 8 7 6 5 4 3 2 1

For my mother,
with much love.

For every evil under the sun,
There is a remedy or there is none.
If there be one, seek till you find it.
If there be none, never mind it.

*Mother Goose*

## Cast of Characters

Sophie Greenway: Managing editor of *Squires Magazine*; part-time food critic for the *Minneapolis Times Register*; wife of Bram Baldric; mother of Rudy.

Bram Baldric: Radio talk show host at WMST in Minneapolis; husband of Sophie Greenway.

Rudy Greenway: Freshman at the University of Minnesota; employed part-time at the Chappeldine Art Gallery; son of Sophie.

Hale Micklenberg: Art critic for the *Minneapolis Times Register*; owner of International Art Investments (IAI); husband of Ivy.

Ivy Micklenberg: Professor of art history at Morton College in St. Paul; wife of Hale.

John Jacobi: Artist.

Katherine (Kate) Chappeldine: Owner of the Chappeldine Art Gallery in Minneapolis.

Louie Sigerson: Lawyer; longtime personal friend of Ivy Micklenberg's.

Max Steinhardt: Doctor of internal medicine; Ivy Micklenberg's personal physician.

Rhea Kiran: Professional dancer; director of the Rhea Kiran Dance Ensemble.

Ben Kiran: Free-lance photographer; Rhea's ex-husband.

Charles Squire: Assistant to Hale Micklenberg at IAI.

Betty Malmquist: Old friend of Hale Micklenberg's.

# Prologue

The drawing was good. It would work. A steady hand reached out to touch the edge—to center it against the easel. Everything was ready. Nothing stood in the way any longer. In the darkened room, the light shining down on the matted pastel lent an almost holy aura to the frozen moment. But this was no icon. This sweet, childish image was born in rage. And if all went as planned, it would send the one responsible for it straight to hell!

# 1

Ivy knew if she could make it through the next few hours, she could make it through anything. She sat in front of her mirror, in the bedroom she had shared with her husband, Hale, for almost two decades, and brushed through her thick, shoulder-length blonde hair. She'd always felt the years had treated her face kindly. Yet, in the past few months, she'd begun to notice worry lines around her mouth and eyes. Even in the rose satin evening dress she'd chosen for the gallery opening tonight, her shoulders looked hunched, her expression pinched and dispirited. It was inevitable, she imagined, this disintegration in her appearance. Her unhappiness, once so carefully concealed, was beginning to show. Not that her husband had noticed. He noticed almost nothing about her these days.

"Where are my onyx cuff links?" demanded Hale as he swung his overweight frame into the bedroom. He'd already showered and carefully groomed his gray mane. The scent of Royal Copenhagen cologne clung to him like a poisonous mist as he strutted about the room. Hale Micklenberg was an unabashedly vain man. Ivy knew most women found him attractive.

"Well?" he insisted, stopping in back of her chair and placing his hands on his hips.

She didn't turn, but stared instead at his reflection in the mirror, trying to remember when everything had changed. In the early days, they had been drawn together by the intensity of their love, as well as a tragic secret. But now, the connections between them had withered. "They're in the dresser, top drawer, left-hand side."

He bent down and brought his face very close to hers, straightening his red bow tie as he gazed into the mirror. "What time is Sigerson getting here?"

She waited for him to move away before answering. "Seven. He wanted to make sure Sarah was comfortable before he left her for the night."

"Comfortable?" Hale snorted. "The woman has a round-the-clock nursing staff."

Ivy's mouth tightened.

Louie Sigerson had been her lawyer as well as her friend for more years than she dared count. His wife, Sarah, had been bedridden since the early Eighties. Her struggle with emphysema was almost over. Louie hated to leave his wife in the evenings, yet unless he got out of that old house once in a while and relaxed, he was going to explode. He needed a diversion to take his mind off his problems. Tonight would be a tonic. Ivy knew watching someone you love die was the grimmest of all human events. Her heart went out to them both.

"I'm not expecting much from this opening tonight," muttered Hale as he slipped on his suit coat. "John Jacobi has all the talent of a university-trained flea."

"I liked what Kate Chappeldine showed me last week," replied Ivy, turning and standing. She held her husband's eyes several seconds too long.

"Well," said Hale, bristling, "whatever. Just so long as you remember it's my opinion that will be printed in next Sunday's paper. I don't want any more of your little scenes."

Ivy could feel the acid welling up inside her throat. She grabbed her purse and left the room before she could say any more. Now was not the time for a fight.

The truth of the matter was, Hale, whose name appeared weekly above the local Art News and Reviews section of the *Minneapolis Times Register*, didn't actually write his own column. Ivy had written it ever since he'd taken over the position ten years ago. To be precise, Hale would hold forth on whatever topic or artist was to be covered that week, but it was Ivy who shaped the ideas into the now famous Hale Micklenberg style of art criticism. Hale knew he needed Ivy, and that realization must have galled him every day of his life. It thrilled her just to think about it. Lately he'd become even more defensive than usual. Well, let him sweat. It would serve him right if she never wrote another word.

Once downstairs, Ivy headed straight for the small wet bar in the living room. Louie would be arriving any minute. Just as she finished pouring herself a mineral water, the doorbell sounded. She took a sip and then crossed into the front hall.

"Come in," she said, a welcoming, yet somewhat impatient look on her face.

Louie Sigerson stepped inside. He was a thin stick of a man, with light brown hair and a weak chin. As he removed his coat, he poked his head into the living room. "You took down all the Christmas decorations."

"It was about time, don't you think? It's almost Valentines Day."

"But you love them so. What's the harm?"

Ivy tossed his coat over a bench in the entryway. "You're just an old softie. I think that's why I like you so much. You embody all the qualities I wish I had, but don't have the energy to cultivate."

Louie followed her into the living room, folding his tall, bony frame into a wing chair next to the cold fireplace. "Where's Hale?"

"Upstairs. Primping." She glided back to the bar. "Can I offer you anything? White wine? Perhaps a shot of prussic acid?"

"You think the evening's going to be that bad?"

She didn't answer; she merely saluted him with her glass.

"Are we still on for dinner after the opening?"

"I made reservations at the Lyme House. The Chapeldine Gallery is just up the street. I'm sure we'll run into lots of people we know. Might as well spread our good cheer around."

He watched her for a moment. "Ivy, what's wrong?"

"What do you mean?"

"You tell me."

She took another sip of mineral water. "Oh . . . you know. It's Hale. It's always Hale. I'm sure you're sick of hearing it."

"Try me."

She sighed, pinching the bridge of her nose. "I just get tired of being . . . invisible. I'm not invisible, am I, Louie?"

"Hardly."

"I'm still attractive."

"Highly." He hesitated. "Want me to break his arm for you? He's had it coming for years."

She didn't smile. "Maybe."

"Just say the word. I've loved only two women in my long life. Sarah and you. I'd do anything for either of you."

"I know," she said softly, gratefully. Again, she checked her watch. "I wish he would get down here. We're going to be late." She stepped over to a series of windows overlooking the front yard. Across the street, she could see snow lying heavily on the rooftops as chimneys puffed smoke into the twilight.

"Perhaps I should run upstairs," offered Louie. "See if I can hurry him along."

"No, stay put. If we're late, his grand entrance will simply have a larger audience." She could feel Louie's eyes boring into her back. Such bitterness was hard for him to take. Especially now, with his wife so ill.

Suddenly a small pane of glass next to her left shoulder burst inward. Then another. Before she could react, Louie screamed, "Get down!" She felt him lunge at her from across the room, pulling her to the floor. Another shot came through the glass, hitting the mantel.

"Be quiet!" he ordered, dragging her away from the window. "Someone out there's got a gun!" He reached up and switched off the overhead light. For a moment they lay motionless in the semidarkness. "Are you all right?" he rasped.

"I think so."

"Just stay down."

Carefully he crawled over to the front door. He turned off the hall light and then took a quick look outside. "I can't see anyone."

"Maybe they're gone," said Ivy. She realized her body was quaking violently. Tiny pinpricks of blood welled up as if by magic on her bare arm.

"Or hiding in one of those fir trees," he whispered. "I'm going to call 911."

"What about Hale?"

Louie crouched near the phone and glanced up the stairs. "I can't believe he didn't hear those shots."

"We've got to warn him not to come downstairs!" Ivy made a move to get up.

At that same moment, Hale came through the swinging kitchen door into the dining room. "Hey . . . what's going on? Who turned off all the lights?"

"Get down!" shouted Louie.

Ivy began to crawl toward him. "Someone took a shot at me!"

Hale bumped into the edge of the huge mahogany table, nearly losing his balance.

She pulled him to the carpet.

"What the hell?" He seemed terribly concerned that his suit might get wrinkled. "Stop it!" He squirmed away from her.

"Some idiot out there's got a gun," said Louie, picking up the receiver and poking in the numbers. "They took several shots at your wife. Didn't you hear anything? Look at the front windows!" Clearing his throat, he spoke clearly and calmly into the mouthpiece, giving the address and a short description of what had just happened. "Are you sure you're not hurt?" he called to Ivy.

"No. Just some small cuts."

He repeated her answer and then urged the person on the other end to send a police car immediately.

Hale crawled a bit farther into the living room. In the soft light streaming in through the windows, the glass littering the Oriental carpet glittered like diamonds. He seemed momentarily at a loss for words.

"I thought you were upstairs," said Ivy, leaning her back against the edge of the dining room arch. She drew her knees up close to her body.

"I . . . was." He paused. "I came down the back steps into the kitchen. Are you sure you're all right?" he asked. He was beginning to sweat.

"I'm fine. Just shaken." For Ivy, the full magnitude of the situation was just starting to sink in. Those bullets had been *close*. She could have been killed!

"For God's sake, man," said Louie, his disgust all too apparent, "your wife needs you! Put your arm around her."

Hale's head shot up, looking as if he'd just been slapped. "Of . . . course." The hesitation in his voice spoke louder than any words. He eased himself over to where she was sitting.

In an instant, Ivy felt trapped, pinned to the wall by his heavy body, bruised by the smell of his cologne. She closed her eyes and turned her face away.

"That's better now, isn't it, dear?" Hale tightened his grip around her shoulders.

Desperately she fought down a wave of nausea. "Much," she whispered. In her entire life, she'd never felt so alone.

# 2

Attempting to rein in her growing impatience, Rhea sipped her red wine and watched the other restaurant patrons talking, laughing, and enjoying their food. Agreeing to meet Ben for dinner had been a mistake. She couldn't understand why she'd let him talk her into it. To top it off, he was late. She was never going to make it over to the Chappeldine Gallery for that art reception if she didn't order dinner soon. Taking one last glance at the front entrance, she opened the menu and began studying it. It would serve him right if, by the time he finally arrived, she was halfway through her meal.

The cannelloni stuffed with scallops and fresh asparagus looked promising. During their short marriage, Luciano's had become their favorite restaurant. Ben loved Italian food. He often said he could eat pasta morning, noon, and night. Since Rhea was too busy with her own career to cook very much, they'd eaten here often. She hadn't been back since—

"I recommend the tagliatelle in walnut sauce," said a voice she recognized immediately.

"You're forty-five minutes late!" Any vestige of politeness Rhea possessed had dissolved into her third glass of merlot.

"Good evening to you, too." Ben gave her his most irresistible smile and took a seat, extending a single, red rose. "I see I can still count on you for a prompt recap of my sins." His fair skin looked flushed, his blue eyes a bit more intense than usual.

Rhea took the flower, holding it to her nose as she studied him. "What? That's it? Don't I even get an explanation?"

He slipped on his reading glasses and picked up the menu. "I was in St. Paul doing . . . a shoot." Again, he grinned. "The freeway was a madhouse. I really am sorry. I intended to arrive at the stroke of seven. Ah, here comes my peace offering."

A waiter approached the table with two tall champagne flutes and a bottle of Dom Perignon on ice.

"I'll pour," he said, lifting the bottle from its cradle.

"I hardly think our final divorce papers merit this kind of celebration."

"Ah, that's where you're wrong." He held his glass high, gazing at her seductively. "To us."

Somewhat reluctantly, she clinked her glass against his and took a sip.

"I'm glad you wore your hair down. You look unbelievably lovely tonight."

"Thank you."

"Well?" he asked after a moment.

"Well what?"

"Don't you want to tell me I look lovely, too?"

Even after all that had happened, she couldn't help but laugh. Maybe she hadn't lost her sense of humor after all. The fact of the matter was, he did look pretty good. "What are you up to? You never did tell me why it was so important to get together tonight."

"I should think the point would be obvious."

"The divorce?"

"Partly." He leaned closer, his dark hair glistening in the candlelight. "I'm a free man now. I can date anyone I choose." He paused for effect. "And I choose . . . *you*."

This was preposterous. "We're kaput, darling. Dissolved. In case you forgot."

"Exactly. We don't have to live together any longer. I think that calls for another toast." Again, he held his glass high. "To . . . the future. Yours, mine . . . and ours."

This time, she let her glass remain safely on the table. "Ben, I think—"

"All right, all right. Still, you have to admit, physical attraction was never our problem."

"No."

"And I, for one, am still attracted." His gaze moved lazily over her body.

She was beginning to feel a certain warmth she couldn't entirely attribute to the wine.

"Our problems were about money, Rhea. Plain and simple. That dance ensemble of yours is like a sponge."

"I'm not going to sit here and let you abuse my career!"

He held up his hand. "I didn't mean to be argumentative. I realize my studio isn't quite on its feet yet, either. I've been scrambling as hard as you. But yesterday I think my luck may have finally changed. Rhea, I closed the deal of a lifetime."

"Really? Do tell." She said the words with little enthusiasm.

He poured himself more champagne. "Hale Micklenberg—*the* Hale Micklenberg—has just asked me to do his newest catalogue. That company of his—International Art Investments—makes a mint every year. I had it checked out before we shook hands. Actually, I'm supposed to start shooting some of his most recent acquisitions next month. The month after, I may be flying to Europe. I've already ordered a ton of new equipment."

Rhea was genuinely happy for him. Even during the worst moments of their marriage, she could never bring herself to hate Ben. He was a good man; he deserved a break. Still, she couldn't help but be a little jealous. As a dancer, she was in her prime. For the past five years she'd tried every avenue she could think of to drum up financial backing. A national tour was what she wanted most in the world. But without money, it was just another pipe dream. Like her marriage.

"Ever met Hale Micklenberg?"

Rhea pushed the champagne away and returned to her glass of merlot. "Several times. I found him . . . attractive."

"And he, no doubt, returned the compliment."

She raised an eyebrow. "You sound like you know him pretty well."

Ben's smile faded. Finishing his champagne in one stiff gulp, he said, "I first met our illustrious Minnesota prairie critic when I was nine years old. I'm sure he doesn't remember me. It was at an arts camp my parents sent me to. Camp Bright Water up near Silver Lake."

Rhea cocked her head. "What was Hale Micklenberg doing at a summer arts camp? Doesn't sound like his style."

Ben laughed. "Remember, this was over twenty years ago. He was a young man then. His wife, Ivy, was there, too—but I don't think they were married yet. They were both on the teaching staff. Ivy taught painting and drawing. Hale"—he stopped long enough to pour himself more champagne—"well, let's just say Hale was already doing his art critic routine. He just didn't have it down to a science yet."

The bitterness in his voice intrigued her. Ben rarely held a grudge. He was too good-natured. "What do you mean? What did he do to you?"

"To me? Nothing. I was smart enough to stay out of his way. But he was an arrogant bastard. I saw him humiliate more than one kid during my two-week stay. Even the other camp counselors weren't immune to attack. I never wanted to go back. Actually, I wouldn't have been able to. They closed the place shortly after my group left. It was never reopened."

"Why?"

"A kid got lost."

"Lost? You mean like in the woods?"

He shook his head. "His name was Eric Hauley. Someone said they saw him on the main road, hitchhiking into Silver Lake—the closest town. Nobody ever heard from him again."

"That's awful!"

"Yeah. I knew him pretty well. He was a couple years older than me. Nice kid. Talented dancer. You probably would have liked him." He held her eyes for a long moment.

This was becoming ridiculous. "Ben, look. I know you didn't ask me here tonight to swap camp stories."

"No, you're right."

"Then what?"

He looked down into his glass. "Rhea, I miss you. Not the arguments . . . but *you*."

She hadn't expected that. He wasn't playing anymore. His sincerity had caught her off-guard. "I don't know what to say."

"Say you're not hungry."

"What?"

"Say that you don't really want to go to that stupid gallery reception." He reached for her hand, squeezing it gently. "Come home with me."

She felt the temperature in the room zoom up several degrees. Perhaps it was merely the wine mixed with candlelight. They'd spent so many wonderful evenings together in this restaurant. Loving him here was like breathing. It felt completely natural.

"What do you say?"

The words burst out before she could stop them. "I miss you, too."

He grinned. "God, you'll never know how much I wanted to hear that." He motioned to the waiter. "Let's leave your car in the lot. We'll pick it up tomorrow."

"All right." If this was a mistake—well, it wouldn't

be her first. Or her last. She finished the merlot while Ben tossed some cash on the table. Then, slipping on her coat, she followed him out into the cold February night.

# 3

After a mad dash from St. Paul to Minneapolis in rush-hour traffic, Sophie managed to speed through a less than satisfying dinner of cold cuts and day-old focaccia and then race upstairs to wiggle into something a bit more formal than her usual business attire. All of this in preparation for the opening tonight at the Chappeldine Art Gallery. Since she was the managing editor of one of the best-known arts monthlies in the Midwest, she felt it incumbent upon her to put in an appearance. And besides, the owner, Kate Chappeldine, was a good friend. After leaving a note on the kitchen table for her husband, Bram, she'd sprinted out the back door to her car. Standing now in front of a small pencil drawing, she was glad she'd made the effort. This was truly one of the best shows Kate had mounted.

"What is it supposed to be?" asked a woman moving up next to her.

Since Sophie was barely five foot one and the woman was a good foot taller, Sophie's eyes rose to her face with a certain annoyance. "Pardon me?"

"That!" said the woman, squinting through a pair of thick glasses. She pointed to a square box hanging on the wall next to the rear exit.

"It's the smoke alarm."

The woman did a slow turn, dipping her chin and lifting an eyebrow. "Who *are* you?"

"Who wants to know?"

"Well!" she huffed, tugging on her black cape. "You're obviously not the owner of this gallery. I was misinformed."

"You were. Kate Chappeldine is over there—standing by the front entrance." She pointed.

"I see. Thank you."

Her tones were a bit too rounded for Sophie's liking. She watched as the woman stomped away. What a hulk. Someone should tell her that throwing a cape over a body like hers was like trying to hide a water tower under a parachute. Not that Sophie and Bram hadn't put on a few pounds in the past couple of years. Since Bram was already big, it just made him look more imposing. Sophie, on the other hand, was short and decidedly round. The words *garbanzo bean* came to mind as she contemplated her future figure.

"Mom?" came a deep voice from behind her.

She turned to find her son, Rudy, dressed in a waiter's uniform, holding a silver tray filled with small wineglasses. "Hi, honey." She beamed. "I thought I'd run into you, sooner or later."

"I'm on a break right now. There's someone I'd like you to meet." A much taller young man stood next to him.

Rudy, like Sophie, was short, with strawberry blond hair, curious gray eyes, and a smile that could melt a snowdrift from ten feet away. The man Rudy had brought for her to meet looked to be in his late twenties. Rich brown hair and beard. Silver wire-rimmed glasses. Quite handsome. "This is John Jacobi. He's the artist. The one who did all the drawings."

Sophie was surprised and delighted. "Kate said she wasn't sure you were going to make it."

"Oh, no," he said, "I wouldn't miss this for the world. I was just a little late." His voice was deep and confident. He had a definite presence. "I had something I needed to take care of before I drove over from St. Paul." He extended his hand. "I'm very glad to meet you. Rudy tells me you're the new managing editor of *Squires Magazine*. My congratulations."

"What do you think of John's drawings?" asked Rudy, rocking back and forth on the balls of his feet.

"They're wonderful." Sophie smiled. "And you've got a big fan in Kate Chappeldine." She eyed her son for a moment. He looked positively ebullient, almost as if he'd done the drawings himself. Switching her attention back to John, she asked, "Do you do animal bones and feathers exclusively?"

"Right now, yes. Everything in the natural, I suppose even the mythic world, can be represented by them. To me, they're like great cathedrals. Awe-inspiring. Intricate. Amazing in their delicacy and simplicity. And each one unique."

Sophie nodded, though she didn't entirely understand. "I'll make sure my husband comes over tomorrow to see what you've done."

"Where *is* Bram?" asked Rudy, holding the tray steady while several people helped themselves to wine.

Sophie sighed. "Remember that state senator he's been trying to interview? Well, the guy stiffed him again. He was supposed to be on tomorrow's show—Bram always reserves Friday mornings for Minnesota politics—but he called the station and said he was going to be in meetings all day. Apparently, talking to his constituents via the airwaves isn't the priority it was during his campaign. Anyway, Bram convinced him to come into the studio tonight. They're taping a program for tomorrow's broadcast."

"Your husband has a talk show?" asked John.

She pulled on the short wisps of hair around her ears. "It's a radio show. Weekday mornings from nine to noon on WMST."

"It's a great program," said Kate Chappeldine, walking up and draping her arm around Sophie's shoulders. "I see you've already met the star of the evening. Wonderful. Except I'm afraid I'm going to have to whisk him off to meet some other guests."

"Of course," said Sophie. She knew Kate was an aggressive businesswoman. John would no doubt be introduced to all the movers and shakers in the Twin Cities art community who were in attendance tonight, not to mention her most valued patrons, and, of course, those with the deepest pockets.

"I haven't seen Hale and Ivy Micklenberg yet," said Sophie, her eyes searching the crowded room.

"They're coming," said Kate. "Ivy stopped by last week. I showed her a couple of John's drawings."

"It would be just fine with me if they both skipped it," said John, shoving his hands deep into the pockets of his jeans. Realizing everyone was staring, he added, "I had a show three years ago at one of the warehouse galleries downtown. Micklenberg tore me to shreds in his column. If he comes, it will just be more of the same."

"Critics," said Sophie, shaking her head. "I guess they're a necessary evil." She was herself an occasional food critic for the *Times Register*.

"I'm not so sure about that," said John, his scowl deepening.

In an obvious effort to lighten the conversation, Rudy piped up, "Well, you know what Osborne said about them."

"Huh?" said Sophie, raising an eyebrow. "Osborne who?"

"John Osborne. He said that asking a working artist what he thinks about critics is like asking a lamppost what it feels about dogs."

John burst out laughing. "Perfect!"

Sophie had to admit it was a great line.

"Come on, you guys," whispered Kate. "There are other art critics around here tonight. Let's not annoy the herd. We want the stampede to go in the right direction. And anyway," she added, giving John's arm a tug, "it's time to get to work."

Still laughing, he extended his hand to Sophie. "I'm very glad we got a chance to talk, even if only for a few minutes."

"Oh, by the way, Sophie," said Kate, "don't rush off before I have a chance to show you something in the back."

Sophie was instantly intrigued. Kate rarely allowed people into the storage area. "I won't." After they had faded into the throng, she moved closer to Rudy and asked, "Where did you come up with that quote about critics?"

Rudy gave her an innocent shrug. "On Bram's desk in his study. It was right next to the one by Sir Thomas Beecham."

"Really. Which said?"

"Well, he called all critics 'drooling, driveling, doleful, depressing, dropsical drips.' "

Sophie put her arm around him, drawing him close. "You actually memorized that?"

"Sure. It's good practice. If I'm going to be an actor, I have to learn to memorize quickly."

"I can tell you're going to be a sublime comfort to me in my old age."

"Thank you." He bowed his head slightly and then breezed off into the crowd.

"Excuse the mess," said Kate, leading Sophie down a narrow corridor that ended at the storage room. "We're already starting to get some of the artwork for the next opening. Space is at a premium." She opened the door. The room was huge, with a high ceiling, a concrete floor, and concrete walls. "That's funny. I don't remember leaving the light on."

Sophie waited while Kate removed a rather delicate

glass sculpture from their path. "Is this where Rudy works?"

"He does most of the unpacking—as well as every other odd job I can think of. Computer entry. Hanging shows. And I'm teaching him about matting and framing. Don't worry, we keep him busy. I really don't know what I did without him."

"I can't thank you enough for taking him on. A university student's hours don't fit into many normal work schedules."

"He's terrific. He's told me some about his early life—growing up in Montana."

Sophie nodded. "His father was granted custody after our divorce. Until this fall, I hadn't seen him since he was thirteen. Norm, my ex, is a minister. He discouraged any contact. Actually, he . . . well, he thought I was possessed by the devil." As soon as she'd said it, she wished she hadn't.

Kate stopped and turned. "He what?"

It always sounded so bizarre when Sophie tried to explain her past to people who had little familiarity with fundamentalist religion. Normally, even with a friend, she just let the subject drop. "I know what you're thinking. It's kind of a long story—I promise, I'll tell you all about it sometime. The problem is, for years, I thought Rudy believed everything his father told him."

At the sound of a throat being cleared, both women turned.

A balding man emerged from the shadows in the back of the room.

"Who let you in here?" demanded Kate, a startled look on her face. "This isn't part of the gallery. Didn't you see the sign?"

The man, dressed in a dark blue pin-striped suit and peach silk tie, stared back at her, a blank look on his face.

Kate moved toward him. "I'm afraid I'm going to have to ask you to leave."

He blinked several times before saying, "Of course." As he stepped around a stack of boxes, he said, "Good evening, Sophie. I thought I might see you here tonight."

Kate looked from face to face. "You two know each other?"

"I'm afraid so," said Sophie, trying to keep her voice cheerful. "Kate Chappeldine, I'd like you to meet Charles Squire."

"Squire? Any relation to Hilyard Squire, the founder of *Squires Magazine*?"

"I'm his son," replied the man.

"Charles was the managing editor before I took over," explained Sophie.

"You mean before Father canned me eight months ago." He removed his matching silk handkerchief and stuffed it back into his vest pocket with a bit more flair. "But, thanks to my catlike persona, I've landed on my feet. I'm now the personal assistant to Hale Micklenberg at IAI. International Art Investments," he added in an effort at clarification.

"I know what it is," said Kate. She seemed momentarily at a loss. "Well, how . . . nice for you. But that doesn't give you license to enter a private area."

"I was just seeing if you'd received any of the Ezmer Hawks pastels yet. I'm curious about his work. I understand he's going to be your next show." Charles spoke of everything with a kind of weary disinterest. It was all part of his charm, as he liked to point out. "Hale is fascinated by the man's work—I should say the *mystery* man. I understand you don't know much about him."

Kate nodded.

"Hale has a kind of proprietary interest, since he feels he discovered him."

"I'm aware of his interest," said Kate.

Charles pulled on his cuffs. "I believe, if Mr. Hawks plays his cards right, Hale might even feature him in the next IAI catalogue."

"Is that right?" answered Kate. "Well, of course when he and Ivy get here, I'd be more than willing to let you all look at what I've received so far."

"Oh. Sorry," said Charles. "I forgot to tell you. They're not coming." With his usual ennui, he examined the fingernails on his right hand. "They're in the midst of a . . . *situation*. Someone took a shot at Ivy through the living room window. Hale called and told me to give you the message."

Sophie and Kate exchanged shocked glances.

"Well, I suppose I should be off. I have a dinner date."

"Is Ivy all right?" asked Sophie. How typical of Charles to leave that part out. She and Ivy had known each other since kindergarten. Not well, but more or less socially.

"Right as rain as far as I know." He gave a quick smirk, which disappeared almost instantly. It was another quirk of his.

"I'm terribly sorry," said Kate. "If there's anything I can do—"

"Awful thing to happen, I agree," replied Charles. "Probably some kind of freak accident. A drive-by shooting. Gangs," he said, with great distaste. "Well, sorry for the intrusion. Oh, and I did *not* see a sign prohibiting my entrance." He opened the door with a small flourish and disappeared down the hall.

After he was gone, Sophie let out a groan. "That guy is such a weasel. He even looks like one. I think it's the tiny black eyes. Everything about him is entirely too . . . oiled. Then again, I suppose living in the shadow of his prominent father hasn't been easy." She leaned against a worktable. "Isn't that awful about Ivy?"

Kate was barely listening. She'd already crossed to the spot where Charles had been standing and was now busily examining it for . . . what? Damage? Weasel droppings?

"Anything wrong?" asked Sophie.

Kate was too preoccupied to reply. She was down on her hands and knees paging through some drawings.

Something had clearly upset her. Sophie eased herself between the matting table and a storage shelf.

"No, just stay there," ordered Kate. She immediately stood.

"Is everything all right?"

"Yes. Everything's fine."

Sophie recognized a lie when she heard one. This was strange behavior coming from Kate. Not that Sophie knew her all that well. They'd met shortly after Kate opened the gallery two years ago. Still, during the last year especially, she'd become fond of this unusual and bright young woman.

"Don't mind me," said Kate. "I just get uptight when I think someone's seen a work before I'm ready to show it. I really don't like people being back here."

"Sure. I understand. So what did you want me to see?" Sophie hoped a change in subject might lighten her mood.

"Oh. Right. It's over here." She slipped an already matted and framed etching out of its brown paper wrapping and held it up. "What do you think?"

Sophie took it from her. "It's amazing. It looks just like my house."

"It is your house. I found it in an antique shop. The shopkeeper said some local guy did it ages ago. The year 1921 was written on the back, as well as the street address. Apparently, the artist lived in your neighborhood. That's all I could find out."

Sophie carried it over to a better light. "I just love it! Tell me the price."

"Don't be silly. It's a gift."

"I couldn't! The frame alone must be worth—"

Kate put a finger to her lips. "I won't hear another word. Sophie, you and Bram have been my best friends ever since I moved here from New York. Especially this past year. I don't know what I'd have done without you.

This gallery has taken much too much of my time, but it's finally on its feet. I can relax a little. I want to make more of an effort with the people who mean the most to me. This is just a small thank-you."

Sophie was deeply touched. "I don't know what to say."

"Say you have the perfect spot for it in your house."

"Of course I do!" She gave Kate a hug. "Bram will be so pleased."

"Good. Now, I've got to get back to the reception. I'll walk you out." She slid the framed etching back inside its wrapper and handed it over.

Sophie tucked it lovingly under her arm. "Say, you'll have to tell John Jacobi the good news right away."

"Good news?" Kate closed the door and locked it behind her, pocketing the key.

"About Hale not coming tonight."

"Oh. Right." For one curious moment, a look of intense satisfaction flashed across her face. "I'll be sure to do that. Don't you forget to give my love to that handsome husband of yours. To think that in this day and age, Cary Grant still lives!"

Sophie hooted. "Only marginally, my dear. And *not* in Technicolor."

# 4

Louie sat under a Renaissance triptych in the Micklenbergs' living room and watched with great curiosity as a police sergeant began his interrogation of Ivy. The man was a burly Swede, mid-forties, with close-cropped, curly blond hair. A notepad rested on his knee. He seemed to be writing her responses down in some kind of shorthand. Ivy was reclining on the antique chesterfield, her head propped up on a silk pillow. Hale sat next to her on a footstool.

The squad car had arrived quickly after the call to 911. After taking a series of photographs—the trajectory of the bullets seemed to be of primary importance—several officers combed the front yard looking for further evidence. If they'd found anything, they weren't talking.

"Now, Ms. Micklenberg," asked the sergeant, "are you absolutely certain you didn't see anyone outside when you were standing at the window?"

Ivy passed a shaky hand over her eyes. "I'm positive. There was no one there—at least no one I could see."

"Where was the focus of your attention? What exactly were you looking at?"

"I don't know," she said wearily. "I suppose the snow on the roofs across the street. Maybe a car went by. I just don't remember. I was thinking about something else."

"What was that?"

Ivy glanced at Hale. "My husband and I were supposed to attend a gallery opening tonight. I was wondering what was taking him so long upstairs. We were going to be late."

The sergeant's eyes shifted to Hale. "You were upstairs when all this was happening, Mr. Micklenberg?"

Hale adjusted his bow tie. "I was. I didn't hear any shots, if that's what you're asking. I'd come down the back stairs into the kitchen to get a bit of cold chicken from the refrigerator. As I entered the dining room, I found Louie and my wife on the floor. They'd turned off all the lights."

"This was after the shots had been fired?"

Hale nodded.

"Do you own any firearms, Mr. Micklenberg?"

"Me? Absolutely not." He seemed insulted. "I don't need them. The security in this house is excellent. As you may have noticed, we own a great deal of rare artwork. I make sure all my investments are protected." He glanced up at his favorite Rauschenberg, which hung like a huge exclamation point on the dark green wall. He'd placed it there lovingly, next to a highly prized Byzantine icon.

"What about that gate house behind the main house?"

"What about it?"

"Do you use it?"

Hale allowed himself a small smile. "Why, yes. It's my office and my showroom. I have more fine art in there than many museums. The security is even tighter."

The sergeant got up and conferred briefly with one of his men. After they were finished, the officer left through the front door.

"What's going on?" asked Hale.

The sergeant resumed his seat. "We noticed some footprints in the snow leading from the front yard back toward the gate house. I just want to make sure one of my men checks it out."

Hale shot to his feet. "I'm going with him!"

"That won't be necessary, Mr. Micklenberg."

Before anyone could stop him, Hale bolted into the kitchen and out the back door.

"Louie," called Ivy, ignoring her husband's hasty retreat, "will you do me a favor?"

"Of course." Louie stood and approached the couch, glad for the chance to stretch his long legs.

"Will you call Max Steinhardt? My doctor. I want him to come over right away."

"The paramedic who was here earlier said you were doing just fine," said the sergeant, his tone a rough attempt at being comforting.

"I'm a diabetic," replied Ivy. "And I'm on several medications. I want my own doctor." She said the words with great firmness. "Louie, you'll find his home number and the number of his service on the wall next to the kitchen phone. Try his home first. And don't take no for an answer. I mean that." Her mouth set angrily.

Louie understood her irritation. Doctors could be a pain in the ass. His wife, Sarah, had seven in periodic attendance. Not that they did anything particularly brilliant. They couldn't even seem to make her comfortable. "I'll do my best."

"Get him here!" she shot back.

The sergeant looked up, startled by the vehemence in her voice.

A bit more calmly, she added, "I need him."

"Of course. I'll only be a minute." Louie quickly ducked into the kitchen. On a whim as he passed the refrigerator, he peeked inside. Sure enough, there was the plate of cold chicken, several bites taken out of one of the drumsticks. At least Hale hadn't been lying about that. Even so, something about the entire evening had struck a faintly discordant note. He couldn't put his finger on just what it was.

Standing now in front of the phone, he found Max's number right where Ivy said it would be. He'd met the good doctor a couple of times over the years, finding him a bit too athletic for his liking. Max had the complete gym body, and from what Louie could discern, the complete gym mind. The man should have been a sports doctor instead of a surgeon. Max Steinhardt was close to sixty, but looked ten years younger. Maybe, thought Louie, this animosity was simple jealousy: Louie looked and felt every day of his fifty-four years.

After several rings, Max's voice answered. "Steinhardt."

"Hello. This is Louie Sigerson."

"Who?"

Louie took a deep breath. "I'm at the Micklenberg home. There's been a . . . shooting. Ivy Micklenberg would like you to come over immediately. She's unhurt, but very upset."

Silence.

"Dr. Steinhardt?"

"Yes. I'm here."

"She insists that you come. I think your presence would be calming. Right now she needs that badly."

"Are you sure she wanted you to call *me*?"

"Does she have another doctor?"

"Many."

"Look, she specifically asked me to call you. And she said not to take no for an answer."

A pause. "I see. Is *anyone* hurt?"

"No. The police are here right now."

Again, silence.

"Can I tell her you're coming?" Louie didn't understand the reticence. Unless . . . Steinhardt was known for being a ladies' man. Of course. He probably wasn't alone.

"Yes. All right, I'll be over shortly. Tell Ivy not to take anything until I come. Hale has a medicine chest that would put a pharmacy's to shame. *I'll* prescribe a sedative, if I determine she needs one. Is that clear?"

"Crystal."

"Keep her off her feet and warm. And tell her— Oh, forget it. I'll tell her when I see her."

"Fine." Louie put the receiver back in its cradle. What a wonderfully caring man. He returned to the living room. Ivy's interrogation was still in progress.

"Do you work outside the home?" asked the sergeant.

"I'm a professor of art history at Morton College."

"How long have you been there?"

"Fourteen years."

Louie could tell Ivy was tired of answering questions. She barely looked at the officer. Instead, her eyes were fixed on the shattered windowpanes.

"Do you have any reason to suspect someone might want to harm you?"

Ivy stopped and looked up as soon as she saw Louie resume his seat. "Is Max coming?"

Louie nodded.

She seemed to relax a bit. "Good. Now, what was the question? Oh, yes. Do I have any enemies?" She appeared to give it some thought. "No, not that I can think of. I'm not a young woman, Sergeant, so I suppose I've made my share over the years. But I can't conceive of someone—" A ringing phone interrupted her. "Louie . . . sorry." Ivy raised a limp arm. "Would you be a dear and get that?"

Again, he rose and walked into the kitchen. He grabbed the receiver before the answering machine could switch on. "Micklenberg residence."

Silence.

"Hello?" He waited for several seconds. Finally a young boy's voice began to speak.

"Who is this?" he demanded.

Without pause, the boy continued, almost as if the words had been recorded.

"Is this some kind of joke?"

The boy just kept talking. Finally the line clicked.

"Damn," muttered Louie. Angrily he hung up and stood leaning against the counter, staring blankly at a bowl of oranges placed decoratively in the center of the kitchen table. Everything in this god-awful museum of a house looked like a still life. How could Ivy stand it? Out in the living room, he could hear her calling his name.

"I'm coming," he hollered. By the time he'd returned to the room, his anger had been replaced by uneasiness. Could a phone call like that, coming on the heels of tonight's shooting incident, be a coincidence?

"Who was it?" she asked.

"I don't know."

"What did they want?"

He scratched his head, giving a self-conscious laugh. "You aren't going to believe this."

The sergeant looked up from his notepad.

"See, I . . . uh . . . remember the verse from when I was a little boy. It's a nursery rhyme."

"What is?" asked Ivy, growing more impatient with each less than satisfactory answer. "What are you talking about?"

"The boy on the phone. It sounded like a recording. He said, 'For every evil under the sun, there is a remedy or there is none. If there be one, seek till you find it. If there be none, never mind it.' " Louie felt like a school kid reciting his lessons. He looked up, realizing everyone was watching.

The room had become still.

"That's it," said Louie, giving Ivy a helpless shrug.

After a long minute, she asked, "Do you think it was a prank call?"

"I don't know."

At that same moment a red-faced and puffing Hale trudged back into the room, followed by two officers. "Everything checks out fine," he said triumphantly, throwing himself into a chair. "No one tried to break into the gate house." He looked from face to face. "Say, what's going on now? Did I miss something?"

A poetry reading, thought Louie, though he had the sense not to say it out loud. Folding his tall frame into the wing chair once more, he leaned his head back and closed his eyes. What an evening. His night out on the town was beginning to feel more like a day at the circus.

# 5

Bram walked briskly down Penn Avenue on his way to the Chappeldine Gallery. He felt loose. Exhilarated. Pleased with himself for the brilliant way he'd handled this morning's program. After airing a rather dull, taped interview he'd recorded last night with Senator Arlo Barrows—an interview in which the senator artfully sidestepped every important question put to him about the Twin Cities' newly proposed light rail transit system—Bram launched into two hours of deadly political satire. He could almost see the radios out there in radioland melting from the heat. Well, it served the old fart right. Nobody liked a politician doing the two-step on taxpayer time.

Smiling at his reflection in a shop window, Bram stopped to straighten his tie. It was funny. A radio personality could live his entire life in relative anonymity—that is, until he opened his mouth. On the other hand, Bram knew he bore a striking resemblance to a certain movie actor. Unfortunately, this legend, as some were calling him these days, was dead. So unless people took him for an unusually animated corpse, he was an obvious impostor. Oh well. Things could be worse. He could actually *be* an animated corpse. Or an actor, forced to repeat *other* people's words on unto eternity. Either option caused him a moment of psychic pain as he continued on down the street.

At the end of the block he swung open a carved wooden door and entered the gallery. It was an old building, long and narrow, with stark white walls and tons of track lighting. Kate Chappeldine was sitting behind the reception desk in the back, talking on the phone. She waved him a greeting and then motioned for him to look around while she finished her conversation. Bram was glad to oblige. He stepped over to a series of drawings, bones and feathers tumbling together, each drawing a different moment frozen in time. He studied them closely, finding their intricacy quite amazing. He was glad Sophie had suggested he stop by and take a look.

"What do you think?" asked Kate, coming up behind him a few minutes later. Her usual tailored blazer and slacks were replaced today by jeans and a sweatshirt. A smudge on her face told him she'd been working in the back.

"Quite impressive." He gave her a warm smile.

Kate Chappeldine was a tall, no-nonsense young woman, with straight, extremely thin blonde hair and a pallid complexion. Viewed from the right angle, she looked a bit like an ostrich. Her personality was well suited to running a gallery. In other words, she was a born diplomat when it came to dealing with egos. Bram envied her patience.

"As a matter of fact," he added, standing back, "I think these drawings are remarkable."

"John will be so pleased." Kate beamed her delight. "He was going to stop by this afternoon. I'd hoped you two might get a chance to meet."

As they continued to talk, the door opened and Hale Micklenberg puffed into the room surrounded by a cold gust of air. He grunted a greeting, taking off his wool coat and whipping a pair of glasses out of his vest pocket. "I need to look at this exhibit," he announced, "if I'm going to include it in my column on Sunday."

Bram watched Kate's good mood turn sour. He knew Hale had that effect on people. He was sort of a modern day twist on Johnny Appleseed, spreading indigestion and heartburn over the countryside.

Kate signaled her apology to Bram with a small shrug and then led the portly, middle-aged man to the far wall. "Perhaps you'd like to start over here. These are some of my favorites."

Hale squinted at the first one in the long row, making no comment. Ten minutes later, after viewing everything in the gallery in total silence, he took off his glasses, and, with a weary sigh, said, "Just about what I expected. The man is an amateur. No depth. No . . . complexity. I suppose to be fair, one would have to admit he does have a certain technical ability. But that's it."

Bram, who'd taken a seat in one of the front chairs, had been watching this inspection of John Jacobi's latest crimes with great interest. "I liked them," he said.

"Did you?" Hale turned and gave him an indulgent smile. "I don't doubt it." He returned his gaze to Kate. "Thank you, my dear. Now, on to more important matters."

She appeared confused. "Important matters?"

"Have you received any more work from Ezmer Hawks?" He rubbed his hands together, a tremor of excitement passing over his solid face.

"Who?" asked Bram, noticing Hale's unusual interest.

"To my mind," said Hale, drawing in his breath for a grand pronouncement, "he's one of the most important artists at work today. His drawings have a rare sense of the primitive. Prairie primitive, I call them."

Bram knew Hale liked to use the word *prairie* instead of the more common term, Minnesotan. Or even Midwestern. It was an affectation, like his red bow ties, which delighted some, but nauseated most.

"So," said Hale, returning his full attention to Kate, "do you have anything new?"

"A few things."

"Wonderful." He started for the back.

"I'd be happy to show them to you, but right now I wanted Bram to finish—"

"Oh, don't mind me." Bram stood, glancing at his watch. "I'm afraid I've got to run. I've got a dental appointment in half an hour. My right molar." He pointed to his mouth.

"Ezmer has an opening here at the beginning of April," continued Hale, as if the subject had never been changed. "You'll want to make sure you stop by to see his work."

"I wouldn't miss it for the world." Bram wondered briefly if sarcasm was becoming his normal tone of voice. Politicians and monomaniacs did that to him. As he turned to say a *sincere* goodbye to Kate, his mind flashed to next week's lineup at the station. "Say, I've got an idea. We just had a cancellation on next Tuesday's show. What do you say the two of you come on to discuss the art scene in the Twin Cities?"

Hale quickly whipped out a pocket calendar and gave it a look. "I believe I'm free that morning."

"It's fine with me," said Kate. "Anything to advertise the gallery."

"Terrific. You know, we might also want to include your wife, Hale. Ivy is quite the authority in her own right."

Hale gave a grudging nod. "I'll ask her."

"And I'll notify my producer. She'll get back to you with the particulars." As he opened the door to let himself out, he hesitated. "Oh, by the way . . . don't prepare anything. I like my shows to be spontaneous."

"Do you now?" replied Hale, a smirk forming. "Well, I'll make you a promise then. This will be one of your *most* spontaneous shows."

For some reason, Bram didn't like the sound of that.

* * *

"I received a few new things from Soldiers Grove yesterday afternoon," said Kate, opening the door to the storage room.

"Soldiers Grove? Is that where Ezmer lives?" asked Hale. "I just knew it was somewhere in northern Minnesota."

She nodded, switching on the light.

He paused in front of a worktable and glanced idly at a serigraph. "How was it you first came across his pastels?"

"About six months ago, I got a package of drawings in the mail. Ezmer explained that he lived in a small town and didn't have access to matting and framing facilities. He said he'd heard about my gallery through a friend, and asked if I'd mat and frame his work, and then send it all back to him. I liked a number of them so much I wrote to ask if I could show them to my customers. From there we've developed a relationship."

"Really? You never mentioned that before." Hale's eyes took in the cluttered room.

Kate quickly stepped to the rear and drew out several matted but unframed drawings. "Mr. Hawks has no phone. Nothing but a post office box. We handle everything through correspondence."

Hale took one of the works and propped it against the wall, studying it for a long moment. "His style is evolving. See here what he's doing with color?" He folded his arms over his chest. "Wonderful. Yes . . . I like it. What else do you have?"

Kate placed the next one in front of the first.

"Ah." He smiled, his pomposity dropping away. He spoke now almost reverently. "It's so simple. The gesture says it all. This moves me very deeply, Kate. It's the innocence. I don't understand it. And yet . . . I want to. You don't suppose he's planning to come down for the show?"

"He hasn't said." She set the third drawing in front of the second. "This is all I've received so far."

"Hmm," mumbled Hale, cocking his head and frowning thoughtfully. "This one is odd."

"Why do you say that?"

He walked over and picked it up, studying it more closely. "Do you see a form in here?" He pointed to the bottom.

Kate moved up behind him. "No, not really."

"Right here," he said impatiently. "Logs and a flame."

Kate shrugged. "Maybe. Now that you mention it, I can kind of see it. Then again, the flames, as you define them, could easily be tall grass. Or wheat. Ezmer uses lots of naturalistic images. Some are more abstracted than others."

Hale's eyes remained fixed on the drawing. "I suppose you're right. It just struck me as . . ." He abandoned the end of the sentence.

"Does the image have some particular meaning to you?"

"No. Certainly not." He rubbed the back of his neck. "It's just . . . ever since last night—"

"Oh, I'm sorry." Kate stood up very straight. "I don't know what I was thinking. I should have said something as soon as you walked in. Your assistant, Charles Squire, told me about the shots that were fired. How is Ivy? Have the police found out who did it?"

Hale took a partially smoked cigar out of his coat pocket and lit up, blowing smoke high into the air. The act of doing something familiar seemed to relax him. "Ivy's fine. Just a little shaken. And the police haven't got a clue. Just between you and me, I don't have much confidence in our boys in blue these days. All they did was come out to the house and ask a bunch of inane questions. For a while, I think they even thought I'd done it." He took several indignant puffs.

"That's awful."

"Damn right it is." He leaned closer, lowering his voice. "I'll tell you a little secret. I went out this morning and bought a gun. Who knows what some people have in their minds."

"Did you buy one for Ivy, too?"

He bit down hard on the cigar stem. "I can protect my own family, thank you very much."

Kate waved the smoke away from her face.

"And anyway—" His eyes returned to the drawing, causing him to lose focus. After a long minute, he said, "You know, I think you're right. I'm reading something into this that simply isn't there." He laughed, taking several small puffs on the cigar.

Kate felt as if she were in the midst of a poker game. She quickly took the drawings and placed them back inside their packing. Show-and-tell was over. "By the way, Hale . . ."

"Uhm?" This time his attention had been captured by an etching. He crouched down to study it.

"I'm afraid I'm going to have to ask you to put out your cigar before we return to the gallery."

He grunted. "I suppose we mustn't annoy the clientele." Tapping the burning tip very carefully against the side of the framing table, he pinched it until it was completely cold and then put it back into his pocket. "These are too fine and entirely too expensive to simply toss in an ashtray."

Kate resisted the urge to cough. "I should be receiving more of Ezmer's works Monday afternoon. If you'd care to stop by."

"I may just do that," said Hale, following her out of the room and back down the hall.

Glancing now at the front window, Kate noticed the sky had turned cloudy. The forecast called for snow late in the day. As she helped him on with his coat, she said, "Try to be kind to our latest exhibitor in your column on Sunday."

"That, my dear, I can't promise. I have to write what I see. And to my mind this John Jacobi should use his talents, such as they are, to illustrate biology text-books."

Kate bit her lip so hard she could almost taste the blood. "Give my best to Ivy."

"I'll do that. See you Monday, my dear."

After he'd gone, she stepped to the window and watched him trot across the street to his Mercedes. Her eyes darted to a second-floor window just above the spot where he'd parked. Hot oil flung through a screen, she thought to herself—or a small bomb dropped right at his feet. Either would do the trick. She leaned heavily against the cold glass wondering where all the assassins were when you needed them.

# 6

Sophie looked up from her book when she heard the back door open. An ancient black mutt asleep in front of her easy chair lifted a rheumy eye and let out an obligatory growl.

"Hush, Ethel. Rudy, is that you?" Sophie glanced at the crackling fire. It was a bitter night. She knew her son had a late class, but for some reason he was later than normal. The clock on the mantel said nearly midnight. Bram had hit the sack more than an hour ago.

Ethel cast a baleful gaze toward the kitchen as Rudy entered the room and dumped his books on the coffee table. "Sorry," he said, moving to the fireplace and warming his hands. "I hope you didn't wait up."

Sophie couldn't help but notice the dejection in his voice. Mothers were supposed to notice things like that.

Not that she'd had much of a chance to be a mother to him—at least not since he was a little boy.

"Want some chocolate milk?"

"Oh, Mom. You think I'm still ten years old."

"No, I don't," she said indignantly. "I think *I* am." She got up and crossed into the kitchen, calling over her shoulder, "Humor me." She got out two mugs and the half-empty quart from the refrigerator. Then, returning to the sofa, she asked, "What's up?"

Rudy gave a deep sigh and dumped himself into a chair.

Ethel decided to show her overwhelming delight in his company by heaving herself up and lurching over to where he sat. She plopped down heavily on his right foot. Absently Rudy reached down and gave her a pat on the head. Ethel smacked her lips in complete contentment. Life was indeed good.

"It's John," said Rudy, raking a hand through his hair. "I ran into him after class. I'd gone over to that new coffeehouse on West Bank with some friends, and as we were going in, he was coming out. I talked him into staying." He took a sip of the milk. "You know, not to change the subject, but Dad would never have let me drink something like this when I was a kid. We ate virtually nothing with refined sugar in it."

Sophie turned up her nose. "Thank God for the revolution."

"You're so different from the way I remembered you."

"I am?"

"I have all these pictures of you in my mind. You always seemed so uptight. And you never smiled much."

Sophie took a small sip. "I was pretty unhappy when I was married to your father. You know," she said cautiously, setting her mug down, "I haven't wanted to pry, but I'm curious. Have you called your dad since you've been here?"

Rudy shook his head.

She took another chance. "Did you have a falling out or something before you came to stay with Bram and me last fall?"

Most of the time, Rudy sidestepped questions about his past. But tonight, he just sat back and let his eyes wander to the fireplace as a shifting log threw a spray of sparks against the screen. "Sort of. He wanted me to go to that Bible college in California. The one where you two met."

"And you didn't want to?"

He shrugged. "You know Dad. He commanded me to go. He told me I had to resist the devil or he'd swallow me whole. My soul was resting in the balance."

Sophie could feel the old acid begin to churn. Inside her head she heard Norm's voice, remembered how it deepened when he wanted to exert his authority. "And what did you say?"

Rudy kept his eyes on the fire. "That I was going to Minnesota to live with you. That I wanted to attend the university—wanted to get a degree in theatre arts. And then I suppose I ducked, waiting for the explosion."

"And?"

He ruffled his reddish-blond hair, sitting up a bit. "I packed my bags and left. I'd decided not to tell him until two hours before my plane was due to take off. I had a friend drive me to the airport."

"And you haven't talked to him since that day?"

"Nope."

Even though Rudy was her son, Sophie didn't know him very well. Since his arrival in September, she'd tried many times to get him to open up to her. There had been a definite thaw in their somewhat stilted relationship, but Rudy was still closed-mouthed about his feelings and his personal life. Sophie had so many questions. What had the years been like living with his father and stepmother in Montana? Where did religion fit into his life now? She knew answers would come in time. Early on she'd discovered that pushing him to talk only made him more reticent. It drove her crazy, this getting to know her son in small fits and starts, but that was simply the way it was going to be. Sometimes, late at night, he did open up a bit more easily and talk about what he was thinking. She waited for those moments like a starving woman, happy for the smallest crumb.

Rudy sipped his milk. "You know, this stuff isn't bad."

Sophie grinned. "Stick around. Wait till you try the pastry cart at the Maxfield Plaza. You know, your grandmother and grandfather want you to come by there whenever you want. All meals are on the house."

"It's kind of nice having a famous hotel and a four-star restaurant in the family. I'll make it a point to stop by more often."

She smiled as she watched him, thinking he looked so much like she had when she was younger. Perhaps his hair was a bit more red, his eyes a tad more deep-set and dreamy, but no one would dispute they were mother and son. The only attribute that seemed to come directly from his father was the lovely, deep voice. That was all right, she guessed, especially since Rudy didn't use it to command and manipulate. He was much too gentle about the way he lived in the world. That was the quality she admired most about him. He was an easy young man to love.

She watched his smile fade. "You're still thinking about your friend John, aren't you? So, what happened after you bumped into him at the coffeehouse?"

Rudy shook his head, his expression turning angry. "It's Hale Micklenberg. John stopped by the gallery this afternoon. Kate mentioned that Micklenberg had been in to see his work. I guess John had just missed him."

"And?"

"Hale hated it. Called it amateurish. Lacking depth. A bunch of other things."

Sophie pulled her flannel bathrobe more snugly

around her body. "I suppose John was pretty depressed."

"Depressed? He was furious! When I ran into him, he was on his way over to Micklenberg's house to nail the guy's knees to the floor. I was afraid he was actually going to hurt him."

Sophie was surprised by the intensity of John's reaction. "But you talked him out of it?"

"I think so. He just needed some perspective. Someone to listen. He'd been driving around since early afternoon. And he hadn't eaten."

Sophie gave him a tender smile. "You're a good friend."

"Yeah." He looked away.

At that moment, Bram shambled into the living room, stretching his hands above his head and yawning. He glanced at the carton of chocolate milk. "Am I missing a party?"

Sophie took a long sip. "The world is passing you by."

"I was afraid of that." He groped his way to the coffee table and grabbed the carton. "Hey. You drank it all."

Rudy stood. "You know, you two are like nothing I've ever experienced before."

"Really?" Bram was intrigued.

Ethel wasn't. With a low groan, she pushed her aging bones upward and wobbled sleepily into Bram's study. There, she would snooze in his easy chair until daylight, when she would drag herself back into the kitchen and resume her slumber in front of the refrigerator. All life, as they say, was a struggle.

"I'm going to bed," said Rudy.

"All right." Sophie tried to keep the disappointment out of her voice. Bram hadn't plotted to interrupt them. He just had. "See you in the morning. Oh, by the way, will you be having breakfast with us?"

Rudy picked up his textbooks and tucked them under

his arm. "I have to be at the gallery by eight. I think I'll just grab something on my way out the door."

"Okay. Sleep well."

"Yeah. 'Night."

Sophie finished her milk and then set the empty mug on the coffee table. If only they'd had a chance to talk longer. If only she knew Rudy better. *If only.* It might as well be her mantra. As she watched him climb the stairs, she did know one thing. There was something he wasn't telling her. Something important. If she'd ever wished for the power to read minds, it was tonight.

# 7

"I don't suppose you need anything from Manning's Farm Supply? . . ." Bram sat sprawled on the couch, reading the Sunday paper and sipping his morning orange juice. George Will huffed at Sam Donaldson on the TV set in the corner.

Sophie raised an eyebrow at him as she stood in front of the dining room table, her briefcase open in front of her. She was trying to find the article she was supposed to have finished editing by Monday morning, hoping beyond hope that she hadn't left it on her desk at the office.

"They're having a great sale. It just seems a shame we can't take advantage of it."

In her mind's eye, Sophie flashed to the garage. The rafters were already stuffed to the gills with all the wonderful sale items Bram simply couldn't pass up. Farm supplies, however, were a new low. "Well, maybe we could stock up on some tractor lubricant. Or get a couple of extra salt licks for the pigs."

"Pigs don't use salt licks."

"Mine do."

He let the flyer drop to the floor. "Is that some kind of veiled comment on my buying habits?"

"I'd hardly call it *veiled*."

He gave her a smirk as he picked up the next section of the paper.

Ethel announced her entrance into the living room with a muffled groan. She held a green tennis ball snugly in her mouth. Eyeing Sophie and Bram somewhat lethargically, she dragged herself over to a rug in front of the fireplace and plopped down. She released the ball and waited as it rolled about three inches from her nose. Then, her head sinking to the floor, she watched it. Suspiciously.

"Soph, did you see this?"

"See what?"

"This review of John Jacobi's work."

"Hale's review?"

"It's got his name on it."

Sophie couldn't help but cringe. "Pretty bad, huh?"

Bram got up and walked toward her, folding the paper to the exact spot. "Read."

Sophie adjusted her glasses as she quoted out loud, " 'If you haven't been to the Chappeldine Gallery to see the newest drawings by local artist, John Jacobi, take the first bus, cab, or horse cart! Rarely have I been more impressed by a body of work.' " Sophie looked up. "I don't believe this."

"It gets even better."

She continued. " 'Jacobi's raison d'être seems driven less by linear development than by successive explorations of variations. The incredible accumulation of detail creates an irresistible sense of energy and animation in essentially inanimate objects. This is a rare tour de force.' "

"All I can say," said Bram, "is that someone must have slipped Hale the bribe or the threat of the century. When I was at the gallery Friday afternoon, he could barely bring himself to look at the stuff."

"Don't call artwork *stuff*."

"Sorry. I meant to say *doodlings*."

Sophie grimaced.

"See. I can learn."

"Only marginally." She finished the article, shaking her head in disbelief. "I don't get it. This is absolutely glowing. Both John and Kate will be thrilled."

"Ours is not to reason why." Bram took the paper from her hand, closed her briefcase, and removed her glasses. Then, putting his arms around her waist, he whispered in her ear, "As I see it, my options are either you or more of David Brinkley."

"David will be heartbroken."

He nuzzled her hair. "Life is hard."

"I know," she said, wishing her briefcase would disappear in a puff of smoke.

Across the Mississippi River at the Micklenberg residence, Ivy was in the midst of a morning bubble bath. She hadn't really relaxed since the night of the shooting. And that call Louie had taken—a young boy's voice reciting a nursery rhyme. What did it mean? Was it just a joke? Last night she'd finally removed the bandages from her arm, seeing once again the tiny marks the exploding glass had made as it cut into her skin. The whole situation was intolerable. She felt angry and frustrated, and at the same time, strangely apprehensive. Something had gone awry.

Suddenly the bedroom door slammed. She fluffed some soapsuds over her breasts and waited for the inevitable.

"I want an explanation, goddamn it!" thundered Hale as he burst into the bathroom. He waved the Sunday newspaper threateningly under her nose.

"Calm down. You're going to have a coronary."

"And," he added, his voice deadly serious, "if that explanation doesn't furnish a damn good reason for this atrocity, you're the one who'll have to worry about an early grave. I mean it, Ivy!"

She could see his fists tighten. For an instant, she was almost afraid of him. "I did it because I wanted to. You're wrong about John Jacobi. His work is wonderful. I refuse to let you ruin the man's reputation in his own town."

Hale glared at her, speechless.

"There's nothing you can do about it. You're a rotten writer. You could never hope to mimic my style this late in the game. Face it. You need me. And from now on, you're going to listen to my viewpoint."

His eyes bulging with rage, he brushed a hand through his silver hair. "Something's going on. And damn you, I want to know what it is!"

She laughed. It was a strangely high, mirthless sound. "I was nearly killed the other night, *darling*. Perhaps even you can understand how it might change one's perspective. I'm simply no longer going to live my life in your shadow." She could see his body grow rigid.

"Meaning?" He spit the word at her.

"*I'm* writing the column, now." She blew a handful of soapsuds at him. "Close the door on your way out."

He stared at her in complete disbelief. Then, crumpling up the newspaper, he hurled it at her head.

# 8

Several hours later, Hale leaned back in his leather armchair and glared at the huge TV screen directly across from him. Sunday afternoon programming was definitely the pits. Nothing but *Columbo* reruns and mind-numbing sporting events. Picking up the remote, he switched it off, glad for the return to silence. He swiveled his chair around and looked out the gate house's second-story window, noticing that Ivy's Porsche was finally gone. Well, good riddance. If he hadn't left the main house himself and come up to his office to bury himself under a pile of work, he might have strangled her right there in the tub. No, a cooler head *must* prevail. Not that he didn't have some very special plans for dear Ivy. But they would have to wait.

The sound of a ringing phone broke roughly into his thoughts. Absently he picked it up. "Micklenberg here."

"Mr. Micklenberg? This is John Jacobi."

"Who? Oh, hell. I know who you are. What do you want?"

"Well . . . I just finished reading your review of my work in the *Times Register*. I wanted to thank you."

Hale inhaled deeply. "The whole thing was a mistake."

"What?"

"Those weren't my words. *My* review was never printed."

"I . . . don't understand."

"No, I'm sure you don't. And I have neither the time

nor the inclination to explain it to you. Have a good day, Mr. Jacobi." He dropped the receiver back on the hook. The nerve of some people. He tore up the letter he'd been working on and tossed it into the wastebasket.

Again, the phone interrupted him. He could feel his temper rising. He had to get out. Take a walk. Do something besides sit and brood. Instead of answering it himself, he let the machine take it. No more morons were going to bother him today. He fiddled with the volume control to make sure he could hear the message. Then, switching off the computer, he stood and grabbed his coat, slipping it on while he listened. After a few seconds a young boy's voice said, " 'For every evil under the sun, there is a remedy or there is none. If there be one, seek till you find it. If there be none, never mind it.' " The machine clicked off.

Hale stood in the center of the room, unable to move. When Louie had recounted a similar incident the other night, he'd found it curious, but in all the commotion, he'd dismissed it as just a prank call. Annoying, but of no particular importance. But now, here it was again. Who was doing this? And more important, why?

He slumped back into his chair, staring blankly at the top of the desk. Someone was trying to rattle him, that's what it was. All in all, it was a puny effort. Having a child read the message was a suitably sinister touch, but it wasn't going to work. Of course Hale knew he'd made his share of enemies over the years. An uncompromising critic always made enemies. And, to be fair, this wasn't the first time someone had tried to pay him back for a bad review. It was just . . . this time, something seemed slightly off-kilter. Perhaps he'd antagonized a genuine weirdo. He wouldn't be human if he didn't admit to a certain fear of such things. Still, the bottom line was, the police had to be kept out of his business. Whatever was going on, he would handle it himself.

Opening a small safe on the floor in back of his chair, he drew out the gun. He checked the clip. Good. It was loaded. He might as well carry it with him. Until this guy, whoever he was, got tired of playing his little game, it was better to be safe than sorry.

Fifteen minutes later, Hale knocked on Betty Malmquist's front door and waited for her to answer. He glanced down at the shopping bag he was holding, pleased that it was stuffed to overflowing with small, beautifully wrapped presents. He'd been collecting them for weeks. He couldn't wait to see her face.

"Hale!" she said, standing back and allowing him to enter. "This is a wonderful surprise! I didn't expect to see you today."

He noticed right away that she was using her walker again. Her little dog, Arthur, scratched at his leg, wanting a pat on the head. Hale bent down and gave him a hearty scratch.

"Come into the parlor," she urged, shuffling slowly under the small arch. He recognized the dress she was wearing as her very best. Even though she rarely got out to go to church these days, Sundays were still special. Hale loved that about her. She reminded him so much of his grandmother.

"I can only stay for a few minutes," he said.

"You're not going to work?"

"Not today."

She eased herself into a chair, patting the back of her white hair into place. Arthur leapt into her lap. "Can I offer you a sweet?" She nodded to a small bowl of lemon drops on the coffee table.

"Sure." He took several. "How's Arthur feeling?"

"Fine, thanks to you. I don't know how I could have afforded his medical bills if you hadn't offered to pay for them."

"We can't have you losing your best friend."

She smiled, lowering her eyes. "I think I have two best friends. I'm a very rich woman."

He lifted the shopping bag onto the coffee table.

"What's that?" She stared at it curiously.

"Just a little something for you—to make those long winter days seem less long."

"Now, what have you gone and done?" Her voice was scolding, but he could see the delight in her eyes.

"There are several dozen small gifts here. I want you to open one every day until they're gone."

"Hale, you shouldn't! This is too much."

God, he loved doing things for her. It gave him more pleasure than just about anything in his life. "Are your grandchildren taking good care of you?"

"Don't worry about me."

"But I do."

"I don't need to be waited on. I'm perfectly able to take care of myself."

"They're getting groceries for you, right?"

"They are."

He hesitated. "Because if they're not—"

"Hale, you mustn't worry." Her eyes moved to the steps leading to the second floor. "I've missed seeing you these past couple of weeks. I always enjoy hearing you at work upstairs."

"I've had a lot on my mind."

She nodded, smoothing her apron. "I suppose you'll be flying to Europe soon. I like to think of you visiting far-off places. I almost feel like I'm doing it with you."

"I wish you could."

"The postcards are wonderful. I have an entire stack in my bottom dresser drawer. Sometimes, on Sunday afternoons, I take them out and look at them."

She was breaking his heart. He'd known for years she wasn't in good health. It was her eighty-seven-year-old body. There was nothing he could do. "Well, I've got to get going. I promise, next time I'll bring some of that Chinese food you love so much. And we can get out the Scrabble board. You owe me a chance to recoup some of my losses."

"You're a dear boy. You . . . haven't *stopped* working, have you?"

"No. Just taking a breather."

"Well, then, I'll look forward to your next visit." She started to get up.

"No. Just sit there. I can show myself out."

"Take good care of yourself then, Hale. I'll keep you in my prayers."

"Please," he said, realizing his voice was almost desperate, "do that. Don't forget me. You'll never know how much I count on those prayers."

# 9

Just after dusk, Rudy sprinted up the stairs to John Jacobi's second-floor apartment. The artist lived in an old fourplex on Grand Avenue in St. Paul—a fairly funky address by even the most discriminating standards. Although Rudy hadn't grown up in the Twin Cities, he was learning fast.

As he approached the door, he touched his hair, making sure the stiff February wind hadn't completely rearranged his look. The weather had become so bitter. And the way he was dressed, he must look like a snowman.

He unzipped his jacket, then knocked. He wished the butterflies in his stomach would fly away and never come back. Having been raised in a religious time warp, so many things still felt unfamiliar to him. He'd never had this kind of freedom before. He even had a car at his disposal whenever he needed one. He relished each new experience, remembering how utterly constricted his life had once been. Never again, he repeated to himself. Never, ever again.

As John opened the door, Rudy could see a table set in the dining room. Springsteen's *Nebraska* CD played softly from speakers affixed to the ceiling above the built-in buffet. Rudy hadn't known what to expect, but this was wonderful. "Hi." He smiled, stepping into the foyer almost reverently. John's artwork was everywhere.

"You're dressed for a blizzard, I see," said John, grinning. "Just toss your gear over one of the chairs."

Rudy quickly took off his heavy coat and muffler, his eyes traveling around the spacious rooms. The furniture was old—circa 1950—but meticulously maintained. The hardwood floors were bare. One entire wall was filled with books.

"Make yourself at home. I've got a few things to finish up in the kitchen before we can eat."

"Can I help?" asked Rudy. The pungent fragrance of garlic wafted from the open doorway. "It smells great."

"I'm making pasta. And a Bolognese sauce. There's a bottle of valpolicella on the dining room table. Help yourself. Unless you'd prefer beer or a soft drink." John watched him for a moment, his expression amused.

"No, the wine's fine." The one perceived vice Rudy's father had not denied himself—or Rudy—was alcohol. Rudy had grown up drinking wine and beer at church festivals.

"Great. I'll just be in here." John crossed to the kitchen and disappeared.

Rudy's attention was drawn immediately to an old upright piano. Two pictures rested side by side on the back. Picking one up, he saw that it was a high school graduation photo. This was the first time he'd seen John without a beard. Even though the face was young, the expression was every bit as determined, the eyes no less thoughtful. He studied it briefly before turning it over. On the back was the photographer's imprint: KEKKONEN PHOTOGRAPHY, DEER RIVER, MINNESOTA. Interesting. John had never said where he was from. The second photo was much like the first. Only this time, the young man was blond. Must be a friend, thought Rudy. He knew John was an only child. Setting the picture back on the piano, he headed into the dining room in search of wine.

"Where's Deer River?" asked Rudy. He stood in front of a chopping-block table, cutting up a cucumber for their salad.

John, who was waiting for the water to boil, glanced over his shoulder. "Why do you ask?"

"I noticed the photos on the piano."

"Oh. Right. Well, are you familiar with northern Minnesota?"

"Somewhat. My mother's family is from Bovey. That's near Grand Rapids."

John smiled. "Is that right? It's a small world. Deer River isn't far from there." He returned his gaze to the pot.

"Do you miss it?"

"Miss what?"

"Your family. Living in a small town. You know. Your roots."

John shook his head. "I miss . . . the woods. My father died when I was eleven. We were quite close. And Mom . . . just a year ago. I don't have any family left, other than an aunt."

"I'm sorry."

"Yeah."

"I suppose you miss her—your mother, I mean. It was such a short while ago." Rudy thought of his father.

Turning around, John nearly knocked his wineglass off the counter.

"Was she ill?"

He shook his head. "It was"—he paused—"a freak accident. Our house sat on about fifteen acres. It was a densely wooded area. She was out back digging potatoes one afternoon when a rifle shot hit her. Best the police could figure was that it was a hunter. We had signs posted near the highway that said it was private property, but it seemed like every year we'd get some yahoo stomping around looking for deer in the fall."

"That's . . . awful." Rudy felt an involuntary shudder. He quickly finished his second glass of wine.

John picked up the wooden spoon and resumed stirring the sauce. "Do you miss your family in Montana?"

Rudy could tell he wanted to change the subject. That was fine with him. "Not really. But sometimes . . ."

"Sometimes what?"

"Well, I mean sometimes I think what I miss most is what I never had. I suppose that sounds funny."

"No," said John. "I know what you mean."

Rudy was beginning to feel uncomfortable with the entire subject. "So," he said, starting on a green pepper, "you must be feeling pretty great about your rave review."

John stiffened. He kept his back to Rudy as he said, "I called Micklenberg to thank him. I don't know why. I should have let well enough alone."

"Why?"

"Are you sure you want to hear this?"

"Absolutely. I'll admit I was surprised to read something so positive, especially after what he said to Kate on Friday."

John gave an angry snort. "Well, get this. Micklenberg said he hadn't written the column."

"What?"

"I told him I didn't understand, and he said he didn't care. He wasn't going to explain it to me."

"Is that usual? Do people like Micklenberg let other people write their columns for them?"

"Not that I've ever heard."

"So what happened?"

John shrugged. "I don't know." He returned to the sauce.

Rudy couldn't decide whether this was good news or bad. "John?"

"Uhm?"

"How much does a good review mean to you? I mean, is it really all that important?"

John pushed a hand into the pocket of his jeans and leaned back against the counter. "Do you want the long answer or the short?"

Rudy smiled. "I think we have time for the long."

"All right. Here goes." He picked up his wineglass and took a sip, giving himself a moment to arrange his thoughts. "I believe that critics," he began, "especially in the area of fine arts, serve a marginal function at best. They have power and can do damage to an artist, or help a career along, but essentially, they're only a guidepost. What I object to most fundamentally is when a critic—any critic—mistakes his own opinion for absolute truth. Opinion, even educated opinion, is still just that. And most important, nothing and nobody should stand between the viewer and his or her personal experience with the work."

"But," said Rudy, popping a slice of cucumber into his mouth, "for instance, I'm taking an art history class this quarter. Value, whether positive or negative, is always being assigned to this artist or that piece of work. Do you consider that wrong?"

"I don't believe it's ever a mistake to learn about somebody's life, or about the time—the social milieu—in which someone worked. And of course I agree that some works of art are more successful than others. But when an authority says that your personal response to any given piece *has* to be the same as his—otherwise you're misguided, naïve, or just plain ignorant—then I have to draw the line."

Rudy nodded. "I think I understand."

John turned down the flame under his sauce. "Once in a class I took, the professor was discussing objective truth versus subjective truth in relation to art. After the lecture, I stopped him in the hall. I told him that it seemed what he was saying was that when enough people get together and decide subjectively that something has value, it becomes objective truth. After that point, no one is supposed to argue about it anymore."

"And?" said Rudy.

"The guy mulled it over and then started to laugh. He said that basically I was probably right."

Rudy shook his head. "Let *me* mull it over for a while."

"You do that," replied John, with another amused smile.

"But what about Hale? Is he going to print a retraction?"

"I have no idea."

"What will you do if he does?"

John lifted the cover off the pot, his eyes momentarily mesmerized by the steam and bubbling water. "Try to ignore it. I'm not always as angry as I was the other night at the coffeehouse. After Kate told me what he'd said, I don't know what got into me. I'm usually able to control my temper better than that." He looked around. "But thanks for being there. I really needed a friend."

Rudy resumed his vegetable chopping. "No problem." He whacked into a stalk of celery.

"Hey, take it easy. Those knives are pretty sharp."

Rudy was feeling a slight buzz from the wine. He stopped for a moment and watched John dump the homemade pasta into the water. Being here felt good. This new independence, coupled with the conversation and the valpolicella, made him almost giddy. As he pulled over a stool and sat down, he made himself a promise. He would help John in any way he could. They were alike. Neither of them had much money, but both had a clear sense of direction—of what they wanted from their future. Nothing was going to get in their way. Not Rudy's father. And certainly not Hale Micklenberg.

# 10

Rhea couldn't believe her eyes. As she stood in front of her one o'clock Dancercize group on Monday afternoon, the double doors to the dance floor opened and in pirouetted Ben, a big grin on his face. He did a little two-step across to the assembled crowd and then, landing on one foot, took a bow. The women began to laugh and clap. Rhea shook her head, placing a hand on her hip.

"I thought I'd find you in here," he said, catching his breath.

"I'm in the middle of a class. I can't talk right now."

Ben pretended a pout. "Just two minutes. That's all I ask."

She glanced at the crowd. "I don't know—"

"Oh, come on. You ladies understand, don't you?" He flashed them a boyish smile.

Rhea knew if she didn't act fast, the entire class would be in shambles. "All right. Two minutes. Then you're out of here."

"Deal."

They moved over to a long wall, covered floor to ceiling with mirrors.

"We still make a handsome couple," he said, his voice dropping to its most seductive register.

Rhea looked at their reflection. She couldn't help but agree. "All right. Make it fast."

"How long does your class last? One hour? Two?"

"Forty-five minutes."

"Great. I'll wait for you."

"Why?" She could see the women watching them. This was becoming embarrassing.

"I want you to come with me over to Hale Micklenberg's office. I thought I'd drop by this afternoon. Get more specifics on what I'm supposed to photograph."

"Why should I?"

"Rhea, the place is incredible! He's set up a gallery in the small gate house behind the main house. He's got artwork in there from all over the world. Didn't I tell you that his column in the paper is just a sideline? Most of his time is spent helping rich assholes decide on the best investments for their bucks. Some of the work he sells to them directly. And I'm going to photograph it all for his latest catalogue. This is the most lucrative deal I've ever cut! I want you to see it for yourself."

She hesitated. Ben had never lacked enthusiasm. Sometimes, however, in his excitement, he overlooked details. Important details—like contracts. "You do have all this in writing?"

"In writing? Nah. Hale and I shook hands on it. With a guy like him, that's all you need."

He was such a hopeless optimist. And she was so easily caught up in his dreams.

"So? What do you say? Are we on?"

Her class was becoming restless. She couldn't stand here and talk any longer. "Sure."

"Great!" He grabbed her and gave her a hug. "And afterward, I'll take you to dinner."

"Fine."

"And after that—"

"Ben," she whispered, with as much force as she dared, "we just got *divorced*!"

"So? That didn't stop us last Thursday night." He wiggled an eyebrow.

He was incorrigible. "We'll talk about it later. You go upstairs to my office."

"Yes ma'am. See you in forty minutes." He gave her a quick kiss and then waved to the class as he box-stepped out of the room.

An hour and a half later, they stood in front of the entrance to the Micklenberg gate house, waiting for someone to answer the bell.

"Are you sure he's here?" asked Rhea.

"When I talked to him on Friday, he said to stop by Monday afternoon. He'd show me around."

Rhea looked up at the second-floor windows. It was a dark, windy day. A light did appear to be on.

"Here we go." Ben smiled. "I can hear someone coming."

The door swung back. A balding man glared at them with undisguised annoyance. "Yes?"

"Hi! I'm Ben Kiran." He thrust out his hand.

The man looked at it as if it had come directly from a toxic landfill.

"This is my wife—I mean my ex-wife, Rhea Kiran. We're here to see Hale."

"Do you have an appointment?"

"What? Well, not exactly. He just hired me to photograph the spring catalogue for IAI."

"I see." The man peered at them distantly. "He never mentioned it to me."

"And you would be?" Ben's smile remained at high beam.

"Charles Squire. Hale Micklenberg's personal assistant."

"Of course." Ben gave Rhea an amused nod. "May we come in?"

"Hale isn't here."

"He's not?" The smile faded slightly. "Well, perhaps we could come in and wait for him."

"He won't be back for several hours."

"Look, I need to get an idea of what I'm supposed to photograph. It's important."

"What did you say your name was?"

"Kiran. Ben Kiran."

"Hmm. Well, I suppose you might as well take a look." He stepped back and allowed them to enter.

Rhea was immediately struck by the size of the first-floor gallery. From the outside, the gate house looked tiny. Inside, the high ceilings and light cream walls made it appear quite spacious. She also noticed the bars on the windows. Not a welcoming sight. "These are wonderful," she said, stepping to a series of Japanese prints.

"Yes, aren't they?" Charles said the words with his usual ennui. After closing and locking the door behind them, he stood butlerlike next to the stairs.

Ben took this as his cue to begin examining the artwork. He strolled around the room as if he owned the place, a finger pressed to his cheek. Rhea could tell he was enjoying himself.

After a few minutes, Charles said, "I don't recall seeing your signature on a contract."

Ben turned. "Oh, Hale said it wasn't necessary."

"I'm afraid, my dear sir, that it is. Have you agreed to do this based on an hourly rate?"

Ben looked confused. "Hale said to just mail him the bill."

"Well, as I am the one who *pays* the bills, I suggest you nail it down a bit better. Otherwise," he said, biting the cuticle on his right index finger, "you're going to be as disappointed as our last photographer."

Rhea watched a frown form on Ben's face.

"I see. Well, then, why don't you show me one of your contracts?" Ben was trying to keep his voice light. No use antagonizing the man closest to the checkbook.

"I suppose I could do that." Charles headed up the stairs. "Please. Follow me," he called after him.

Ben held out his hand for Rhea and together they climbed to the top.

The second-floor office was lavishly appointed. Hale Micklenberg was a man who spared no expense making himself comfortable. An entertainment center sat directly across from a massive oak desk, complete with huge TV screen and stereo speakers. Charles had apparently been listening to some music before they'd arrived. A Bach fugue was just ending.

Switching off the CD with the remote, Charles sat down behind the desk and opened one of the side drawers. He removed a contract and handed it to Ben. "I assume you'll want a few moments to look it over."

Ben nodded, sitting in one of two leather chairs.

Rhea crossed to the window and looked down at the street. "You're about to have more visitors."

"What?" With an annoyed growl, Charles leapt to his feet and peered over a filing cabinet. "Oh, drat. Not the Kingfields. Hale's supposed to handle them." He shot an irritated glance at Ben. "If you'll excuse me for a few moments?"

"Of course." Ben didn't look up, he merely waved a dismissive hand and flipped to the second page. After Charles was gone, he quickly finished the rest and then tossed it on the desk. "Standard stuff. I'll just have to talk to Hale about a couple of the particulars. But it's no problem."

Rhea wasn't so certain.

"This is a pretty great office, huh?" He rose and moved over to examine the stereo system, running a finger over the CD collection. "Typical. No Clint Black. No Jerry Jeff Walker. Micklenberg probably hates country-western music. Not up to his artistic standards." He turned around, his eyes falling to the computer. "And will you look at that? Top of the line." He stepped to the desk and settled himself behind it. "This is a honey."

"I don't think you should touch that," said Rhea nervously. "Mr. Squire could be back any minute."

Ben gave her another smile as he flipped through the disk file. "Chuckie doesn't scare me. Here we go: taxes for 1994. Should be interesting."

"Ben!"

"All right! Just calm down." He put it back. As he rolled the chair to the side, his right foot hit something heavy. "What's this?" He turned to look. "Rhea, it's a safe. And it's open."

Rhea could feel her body begin to quake. "Ben, I don't like this. Let's go."

He held up another disk. "Why isn't this in the file with the rest of them?"

"I don't know. Just put it back."

He scratched his chin. Checking through the top drawers, he drew out a small package. "These disks are empty. I think I'll make a copy."

Rhea could feel her blood pressure rising. "Put it away!"

Ignoring her, Ben slipped the blank disk into one slot, the disk from the safe into a second. He punched a few keys and sat back. "Shouldn't take long."

"You know, you're crazy. You're going to get us in big trouble!" She moved cautiously to the stairs. "I can hear them talking."

"Great. Tell me when they stop. Say, while I'm at it, I might just as well make a copy of those 1994 tax returns. You never know when you're going to be struck by a bout of insomnia and need some late night reading."

"Ben!" She could hear the door downstairs being opened.

He removed the first disk and replaced it with the second.

"Squire is letting them out. He'll be back up here in less than a minute."

"Plenty of time."

She glared at him. "Put it all back the way you found it!"

"I will."

"Now!"

"My, my. Haven't we become bossy in our old age."

Rhea listened at the door. "He's coming!"

Ben leaned over and put the first disk back in the safe. Then, sitting up straight, his hand poised above the keyboard, he waited.

"Hurry!" Rhea was frantic. What if they were caught? How could they explain what they were doing?

In an instant it was done. Ben dropped the 1994 tax disk back in the file and slipped the copy he'd just made into the pocket of his jacket. As Charles Squire reentered the room, Ben was sitting calmly in his original chair.

Rhea felt like a dishrag. She fell heavily against the doorframe.

Charles gave her a quizzical look.

"Well," said Ben, standing up, "the contract looks fine. I'll stop back when Hale is here and we can sign it."

"All right. I'll give him the message." Charles sat down behind the desk, crossing his legs and rearranging the silk handkerchief in his vest pocket.

"Great." Ben took Rhea by the arm. "See you around."

"I suppose that is inevitable." Charles made a bridge of his fingers as he sat back, his eyes rising wearily to the ceiling.

# 11

Hale paused in front of the gallery window, taking a look inside. Kate Chappeldine appeared to be nowhere in sight. Instead, that son of Sophie Greenway's—what was his name?—was sitting behind the reception desk in the back. The kid looked like one of Santa's elves. Come to think of it, so did Sophie. Well, thought Hale sourly, this might just turn out to be a waste of time.

Entering through the front door, he unwrapped the wool scarf from around his neck and trudged to the rear of the room.

Rudy looked up from his notebook as he approached. "Mr. Micklenberg."

"Good afternoon. I can't remember your name."

"Rudy."

"Right." Hale eyed one of the textbooks on the desk next to him. "Freshman composition. I remember that. I've always loathed creative writing."

"But you do it so well."

"I do?"

"Your column."

"Oh. Right." He strolled around behind the desk, fingering a crystal paperweight. "Is Kate here?"

"She's in the back. If you want, I could go get her for you."

"Do that." Hale flipped open a tattered copy of *Under Milk Wood*. "Dylan Thomas, huh?"

"I'm also taking a poetry class."

"Uhm."

"I'll be right back."

As Rudy scrambled to his feet and dashed into the hallway, Hale made himself comfortable behind the desk. "What's this?" he said under his breath. He picked up Rudy's notebook and began reading. It was a poem. The first line was so ridiculous it made him snicker. By the time he was halfway through, he was doubled over with laughter.

"What's going on in here?" asked Kate as she entered the gallery a few moments later. Rudy was right behind her.

Hale pointed to the notebook and shrieked: " '. . . as comfortable as a blueberry muffin in a brown paper bag'!" His face had turned beet red. "And listen to this one." Again he quoted: " '. . . if I could crawl into the bowels of your heart and remain there, a passionate pilgrim'!" He pounded the desk and roared. " 'The bowels of your heart'! 'A passionate pilgrim'!"

Kate turned around. Rudy's face had become almost as white as the gallery walls. The fury in his eyes told her everything. "Rudy . . . I—I'm sorry." She didn't know what else to say.

Without a word, Rudy ripped the notebook out of Hale's hands, picked up his coat and textbooks, and stomped back into the hall. Kate could hear the rear door slam as he left.

Hale continued to giggle uncontrollably. "That kid is quite the poet."

"Shut up."

He took out a handkerchief and wiped the tears from his eyes. "What did you say?"

"I said shut up!"

His smile evaporated.

"You humiliated him! Why?" She slammed the ruler she was holding down on the desktop, sending the crystal paperweight crashing to the floor.

Hale straightened his bow tie. "Oh, come on. I was

just having a little fun. Even you have to admit it was god-awful drivel."

"It was private."

"Then why did he leave it out here in plain sight?" He rose, coming eye-to-eye with her. Nobody, especially a woman, was going to make him feel like a criminal for simply having a little fun. He refused to blink.

"Why are you here?" Kate stood her ground.

Very calmly, he replied, "You mentioned you were going to be receiving more works by Ezmer Hawks on Monday. Since today is Monday, I thought I'd stop by to see them. That is," he added, his voice taking on a calculated sneer, "if that meets with your approval."

She hesitated. After several seconds, she said, "All right. They're in the back." Turning abruptly, she left the room.

"Here's the first one," she said, placing it carefully on an easel. It was another pastel. Heavy on the blues and violets.

Hale stood back, an approving smile pulling at the corners of his mouth. "Good . . . good. Next?"

Kate placed a larger drawing in front of the first.

He scratched his chin. "These are even more naturalistic than the group you showed me the other day. But I like them. In a strange way they remind me of—" He stopped, a frown forming.

"Of what?" asked Kate.

He gave his head a small shake. "Never mind. Are there more?"

"Two." She hoisted the next one up.

"Uhm. Do you see—?" He stepped up to it and took out his reading glasses. "Here." He pointed. "What does that look like to you?"

She shrugged. "I don't know."

"Sure you do!"

She leaned over to examine it more closely. "Well, it

looks kind of like a sphinx—with fire between its paws."

Slowly Hale removed his glasses. "Exactly," he whispered.

"Does it mean something?"

He didn't answer. "Show me the last one."

She placed it on the easel.

Instantly his hand flew to his mouth, muting the sound of a gasp.

"Is something wrong?"

He closed his eyes, feeling as if an ancient videotape was unwinding inside his brain. That horrible camp. That wretched barbecue pit. He could see it all. His heart began to pound. "Look at it! It's that sphinx again, only larger. And look at the flames. There's a face in it!"

Kate stood back, shaking her head. "I have to tell you, I don't see it."

"You're a complete idiot! Just use your eyes!"

She moved behind him and took him firmly by the arm. "Look, I think you've been under a great deal of stress lately. Someone took a shot at your wife. That's got to be hard. Why don't you come over here and sit down."

"Yes," he said, running a hand over his eyes. Maybe, for once, Kate was right. He let her lead him to a chair.

"I've got a bottle of brandy around here somewhere." She began to rummage through a box on the floor.

"Yes. Brandy. That's a good idea." He took out his handkerchief and wiped the sweat from his forehead.

"Here," she said, finding it under some polishing rags. She moved to the sink and began washing out a coffee mug. "How much would you like?"

"A stiff one." He sneaked a peek at the last drawing. The image was still there. Damn her! Why couldn't she see it?

Kate handed him the cup.

Though his hand shook badly, he took it, finishing it in one gulp.

"Feel better?"

"I think so." He took a deep breath. "Yes. Better."

"Would you like me to call Ivy? Perhaps she should come get you."

"No." Ivy was useless. Besides, she was never home. "She teaches a class on Monday evenings."

"I could call her office. Or leave a message with Morton information."

He shook his head. "I'm fine." He stood, steadying himself on the edge of the framing table. "But I think I should be going."

"Do you want me to call you when we receive more of Ezmer's work?"

"Yes. Immediately." He moved to the door, keeping his eyes away from the easel. "Where did you say Hawks was from?"

"I don't know exactly. Somewhere up near Soldiers Grove. At least, that's the post office he uses."

Hale nodded. He turned to go, then hesitated. "How old is he?"

"To my knowledge, nobody's ever seen him. He's kind of a recluse."

He felt a spasm in his stomach. "You don't find that odd?"

"I suppose it is."

"You suppose! That's all you can say?"

"Lots of talented people have quirks. It goes with the territory."

He gave her a freezing stare. "When you want to reach him, how do you do it?"

"I send all correspondence to a post office box in Soldiers Grove. He usually writes back within a week."

"Would you give me that box number if I asked you for it?"

"I suppose so."

"Good."

He left without a backward glance.

# 12

Late Monday evening, Dr. Max Steinhardt pulled his Lincoln Town Car into the Micklenberg driveway and slipped the engine into neutral. "Well," he said, reaching over and putting his arm around Ivy, "I guess we better call it a night. Unless you want me to come in."

Ivy glanced at the gate house. The light was on in Hale's second-floor office. "No, he's home. I think we better not chance it."

"All right. But one of these days, this farce is going to end."

She smiled at him, touching his cheek. "I don't know what I'd do without you."

"Don't even think about it." He kissed her with a strength she found intoxicating. "Everything's all set now, right?"

"Don't worry."

"We'll never have what we really want unless we're strong."

Ivy knew that if Max admired anything in this life, it was strength. His sixty-year-old physique was living proof. Never, in all her forty-five years, had she been so attracted to a man. The fact that he worked out every day at his club gave his body a tautness men twenty years his junior would envy. At this stage of her life, she never expected that sex would take on such importance. Yet, there wasn't a thing about Max she didn't find utterly . . . delicious.

"Call me if you need me." He gave her another lingering kiss.

"I will."

"And don't antagonize Hale any more than you have to. It's not smart."

"But it's so much fun." She winked as she opened the car door. "Later, my love." She bounded up the steps to the back door, giving him a wave as he sped out of the drive. Again, she looked at the gate house. If she was lucky, Hale would stay there all night. And rot.

After pouring herself a glass of orange juice in the kitchen, Ivy grabbed her purse and headed up to her bedroom. As she switched on the light next to her bed, she noticed the time. Nearly eleven. Even though she'd been up since dawn, she wasn't the slightest bit tired. She wondered how Louie was—and how Sarah was doing. She and Max had run into him yesterday evening coming out of a downtown restaurant. She wondered if Louie knew about them. If he hadn't known before last night, he probably knew now. Oh, well. It didn't matter. Louie despised Hale. Twenty years ago, if it hadn't been for Hale Micklenberg's youthful charm, she might have married Louie. No, he would keep his mouth shut. The one person in the world Ivy knew she could trust completely was Louie Sigerson. She decided to give him a call. It was late, but she knew he would be up. Besides, she had a favor to ask.

The phone rang several times before he answered.

"Hi," she said, kicking off her shoes and lifting her feet up on the bed. "How's Sarah?"

"No change." He coughed several times, clearing his throat.

Ivy wondered if he'd been crying. These days, when she called, she never knew what she might be interrupting. "What do the doctors say?"

"Well, she's in no immediate danger. But—" His voice broke.

Ivy waited, her heart aching for him.

"It won't be long."

She could feel herself begin to tear. "If I could do anything to change this for you—"

"I know. No one can."

She could hear him blowing his nose. "How are you?"

"Oh, about the same. The nights get pretty long."

"Are you taking some time away from the office?"

"I went in this morning, but I can't concentrate."

"I understand."

"It's just—sometimes I need something to take my mind off what's happening at home. You know." He sniffed.

"Then I think I might have just the ticket. I was hoping you'd be able to give me a ride over to WMST tomorrow morning. Hale and I are scheduled on Bram Baldric's radio show."

"Won't you be going with Hale?"

"Not if I can help it. And the brakes on my car have been acting funny. I took it into the shop this afternoon." She switched on the TV with the remote. Jay Leno was doing his monologue.

"Okay. I've got the picture. What time?"

"The program begins at nine. We should be there about ten minutes before it starts."

"Fine. I'll pick you up at seven-thirty and we can catch a bite of breakfast first. What do you say?"

"You're a lifesaver." Even though she couldn't see his smile, she could feel it. At least she'd given him that much. "See you in the morning."

# 13

"Are you sure you're feeling all right?" asked Louie, holding the door to the radio station open for Ivy as she passed in front of him. "I'd hoped some ham and eggs might give you a little more energy."

"I told you. I had a restless night." She led the way to the elevator. The studio was on the third floor.

"Is it your back again?"

She nodded. "I took several painkillers about one A.M., and then again at six. I think they're starting to wear off."

The elevator doors opened and they stepped on.

"Do you feel well enough to do this program? I'm sure Bram would understand if you backed out." All during breakfast, Ivy had seemed unusually preoccupied. Louie wasn't convinced it was simply a bad back.

"You know how I feel about commitments. I'll get through it." As soon as the doors reopened, she crossed to the reception desk.

Louie folded his thin frame into one of the chairs provided for visitors. The radio show just prior to Bram's was being broadcast over two speakers positioned at either end of the room. A man and a woman were discussing the British royal family. Louie stifled a yawn. Chuck and Di always did that to him.

"Ivy! Glad you could make it." Bram emerged from one of the far doors, a welcoming smile on his face. "Hale and Kate are already here. Hang up your coat and come with me."

Ivy handed her things to Louie. "You remember Louie Sigerson."

He thrust out his hand. "Of course. Good to see you again. Come on back with us and you can watch through the glass."

"Fine," said Louie, taking Ivy by the arm. She was really beginning to worry him. She seemed terribly unsteady. Even Bram seemed to notice.

"I promise you," said Bram, striding quickly toward the end of the hall, "this will be completely painless."

Ivy gave him a faint smile. Before she disappeared behind the heavy door, she whispered to Louie, "Be a dear and call Max. I'm really not feeling well."

"Perhaps I should take you to a hospital," he said, trying not to sound upset. He didn't want to frighten her.

"No, just make the call." Her voice was firm, but Louie could hear the uncertainty.

"Of course. Don't worry. I'll go find a phone right away."

She gave him a peck on the cheek.

He watched for a moment as Bram handed her a pair of earphones. Kate and Hale were already seated behind a round table. As soon as the ON AIR light came on, Louie dashed back to the reception desk and asked where he might find a public phone. The woman pointed to one near the elevators.

He knew it was best not to question Ivy any more than necessary. She was terribly high-strung. Pushing her to do something she didn't want to do would only make her more anxious. Still, he was worried. Whatever it was that was bothering her, it hadn't just started this morning. Something had been brewing for months. Hale was no help at all. When it came to emotions, he had all the sensitivity of a mollusk. And Louie had been so preoccupied with Sarah, he hadn't been any help, either. It was only logical that Ivy would turn to someone else. And Louie felt certain he knew who that someone was.

Opening the phone directory, he began his search for the office of Dr. Max Steinhardt.

Louie waited in the main reception area, listening to the radio broadcast while watching the elevator doors. Max said he would be right over. In the meantime, Hale was being his usual tedious self, waxing on and on about various galleries around the country. God! It was beyond him how Ivy could put up with a man like that all these years. Hale presented himself with complete confidence, but Louie knew better. He'd never met a human being before with so many malicious insecurities.

Kate Chappeldine spoke about her new gallery, and about how she'd grown up in New York City. Her father, Ross Chappeldine, played second violin for the New York Philharmonic. She explained that she'd picked Minneapolis as the place to start her gallery because of its national reputation for being a leader in the arts.

So far, Ivy had said very little.

Just as Bram started to elaborate on the local art scene, Max emerged from a side door. He'd obviously taken the stairs.

Louie raised a weary eyebrow and stood. How utterly predictable the man was. He probably had barbells in his pockets. "Over here," he called, motioning for him to follow.

"Where's Ivy?"

"In the studio. She's on the air right now."

Together they rushed down the hall.

"You said on the phone that she'd taken some painkillers for back pain." Max removed his gloves and stuffed them into the pocket of his coat. He was carrying a medical bag. "Do you know what she took—specifically?"

Louie shook his head. "No clue."

They came to a full stop in front of the glass. Ivy

noticed them immediately and gave a small wave. She took out a pen and notepad and began writing. When she was finished, she handed it to one of the technicians, who pushed it under the door.

Max picked it up and read out loud:

Thanks for coming. My back is still hurting me. Could I have two more of the pain pills? They're in the gold pillbox in my purse. When I'm done in here, Max, could you check me over? I feel kind of funny.

"Where's her purse?" He looked around.

"It's right here under her coat." Louie handed it to him.

He opened the clasp and began rummaging through the contents. "Okay. Here's the box. Now." He stopped cold when he saw the pills.

Louie could see a look of intense distress pass across his face.

"These aren't pain pills," he said, watching Ivy for a moment through the glass. Her head was resting between both hands, her eyes closed. Bram appeared to be watching her, too.

"What's wrong?" pleaded Louie.

"Those pills—they're Lasix!"

Louie didn't understand. "So?"

"They're a diuretic, man. She's a diabetic! How many did she take?"

Louie had to think back to their conversation. "Four. Though I could be wrong. She said she took two in the middle of the night, and then two again this morning."

The ON AIR light went off as the national news came on. Bram rose instantly and moved to Ivy's side, motioning for Louie and Max to come into the room.

"We've got to get her to a hospital," said Max as he entered and knelt down next to her. He started to take her pulse. "Someone call 911 and tell them it's an emergency. And get me a glass of water."

Bram quickly left the room, returning a few moments later carrying a pitcher and several mugs. "The receptionist is making the call."

Max nodded, reaching into his medical bag and taking out a syringe and a vial of clear-looking liquid.

"What's that?" asked Hale, who had remained silent during all of this. He moved closer to Ivy.

"It's potassium." Max worked quickly, pushing up her sleeve. "Give her some air," he barked, glaring at Hale.

Hale stiffened. "She's my wife, goddamn it! I demand some answers."

"I feel so light-headed," said Ivy, holding her stomach. "And a little nauseous."

"Bend your head down between your legs." Max helped her into the correct position.

Louie, who had stayed near the door the entire time, continued to watch with a sinking sense of déjà vu. For eleven years, his wife had been worked over by doctors. Nothing had helped. She was dying, and there wasn't a single thing he could do about it. And now, here was Ivy, sick in a way he didn't understand. It took every ounce of willpower he had to stay in the same room with her. He felt ashamed of himself for such a cowardly reaction, but there it was. Even though he loathed the timid, useless man he'd become, he couldn't help himself. He was revolted by illness. He wanted to turn his back on all the pain and just run—as far and as fast as his feet would take him. "Is she going to be all right?" he asked, his voice barely audible.

Max looked up, glancing from face to face. "She's going to be fine. Absolutely fine."

"Back on the air in two minutes," said one of the technicians.

"Where are those paramedics?" demanded Hale.

"There's a fire station less than half a block away," answered Bram, his eyes rising to the clock. "They should be here any second."

Max grabbed the pillbox and shook the pills out into his hand. "Damn," he growled, looking up at Hale. "I can't believe this."

"Here they are," called the technician.

Two burly men rushed into the room carrying a portable stretcher between them.

Max took over. "I'm Dr. Steinhardt." He stood back as they made Ivy comfortable. "I want her taken to Northwestern. I'll ride with you in the van."

Hale stood next to her as they covered her with blankets. "I better come, too."

"No room," said Max. He held Ivy's hand as they wheeled her out.

# 14

Ivy was awakened from a fitful sleep by the sound of footsteps. By the time she was able to focus on the source, they'd stopped. But they'd come close to her. She knew that much. The hospital room in which she'd spent most of the day was now dark, yet she could sense a presence. Someone was on the other side of the curtain. For a split second, she had the urge to cry out. Instead, she asked—very softly: "Who's there?"

The curtain fluttered. The face of Kate Chappeldine appeared above her bed.

Ivy grasped for the cord and turned on the light.

"Is this a bad time?" The young woman was holding a small bouquet of daisies.

At the sight of the flowers, Ivy heaved a sigh of relief. She felt silly for her reaction. What could she possibly have to fear from Kate? "No, I'm delighted to see you. I was going a little stir-crazy." She adjusted the bed to a sitting position.

Kate handed her the bouquet. "How are you feeling?"

"Much better. The doctors just wanted to keep me overnight for observation. I should be released first thing in the morning." She gave her a sheepish smile. "I guess I must have mixed up my pills. Although—"

"Although what?"

"Well, I don't believe any doctor I've ever had has prescribed a diuretic. Hale said he used one years ago, but he assured me he'd thrown the bottle away. I just don't understand how they could have gotten into my medicine cabinet."

Kate's eyes narrowed. "I don't mean to upset you, but don't you see any connection between this and someone taking a shot at you the other night?"

"Well . . . actually," said Ivy, straightening her robe, "I did consider the possibility."

"And?"

"What do you want me to say? That someone is trying to—to murder me? I won't accept that. It's too crazy!"

"Is it?"

"Yes," she said, though she knew her voice carried little conviction. "Look, nobody has access to my medicine chest except me and—" Her attention strayed to the window.

"Have you informed the police about what happened this morning?"

"Well, Max did say something about calling them." She slid farther down in the bed. "I can't handle this right now. Could we change the subject?"

Kate hesitated. "Sure," she replied after a few seconds, pulling up a chair and sitting down. "Has Hale been in to see you?"

"For a few minutes. He couldn't stay."

"You two lead very busy lives."

She sighed. "I suppose we do."

"IAI must take up a lot of his time."

"It does. But you know something? Years ago, it didn't seem to matter. We always made time for each other. We loved being together. But then he started having to work evenings. Weekends, too—though I could never locate him if I needed something. Once upon a time, this would have been hard for me to admit, but now . . . well, I guess I just figure he's seeing other women."

"You're brave to be able to talk about it so calmly."

She gave a small shrug. "I don't have any proof, mind you, and he denies it vehemently, but what else am I to think? Thank God for my friends. Louie was here today for over an hour."

"Louie?"

"Louie Sigerson. My lawyer. We've been close for many years. He's having a rough time right now. His wife is dying of emphysema."

"I'm sorry."

"Sometimes I get so worried about him. He buries everything deep inside. I don't think he sees how all of this has affected him." She glanced at Kate out of the corner of her eye. Why had she come? Was it simple kindness—or did she want something? "He's shut himself off from everyone—except me. I wouldn't *let* him shut me out. We've always had a very special bond. But I'm not enough. I wish he would just bust loose. Get drunk. Smash his best china. Find a woman. Anything to let off some steam."

"But he won't?"

Ivy shook her head. "At least I got him to promise he'd come to our annual Piero della Francesca birthday bash. If nothing else, it'll get him out of the house. You came last year, didn't you?"

"I did." Kate smoothed a wrinkle in her dark wool slacks. "It was quite a party."

Ivy's smile turned wistful. That had been the first time she and Max— No! Now was not the time to daydream. She had to keep her wits very carefully about her. Especially with Kate. For some reason, the young woman's scrutinizing stare unnerved her. "Anyway, you should have your invitation in the mail any day. This year we're going to celebrate Piero's birthday on the twenty-second. That's next Friday night."

Kate looked up at the TV set in the corner. The six o'clock news was on, though the sound had been turned off. "Where did you get the idea to celebrate his birthday?"

"Actually, nobody knows when he was born. Since both Hale and I love his work, we decided one winter that his birthday would make a great excuse for a party. We've been doing it ever since."

"Well . . . I'm looking forward to it. Who else will be there?"

"Oh, all the usuals. Friends from the *Times Register*, as well as other business associates of Hale's. Some colleagues of mine from Morton. Sophie and Bram. And Charles Squire—he's Hale's new assistant. By the way, I was hoping that artist you're featuring . . ."

"John Jacobi?"

"Yes. I was hoping he could come. If I send an invitation to your gallery, would you pass it on to him?"

"I'd be delighted to. But are you sure Hale would want him there?"

Ivy waved the question away. "Don't worry about that. On all important matters, Hale's opinion doesn't count."

They both laughed.

"Well," said Kate, rising and dragging the chair back against the wall, "I suppose I should be going. I've got to get back to the gallery."

"You were a dear to come. By the way, how did the rest of the show go this morning? I was so embarrassed, leaving you in the lurch like that."

"Don't give it another thought. Everything was fine. Actually, some guy called in and wanted to talk about NEA grants. We spent the rest of the time arguing about Jessie Helms and Robert Mapplethorpe. Bram loves that kind of controversy. He says it makes for great radio."

"I'm glad I missed it."

"Yeah. I could have skipped it myself. Anyway, I'm happy to see you're feeling better. And look, I don't want to upset you, but please promise me you'll be careful."

Ivy raised her hand. "You have my word. But don't upset yourself. And don't give it another thought. Nothing's going to happen to me that I can't handle."

# 15

"I don't suppose my son is still here?" asked Sophie as she bustled into the Chappeldine Gallery late the following morning. She had several hours to kill before she needed to be back to her office.

Kate looked up from a stack of paperwork. "You just missed him. He had a study group he wanted to attend before his afternoon class." She tossed her pencil on top of the desk and stretched.

"Nuts. I was hoping to interest him in a bite of lunch. Oh, well. I guess I'm doomed to eat alone. Unless . . . ?" She raised an eyebrow, giving Kate a hopeful look.

Kate glanced at her watch. "I wouldn't be able to leave for another half hour."

"No problem." Sophie pulled up a chair and sat down. "So. What's new?"

"Not much."

"You look kind of tired."

"Really? I guess I haven't been sleeping too well lately."

It was a common malady, thought Sophie. She'd been tossing and turning herself. Mostly she was concerned about Rudy. "Are you going to the Micklenbergs' party next Friday night?"

"You must have gotten your invitation. Me, too."

"You don't sound thrilled."

"I'm not. The Micklenbergs aren't exactly my favorite people." She shook her head. "I'm really sorry about what happened to Rudy the other day."

"Excuse me?" Sophie pricked up her ears.

"Didn't he tell you?"

"He didn't tell me anything." Not that she hadn't wondered what was going on. On Wednesday afternoon, Rudy had come home from work and bolted up the stairs without so much as a word. He'd slammed his bedroom door and hadn't come out until the next morning. Sophie tried to get him to talk, but he refused. Ever since then, his moodiness had concerned her, but she knew she was helpless in the face of his continued silence. At least now maybe she'd find out something. "What happened?"

"Well, Hale stopped in to see some work I'd just received from an artist in northern Minnesota. Rudy was sitting at the desk here, working on his studies. He offered to run back to the storage area to get me. While he was gone, Hale started reading a poem Rudy had written—a love poem, I suspect. When we returned to the gallery, Hale was laughing so hard I thought he was going to fall off the chair. He even quoted some of the passages out loud."

Sophie could feel the muscles in her neck tighten.

"Needless to say, Rudy was furious. He grabbed his

books and left. He hasn't mentioned it since, but I know it's still bothering him."

God, how painful, thought Sophie. She remembered her own youthful attempts at love poetry. To have one read out loud and then laughed at . . . "Hale Micklenberg is a menace," she muttered angrily.

"In more ways than one."

She looked up. "What do you mean?"

"Didn't you hear what happened to Ivy yesterday?"

"Sure. Bram called me as soon as the program was over. Ivy took the wrong medication. I guess it could have been quite serious."

"You're damn right it could. Except, there was no reason for that drug to even be in her house."

"What are you saying?"

"Think about it, Sophie. First, someone takes a couple of shots at her. Then, she takes a drug that could have been fatal. But how did the drugs get mixed up? Who brought the drug into the house in the first place? Not Ivy."

"You think Hale had something to do with it?"

"He had tons of opportunity. And he's a hateful man."

Sophie didn't disagree.

"Like a lot of critics, he's a frustrated artist. He can't create himself, so to feel powerful, he places himself above those he can't hope to emulate."

"So? What's that got to do with . . . ?"

"Hurting Ivy?"

Sophie nodded.

"I don't know specifically, but I think it's all part of his malevolence—and his desire to control."

Sophie didn't feel comfortable jumping to such a broad conclusion. Besides, she distrusted this kind of off-the-cuff psychology on general principle.

"Speak of the devil," whispered Kate.

Both women looked up as Hale strode briskly into the gallery, a cigar clenched between his teeth.

"Good morning, ladies." He whisked the cigar out of his mouth as he came to a stop directly in front of them.

"I'm sorry," said Kate, pushing an ashtray toward him, "but you're going to have to put that out while you're in here."

Giving an annoyed grunt, he tapped the ash off the end and then lovingly crushed the tip against the glass. "I'm here to see Ezmer's latest installment." His normal grandiosity was noticeably absent.

"Sure," said Kate, rising from her chair. "It's in the back, still boxed up. I haven't looked at it yet myself."

"Ezmer?" asked Sophie, a questioning look on her face.

Kate reached into the top desk drawer and drew out a letter. "Ezmer Hawks. That artist from northern Minnesota. I've featured his work here before."

The light dawned. "Oh, sure. The one who does pastels." Sophie found the man's work rather childish. She'd never paid it much attention.

"Well?" said Hale, his expression full of impatience. "Let's get on with it."

"Of course. But first, this is for you." Kate handed him the letter. "It came in the morning mail."

"What is it?"

She shrugged. "It's from Mr. Hawks. It's addressed to you."

Hale's hand shook ever so slightly as he ripped it open. Taking out his reading glasses, he remained silent while studying the contents. When he was finished, he folded it and stuffed it into his pocket.

"I didn't know you two were corresponding," said Kate.

"We're not." His voice was cold. "I want to see that drawing. Now."

"Certainly. Sophie, you're welcome to come with us." Kate moved around the desk and headed into the hallway.

"Don't mind if I do." She was entirely too intrigued

by Hale's strange behavior to turn the invitation down. Picking up her purse, she followed them back to the storage room.

As Kate unwrapped the small package, Sophie stood near the door and watched. Hale seemed uncharacteristically nervous. He kept fidgeting with his bow tie. His hands dipped in and out of his pockets. Finally Kate pulled the drawing free and handed it to him. At first, he just stared at it. No reaction. After another few seconds, Sophie noticed a muscle in his cheek begin to twitch. His forehead had become bright with sweat. Something truly extraordinary was happening and she had no idea what it was.

Crossing to where he and Kate were standing, she peered at the small pastel. It was more realistic—and at the same time, more surrealistic—than any she'd seen before. It appeared to be the frame of a door set directly at the edge of a cliff. Below was a river.

Slowly Hale handed it back. "Thank you," he said, his voice strangely flat. He took off his glasses and put them away. "I have to go." As he reached the door, he turned. "What's that box number? The one in Soldiers Grove?"

"Ezmer's?"

He nodded.

"Box 183. It should be on the letter he mailed you. Why?"

He opened the door. "None of your goddamn business."

# 16

Several hours later, as Hale sped out of Moose Lake on his way to Soldiers Grove, he thought again of the note he'd received earlier in the day, the one from Ezmer Hawks—if that was his real name. He no longer believed it was. It had said, very simply: "Childhood memories. What would life be without them? Glad you like my drawing better than you did my dancing." Shivering inwardly, Hale realized the message could only be from one person. The only problem was, that one person was dead. With his own two eyes, he'd seen the boy fall from the cliff. There was no plausible explanation for what was happening now. Nothing that would explain the drawings or the phone calls.

He thought again of the boy's voice. " 'For every evil under the sun, there is a remedy or there is none.' " Someone was trying to drive him over the edge. He laughed at the absurdity of his own image. Over the edge—terrific! If he didn't keep his wits about him, he might really self-destruct. His only hope was to find this recluse, this Ezmer Hawks, or whatever his real name was, and demand some answers. Glancing at the glove compartment where he'd stashed his gun, he felt certain that today, no matter what it took, he was going to put a stop to this terrorism once and for all.

An hour later, the Soldiers Grove water tower appeared in the distance. He was almost there. The first order of business was a phone directory. Perhaps this Hawks character had a published street address. It was worth a try. He pulled into a gas station and got out. The cold wind felt bracing after the overheated car. After perusing the local directory, he slammed the book in frustration. No Ezmer Hawks was listed. The station attendant pointed the way to the post office across the street.

Once inside the small building, Hale quickly found box 183. He bent down and looked through the glass, but it was empty. Only one other person seemed to be around. A man standing behind the front counter. Mid-sixties. Balding. He looked as if he'd lived his entire life in the small town and probably knew everyone. Hale approached cautiously. He wasn't sure what was the best tactic.

"Can I help you?" The postal employee gave Hale the once-over.

Hale smiled easily. He knew his cashmere overcoat and heavy gold jewelry probably pegged him as a rich outsider. It gave him a certain satisfaction—since he'd grown up in a town very much like this one and didn't like being reminded of it. "Yes," he said, feeling in his back pocket for his wallet. "I'm looking for someone."

The man merely stared.

"Ezmer Hawks. Do you know him?"

"Ezmer Hawks," he repeated, shaking his head. "Can't say that I do."

"He rents a box here. Box 183."

"Well then, I'm sure we've met. I just can't place the name."

Hale was becoming impatient. "He's not listed in the phone book."

"Is that right?"

"I don't suppose there's any way you could give me his address."

The man shook his head. "Nope. We're not allowed to give out that information."

Hale laid his wallet on the countertop.

The man's eyes fell to it.

"You're sure?" he said, pulling out a fifty-dollar bill.

"Well, that's policy. But then, I hate bureaucrats, don't you?" He reached for the money. Taking out a ledger, he flipped a few pages until he found the address. "Hmm. Here it is." He found the spot with his finger. "That's funny."

"What's funny about it?"

Again, the man glanced at the wallet. "Nothing. The address is 4712 East Pine Lake Road." He wrote it down on a notepad and handed it to Hale. "Make a left when you get back on the highway. The road is about a mile out of town. Turn right and follow it until you get to the house. The road parallels the lake, so you can't get lost."

"Thanks." Hale returned the wallet to his back pocket with a small feeling of triumph. Money could buy almost anything. Even answers from Ezmer Hawks.

Fifteen minutes later, he spotted a mailbox along the side of the road. He pulled his Mercedes over and got out. The name on the box was Westman, but it had been scratched out. What was most important were the numbers 4712. This had to be the place. He grabbed his gun, stuck it in his belt, and headed down the snowy path to the house. From a distance, it didn't look particularly inviting. It was hand-built and tiny, with shingles instead of wood siding. Huge icicles hung from the roof. As he got closer, he realized some of the windows were broken. And no one had shoveled any of the walks. The latch on the front door was rusted, coming off in his hand as he opened the door. Stepping into the dank front room, he saw the place was deserted. "Damn!" he exploded, realizing he'd been sent on a wild-goose chase. He kicked an old pot across the floor.

If this was the address in the post office log and no other address existed, he was at a dead end. He felt in his pocket for the letter Kate had given him. Sure enough, it was a Soldiers Grove postmark. Hawks had to be here somewhere. Perhaps if he went back to town and spent a few minutes asking around, he might put an end to this little game of hide-and-seek. It was worth a try.

Francie's Cafe was located on Soldiers Grove's main drag. On one side was a hardware store and on the other, the Soldiers Grove Washateria. Directly across the road was Dave's Feed and Seed. As he entered the building, he noticed a familiar form sitting at the counter. The man's face was partially obscured by a newspaper, but Hale recognized him at once. It was John Jacobi. The sight of the young man startled him into paralysis.

After considering the situation a few moments, Hale decided to sit down next to him. Play it cool. He grabbed a menu and began looking it over.

John read for a few more minutes and then lowered the paper, his hand finding his coffee cup. As he did so, he noticed Hale sitting right next to him. "Mr. Micklenberg!"

"Small world, isn't it?" Perhaps young Mr. Jacobi was the answer he'd been looking for. If he was, it explained a lot. "What are you doing here?"

John seemed momentarily at a loss. "My . . . aunt lives in town. I come up fairly often."

"Quite the family man."

John seemed confused. "She collects bones and feathers for me—objects she finds in the woods. They're my models. I need them for my work. I come up here every now and then to collect them—and to have a piece of her pie."

"That's all?"

"I beg your pardon?"

"That's your only reason for coming to this thriving metropolis?" Hale noticed the waitress give him a nasty look. He glared at her until she turned away.

"Why do you ask?"

"Oh, I think you know."

John put the paper down. "Look, I don't have any idea what you're talking about."

"No?"

"No. And what I do with my time is *my* business." He held Hale's eyes.

Hale could sense the threat. He knew he'd hit pay dirt. "I got your message this morning."

"What message?"

"The one about childhood memories." He watched him for a reaction, daring him to come clean. After a few silent seconds, he decided that the young man was a pretty fair actor. But not good enough. "Now I've got a message for you." He leaned very close. "I want you to back off. I don't know what your game is, but I'm onto you. Stay away from me. No more phone calls. No more cute little camp drawings. You got that?"

John leaned away. "You're not making any sense."

"Maybe." He glanced briefly at a man eating a bowl of soup at the far end of the counter. "You'd be about the right age."

"For what?"

"But you're not him. I know that much. I'd recognize him anywhere—even twenty years later."

"Mr. Micklenberg, don't take this wrong, but you're . . . babbling."

Hale gave an angry snort. "What were you? Friends?"

John blinked.

"You can't know anything. I don't even know why I'm bothering to talk to you."

"That's a good point. Maybe you should just order some chili and mind your own business."

"You must be independently wealthy to be able to take time off anytime you please and drive up here."

"I have a job."

"Really? Doing what?"

"I work for the Bergdorf Brewery in St. Paul."

Hale stifled a laugh. "The working man's artist. God, it takes me back to the Sixties. And you know what, kid? It still nauseates me."

"It's an honest day's work. You'd be surprised. There's an art to making a good beer. Like other things."

"What do you mean by that?"

"Whatever you want it to mean."

"Don't toy with me."

"Is that what I'm doing?" A small grin appeared.

"I can play rough. I've got enough money and power to destroy you a hundred times over, so don't push me. Right now I've had about all I can take."

"Is there something wrong?" asked a tall, heavy-set woman who'd just stepped out of the back. An immaculately white apron covered a floral print dress.

Hale raised an eyebrow, wondering if this was Francie, the owner of the restaurant. "No, nothing's wrong."

"Johnny, what's going on? Who is this guy?"

John pushed his coffee away. "Aunt Francie, I'd like you to meet Hale Micklenberg. He was just leaving." Another grin.

Francie took the menu from Hale's hand and slipped it under her arm. "Good. I think we just ran out of everything."

Hale stiffened. "Well, so much for small town hospitality."

"Yeah, you can't count on anything these days." She leaned a heavy arm on the counter and waited.

Hale's frown deepened. He turned one last time to John. "Just remember what I said." After looking at the long row of homemade pies behind the counter and hearing his stomach growl, he stood and straightened his coat. It was nearly four P.M. Even though he hadn't eaten since breakfast, he'd be damned if he'd buy a piece of *that* woman's pie. It was probably poison.

"I suggest," said John, folding the newspaper with

great care, "that you go home and call your therapist. You seem pretty uptight. Sometimes it's best to talk things out—get whatever's bothering you off your chest."

Hale could feel his blood pressure rising. He had to leave before he did something stupid. And anyway, if it became necessary to take care of John Jacobi, he didn't want any witnesses. "I'm glad we had this conversation. It was clarifying."

John nodded, glancing at his aunt out of the corner of his eye. "It was."

Was that amusement in the young man's face?

"Good afternoon, Mr. Mickel*baum*." Francie smiled, nodding to the door. "Have a safe drive home."

# 17

The following Thursday evening, the phone in the Micklenberg home began to ring. Ivy, who was sitting in the living room watching the snow accumulate on the fir trees in the front yard, jumped at the sound. She wondered, as she dashed into the kitchen to pick it up, just who it might be. "Hello," she said into the receiver.

For a moment the line was silent. Then: "Ivy? Is that you?" The voice was hoarse, barely audible.

"Louie!" She knew instantly something was wrong. "What is it?"

"It's Sarah." His voice broke. "She . . . died this morning."

Ivy could hear him crying. Her own heart sank inside

her. Very softly, she said, "I'm so terribly sorry. Louie . . . are you all right?"

"Yes." He sniffed.

"Where are you?"

"At home. It happened just before five A.M. I was with her."

"That's good. I know that's what you both wanted."

Another sniff. "I've spent most of the day arranging the funeral."

"You shouldn't have done that alone. Why didn't you call me earlier?"

"I . . . couldn't."

"I'm coming over to get you."

"Why?"

"I can't stand the thought of you rattling around that old house, all by yourself. I want you to stay here for a few days. Until you feel stronger."

"I couldn't bother you like that."

"Louie, get real! It's no bother. In case you've forgotten, we have *six* bedrooms. I think we can spare the space."

"But your party. It's tomorrow night. You must be going crazy trying to get everything done."

"Have you ever heard of caterers and cleaning services? I hire the very best."

"But what about Hale?"

"What about him? He flew to Chicago yesterday for a meeting. I'm not even sure when he'll be back."

"I . . . don't know."

She could hear the hesitation. She also knew he wanted to come. "Well, I do. Pack a small case and I'll be over to pick you up in half an hour."

"Ivy . . . I . . ." Again, he sniffed. "Thanks."

An hour later, Louie was seated behind the Micklenberg kitchen table watching Ivy make an omelette. "I don't know why I merit this kind of attention."

She glanced over her shoulder. "Just lucky, I guess."

He smiled. It was the first time all day he'd allowed himself to relax. "She's going to be buried at Lakewood. It's what she wanted. The funeral is next Monday."

"Is there anything I can do to help with the arrangements?"

He shook his head. "Sarah's sister is inviting everyone over to her house after the service. She's taking care of all that."

"Good." Ivy placed the omelette on the plate with two pieces of toast. Turning off the gas, she crossed to the table and set the food in front of him. "Now. Eat."

"I don't know if I can." He put his hand on his stomach.

She eyed him cautiously. "You know what you need? A stiff shot of brandy."

"I don't drink."

"Well, I think today is an exception." She left the room and returned a moment later carrying a bottle of Armagnac. "This is Hale's favorite. I'm sure it's good." She got down a glass from the cupboard and poured several inches. "Come on now," she said, handing it to him, "bottoms up."

He stared at it suspiciously. Finally, closing his eyes, he took a gulp. "Agh," he said, making a sour face. "How do people stand this?"

"Just wait." She gave him a patient smile. "One more time."

"Really?"

"Trust me."

He lifted the glass and took another sip. "Well, that was a little better—I guess." He began to feel a pleasant, warm sensation in the pit of his stomach. "I will say, the food does smell awfully good."

She sat down across from him, resting her chin on her hands. "You're going to be all right, you know."

He nodded, taking another swallow. "It's hard to admit this, but—"

"But what?"

"Well." He closed his eyes. "I'm . . . glad she's gone." There. He'd finally said it. "She was suffering so terribly these last few years. And I—"

"And you've been a saint."

"Don't say that."

"No? You never stopped loving her—or taking care of her. The personal cost to you had to be immense. Of course you'd feel relief. You wouldn't be human if you didn't."

Louie couldn't believe what he was hearing. She actually understood. He covered his eyes with one hand and started to cry. "I've felt so guilty these last few months. I just wanted it to be over."

She reached for his hand. "You were a wonderful husband. Don't ever forget that. Nobody should have to live forever in a situation that makes them miserable."

He wiped away the tears. "No?" He took another sip of his drink, realizing he was beginning to feel unnaturally loose, his normal reticence dropping away. "What about you and Hale?"

She withdrew her hand. "What about us?"

"You aren't happy. I know about you and Max. Why don't you just divorce the bastard and get on with your life?" He couldn't believe he'd said it, though he knew she'd been unhappy for years.

She leaned back in her chair and folded her arms. "It's not that simple."

"Why not?" He poured himself more brandy.

"You remember that prenuptial agreement we signed?"

"The one your father insisted on? Sure, I helped draw it up."

"Well, when we were first married, I was the one with the money. I had the trust fund. I own this house. I put him through school. I supported us for years while he looked around for the right job. But now, as they say, the shoe is on the other foot. His art investment company earns millions each year. If I divorce him, we both walk away with only what we brought into the marriage. That means I get the house and the trust fund—which, by the way, is almost gone—and he keeps IAI. Get the point?"

As a tax attorney, Louie could hardly miss it. "But you're not happy! Doesn't that outweigh everything else?"

"God, you're more naïve than I thought."

That stung.

"I want it *all*, Louie. Max and the money."

"But, how? I don't see—"

"Eat your omelette before it gets cold."

He looked down at the plate. "Right." He took a bite, then another sip of brandy. As his eyes strayed to the window, he noticed Hale's car pull into the drive. "I think we're about to have company."

Ivy stood and walked to the door. "Damn. I was hoping his plane would crash."

"Don't say such things!"

"Why not? It's the truth. You know Louie, you suffer acutely from being born a Norwegian Lutheran. It's Minnesota's most common birth defect. You're too *nice*."

For some reason, her comment struck him as hilarious. He burst out laughing.

Hale puffed into the kitchen carrying a suitcase. "What's going on? What's so funny?" His eyes fell to the bottle of Armagnac.

"My wife just died," said Louie, wiping a hand across his mouth.

Hale glared. "Really? And I suppose mass starvation sends you into giggling fits."

Louie steadied himself on the table, trying to regain his composure. "No," he said softly.

"I've invited him to spend a few days with us," announced Ivy. "This is a hard time. He shouldn't be alone."

Hale grunted, dropping the suitcase next to the refrigerator and removing his coat. "Listen, Louie. Be a good boy and disappear for a few minutes. Ivy and I have something we need to talk about."

"We do?" She raised a skeptical eyebrow.

"Of course," said Louie. He scrambled to his feet.

"Why don't you take the bottle with you. It will help ease your . . . sadness."

Louie squared his shoulders, ignoring the sarcasm. "Don't mind if I do." He grabbed the brandy, realizing for the first time how light-headed he'd become. His body felt positively fluid as he glided into the living room. "Toot, toot," he whispered, chugging around the coffee table. He stopped in front of an easy chair and dumped himself into it. Then, leaning his head back, he closed his eyes. So many emotions were pulsing through his brain, he couldn't focus on just one. But the pain had definitely eased. The relief was so intense, he felt almost giddy. Remarkable that he'd never tried brandy before. Ivy was right. He was too much of a puritan. Well, things were going to change. He wasn't sure just how, but the life he'd known for the last ten years was over.

As he surveyed the room, he decided the first order of business was a little eavesdropping. He was curious about what Hale had to say to Ivy. Never before would he have even considered doing something so—so unethical. Well, what the hell! This was the new and improved Louie Sigerson. He crouched down and crept silently back to the kitchen. As he oozed to the carpet and peeked through a crack in the door, he could hear Ivy speaking:

"They *what*?"

"I said, the police picked me up as soon as my plane landed!" Hale cracked a knuckle.

"They were actually waiting for you at the airport?"

"You're damn right they were. And they took me

downtown for questioning. Me! Riding in the back of a squad car!"

"What did they want?" Ivy leaned against the counter.

"Don't play dumb with me. You know exactly what they wanted."

"Look, I don't have a clue what you're talking about."

"No? You don't remember those shots fired at you the other night—or the Lasix that got into your pillbox? Seems the police think I'm trying to murder you. Your friend Max's been talking to them. From what I could gather, he's been pretty convincing."

Ivy stared at the half-eaten omelette. "What did you tell them?"

"That I'm completely innocent! I demanded to have my lawyer present. Except, he was in court and couldn't be reached."

"But they don't have any proof."

He snorted. "Oh, that's just a minor technicality. This is too delicious a story to simply let drop. Just picture it. 'Wealthy art critic makes two vicious attempts on loving wife's life. Details at ten.' "

"What are you going to do?"

"What do you think? Find the best private detective in the business. Have him prove you're setting me up."

"Why would I do that?"

He gave her an evil sneer. "You presume I don't know about you and Max? I'm not blind!"

"But it's not true! I had nothing to do with it. I was the victim!"

"Cut the crap, Ivy. Maybe you're even behind that Ezmer Hawks shit at Chappeldine."

"The what?"

"Those cute little camp scenes? Reminiscences of Camp Bright Water. And that kid who calls us all the time, reciting his favorite poem? Nice touch, sweetie, but it won't work."

"I had nothing to do with that! I got one of those calls, too, in case you don't remember. The night of John Jacobi's opening."

"So what? It's just a cover."

Her eyes opened wide. "You think this has something to do with—with Eric?"

"You're damn right I do. Except he's dead. And the only other person who knows the truth is you."

"I've spent my life protecting you!"

"You were protecting your future, sweetie, not me."

"How can you say that!"

"As I think about it, it makes more and more sense. You're behind everything. You get rid of me, and in the process, get your hands on my entire estate."

Ivy began to back toward the door. "You've lost your mind! You're like talking to a crazy man."

"I never thought of you as having a very subtle mind, Ivy. Maybe I should reconsider. But just remember: I'm onto you, sweetheart. You try anything else and I'll break your arms. I'll break your boyfriend's arms, too. If you think that's an idle threat, try me." He picked up his suitcase. "I'm sleeping in the gate house from now on. I can't stand to be in the same room with you. Tomorrow, I'm going to file for divorce."

She gasped.

"Don't tell me you're surprised?"

"I . . . but—"

"You want that musclebound surgeon? Well, you can have him. But you'll leave this marriage with nothing."

"The police were right! You are behind those attempts on my life! You can't stand the idea that I've found someone who really cares about me."

His smile was full of bitterness. "Maybe so."

"But you must be reasonable!"

"Why?"

She rubbed the back of her neck. "Because . . . what about the party tomorrow night?"

He laughed. "Always the perfect hostess. Don't

worry. I won't embarrass you. As a matter of fact, I intend to play the loving husband all evening. In the end, I'm going to look like the wronged party, not you. And it'll be the truth—because that's what I am!"

She groped for the edge of the counter. "That's ridiculous. When everything comes out about all your women friends—"

"What women friends?"

"How stupid do you think I am? I know you've been sleeping around for years."

"You're nuts!"

"Am I? Where were you all those nights and weekends when you couldn't be reached?"

"None of your goddamn business."

"See! You admit it."

"I admit nothing. You may not believe this, Ivy, but I've been faithful to you. To our marriage."

"I don't believe you!"

"That's your choice."

"You never loved me!"

"And what if I didn't?"

"Say it! Say you never loved me."

"Why?"

"Because it's important!"

He glared at her.

"I hate you!"

" 'For every evil under the sun—' "

"Don't!" She ducked her head, covering her ears.

"Can't even take a simple nursery rhyme? You're getting soft, darling." He started for the door. "By the way, just for the record, I did love you. Once. More than anything in the world."

"Get out!" she shrieked.

As the door slammed behind him, she picked up a bowl of oranges and hurled it at the wall. The fruit fell to the floor with a dull thud. Sinking into a chair, she wrapped her arms protectively around her chest. Her sobs came in small fits. "Damn you," she repeated, over and over again. "I'll get you for this. I'll get you!"

# 18

"How do I look?" asked Bram, brushing a piece of lint off his otherwise immaculate tux. He tugged on his French cuffs. "Well?"

Sophie handed her coat to one of the Micklenbergs' hired staff. Piero della Francesca's birthday party was in full progress. Turning her attention to her husband, she raised an eyebrow suggestively and whispered, "Straight out of *Masterpiece Theatre*."

"You mean like an English butler?"

"I didn't say that."

"No, but—"

"You look wonderful. And yes, I'd like my tea in the library in fifteen minutes." She took his arm and together they made their grand entrance into the living room. "I will say I'm glad you shaved off that beard you were growing last fall."

Bram stroked his smooth cheek. "Yeah. It made me look too much like a bear."

"More like a woodchuck." She made a quick perusal of the standing-room-only crowd, noticing that her son was nowhere in sight.

"Maybe he's not coming," said Bram, grabbing a handful of cashews from a large, crystal bowl.

"Who?"

"Rudy. That's who you're looking for, right?"

She harrumphed. "Who made you so smart? Actually, he did say he might drop by later with John."

"Figures. You can hardly expect an eighteen-year-old male to escort his mom to a party." He popped a cashew into his mouth.

"I suppose. In some ways, I wish he'd skip it altogether."

"Because of what Hale did to him?"

She nodded. "He's still angry. He doesn't talk about it, but I know he is. I love him, but he's got a terrible temper."

"Sort of like his mother."

"I beg your pardon?"

"Come on, Sophie. Stop worrying. Rudy and John will probably spend the entire evening swilling java in some campus coffeehouse. He's a smart kid. You must learn to trust his instincts."

"I do. It's just—he's so young."

"Don't let *him* hear you say that."

She adjusted the belt on her best basic black dress. "You know something else? I'm glad Rudy and John have become such good friends. He needs someone to confide in."

"You mean until he learns to confide in you?"

"Don't be silly. I'm not asking to be his *buddy*. But for a mother, he could do worse."

They came to a stop in front of the fireplace. On the mantelpiece above it rested a framed picture of Piero della Francesca, a garland of white roses surrounding the grim likeness.

"He doesn't look particularly happy," said Sophie, cocking her head.

"You mean he's not smiling. Lots of people don't smile as much as Americans do. In fact, some cultures find our constant need to grin not only excessive, but cloying."

"Thank you for that *Reader's Digest* moment." She noticed Kate Chappeldine waving at them from the dining room. "I think we're being summoned." Taking Bram by the arm, she screwed her face into a scowl and then said, "Come on, honey. Let's go have some fun."

He rolled his eyes.

As they approached, Sophie saw that Kate wanted to introduce them to the couple she was standing with. They were a handsome pair. The man was tall, with dark hair and light blue eyes. A definite hunk. The woman was also tall, with an exotic, almost Middle Eastern face, long brown hair, and a decidedly athletic body. The clingy red dress she wore accentuated every curve.

"Sophie, Bram"—Kate beamed—"I'd like you to meet Ben and Rhea Kiran. Ben is a photographer. He tells me he's going to be shooting Hale's summer catalogue. I thought he looked awfully familiar, but we can't place where we might have met. And his wife is the creative director, choreographer, and lead dancer for the Rhea Kiran Dance Ensemble."

"Of course!" Bram extended his hand to them both, though he kept his attention on Rhea. "I was almost positive I'd seen you somewhere before. Sophie and I had the pleasure of attending one of your performances last spring at Northrup Auditorium. You were wonderful."

"Thanks," said Rhea, taking a sip of champagne. "That's always nice to hear."

"You've got incredible elegance," continued Bram. "I suppose you've studied a long time."

"Since I was a child."

"Your parents no doubt encouraged your talent."

"Actually, it was my brother. He was a terrific dancer himself."

"Really?" said Ben, turning to her. "I didn't know that."

"Is your company still performing?" asked Sophie.

"Locally, yes. Unfortunately, what we really need is to mount a national tour. But that takes backing. And to get it, we need more visibility. Which means we need to tour—but we can't tour without the money. You get the point." She gave a frustrated shrug.

Sophie noticed Ben put his arm around his wife's waist. Newlyweds? she wondered. They still had a certain glow about them. "Well," she said, selecting a canapé from a tray on the dining room table, "maybe your husband can pad his expenses and soak Hale for a few extra pieces of gold."

Ben laughed. "Don't think it hasn't crossed my mind. Oh, by the way, we're not married. Actually, Rhea and I just got divorced."

Sophie's hand froze midway to her lips. "Really?"

He gave her an amused nod.

"Have you known Hale long?" asked Bram.

"We go way back," said Ben. "He was one of the counselors at an arts camp I attended one summer—back in 1971. I think he might even have met his wife there that same year. At least, I know they weren't married yet."

Bram snorted. "An arts camp! I can just see Hale stomping through the woods with thirty screaming kids in tow, trying to find true north."

Again, Ben laughed, glancing at Kate. "Is something wrong?" he asked, reaching out to steady her.

"Wrong? No. Just a little too much champagne." Her smile was apologetic. She turned as another man strolled up.

"Hi," said the man, his voice excessively cheerful. "I'm Steve Nelson."

Bram shook his hand, making the rest of the introductions.

"Nice party," said Steve, eyeing a bowl of fresh strawberries on the buffet table.

Sophie followed his gaze, her stomach giving an involuntary growl. The Micklenbergs were known for providing a tempting array of buffet treats. An ice sculpture formed the centerpiece for the table, surrounded by mounds of shrimp and carved crudités. Next to it was a long silver tray of dipping sauces. Curry. Peanut oil, vinegar, and hot peppers. A spiced Cajun mayonnaise. A cocktail sauce with plenty of sliced lemon. Her eyes moved to the caviar and a lovely crock of anchovy butter. Thick slices of a dark Russian rye sat next to it. And next to that, a large wheel of baked Brie covered with caramalized brown sugar and toasted walnuts. Home-baked mince pies with brandy sauce completed the menu. Sophie knew there were other tables scattered here and there around the house. Each with a different assortment of goodies. It was all she could do to bring her attention back to the conversation at hand.

"Lots of great artwork in this house," continued Steve, still surveying the scene. "This is really neat for me because I'm going to be photographing Hale's new summer catalogue."

Sophie blinked. She looked immediately at Ben. At first, he just stared. Then, his back stiffening, he said, "Excuse me, but what did you say?"

"Me?" Steve hesitated. "Well, first I said it was a nice party."

"No, the part about the catalogue."

"Ah . . . Oh. That I've been hired to photograph Hale's summer catalogue."

"Who hired you?"

The man looked from face to face, obviously hoping someone would offer him a clue to what was happening. "Hale hired me," he said somewhat defensively.

"Have you signed a contract?"

"It was a verbal agreement. How come you're so interested?"

"Because"—Ben smiled, his voice ominously pleasant—"Hale hired *me* to do that shoot. Several weeks ago. One of us is being screwed."

"Well, it's not me! I've got a firm commitment!"

Ben's face flushed with anger. "So do I!"

Rhea put her hand on Ben's arm, whispering, "It's not his fault. Just let him go."

"I'm not the least bit worried," said Steve, backing away. "Hale is a man of his word. Unlike some people."

Ben's fists tightened.

"Why don't we go find you some champagne," said Bram, starting to walk Steve toward the east sun room. "I think we all need to cool off."

"I'm not going to let Hale get away with this," insisted Ben, his eyes searching the crowded room. "That asshole's got to be around here somewhere. It's *his* goddamn party!"

"Just calm down," replied Rhea, leading him out of the dining room. "We'll get this sorted out, don't worry." She gave Sophie and Kate a small wave goodbye.

After everyone was out of earshot, Sophie muttered, "Hale strikes again."

"So it would seem." Kate didn't even try to hide the acid in her voice. "That man should be put away—or put out of his misery. One of these days, someone's going to do it!"

"Hey, come on," said Sophie. "They'll work it out." She put her arm around the young woman's shoulders, surprised by the intensity of her reaction.

"At whose expense?" Kate ran a hand through her thin blonde hair.

"Well . . . let's hope it's at Hale's."

"Fat chance." Her mouth set angrily.

"Come on, Katie. It's a party. Let's forget about that gasbag for the rest of the evening and have some fun."

Kate just stared straight ahead. "Of course," she said somewhat woodenly. "You're right. Listen, there's something I forgot to do. Gallery business. You understand. I'll catch you later, okay?"

"Okay. But what—?"

"Tell Bram to save me a dance. I'll meet you all in the conservatory in half an hour."

There was no use arguing. "We'll be there."

Kate swept to the front door and out into the cold night.

"Not smart," said Sophie under her breath. "Not smart at all." She didn't know what Kate was up to, but she hoped it had nothing to do with Hale Micklenberg.

Rudy and John entered the Micklenberg mansion an hour later. Neither had bothered to dress for the affair.

"I'm only here because I'm curious," said John, handing his leather jacket to a man standing next to the front door.

Rudy did the same. "I don't even have that excuse." His eyes took in the noisy scene. "It's amazing how many friends you have when you've got money."

"I hardly think we qualify as friends."

"Good evening, gentlemen," said a man carrying a tray of champagne. He was tall and lanky, with thinning brown hair and a weak chin. By the leather patches on his sport coat and the distracted look in his eyes, Rudy pegged him as a professor.

"Don't I know you?" asked John. He took one of the flutes.

The man bowed slightly. "Louie Sigerson. I'm a friend of the family's." He set the tray down on a small table and took a glass himself, lifting it to his lips. "If you play butler, you get the entire tray all to yourself. Quite a deal."

Rudy could tell he wasn't exactly drunk, but he wasn't exactly sober, either.

"Sure," said John. "I remember. We met at the Chappeldine Gallery. You came in to see my show several days after the opening. I'm John Jacobi."

"The bone and feather man," said Louie, extending his hand. "How nice to see you again. What are you working on now? A rabbit femur perhaps? Detailed duckdown?"

John began to laugh. "And this is Rudy Greenway."

"Greenway? Any relation to Sophie Greenway?"

"I'm her son."

"How wonderful! But then, at your age, you'd hardly be her father." He emptied his glass. "I didn't realize she had any children."

Rudy hated these introductory conversations. He never knew what to say. "Yup. She does."

"Yup?" repeated John, making his face into a question mark.

Rudy glared at him.

"Well, I'm off to forage for nourishment," announced Louie. "You know, I've never eaten cheese puffers before. But I'm turning over a new leaf." He held up the empty glass of champagne in a kind of salute.

"Terrific," said Rudy, stuffing his hands into the pockets of his jeans.

"You boys have a good time." Waving over his shoulder, he drifted off into the living room.

"Quite a character," said John, watching him put his arm around Ivy Micklenberg and give her a peck on the cheek.

"Let's find the cheese puffers before he eats them all," said Rudy, rubbing his hands together hungrily.

"Actually, they're not really called cheese *puffers*. It's cheese puffs."

"Mmm." Rudy nodded.

"You've never tried them, either?"

"Dad wouldn't let us eat junk food."

"No? Figures." He put his hand on Rudy's shoulder and gave him a knowing look. "Come with me, then. And prepare yourself for a sublime culinary experience."

Ben left Rhea sitting on the couch in one of the sun rooms, talking to a man named Louie Sigerson. He seemed quite interested in modern dance. At least, while he was gone, she was in good—as well as safe—company.

He'd seen Hale several times over the course of the evening, but felt slugging him in the stomach in the presence of so many witnesses might be counterproductive. Instead, he'd formulated a more reasonable plan of attack.

He was going to have a little chat with Charles Squire.

"Hey, Chuckie," he called, finding him standing under the dining room arch. "Remember me? Ben Kiran?"

Charles lowered his chin and raised an eyebrow. "How could I forget?" He'd been talking confidentially to a young woman, his hand almost, but not quite, touching her face. Not much of a ladies' man, thought Ben as he grabbed him by the arm and led him into a dark, deserted hallway between the back stairs and the rear entrance.

"Excuse us," he said, smiling over his shoulder at the young woman. "I'll bring him back in just a minute."

"Take your time," she said, giving him the once-over. She obviously liked what she saw.

"Hey, take your sweaty hands off me!" insisted Charles, a surprised look on his face as Ben shoved him, face first, against the wall, one arm pinned behind his back. "What are you doing?"

"I want some information."

"Try the public library."

Ben twisted the arm.

*"Agh!"*

"Just shut up and listen then." He looked around to make sure they were alone. "I met a guy tonight by the name of Steve Nelson. Ring any bells?"

"Possibly."

"I want to know what kind of game you and Hale are playing?"

"Game? On the contrary. I think Mr. Nelson may simply have made Hale a better offer."

"How could he? We never settled on a final price."

"Then . . . perhaps it boils down to personalities. Hale usually doesn't hire thugs."

On that last word, Ben twisted the arm even harder. Charles grunted with pain.

"Have you ever had a broken bone, Chuckie? It's no fun. I suggest you show a little more respect."

Biting his lower lip, Charles gave a nod. "What do you want?"

"I want you to give Hale a message. Tell him I know what he's up to. I've got a copy of a very interesting disk. The one he keeps in his safe."

"The what?" His eyes grew wide.

"As I see it, Chaz, old boy, it's *your* ass that's on the line—because you left me alone in his office. You better be pretty persuasive when you tell your boss to drop Nelson down a manhole. I'm the only one who's going to do that shoot. Got it? We'll talk about money later. You understand, of course, that my services don't come cheap. Especially now."

Charles made a sour face.

"So? Are we perfectly clear on this?"

"Perfectly," he gasped.

Ben let him go. To be honest, the guy gave him the willies. He was the only man he'd ever met whose expression was both vacant *and* piercing.

Charles rubbed his shoulder.

"Sorry about the arm, but I had to get your attention. You know, Chuckie, you could be in some pretty hot water. I suggest you play your cards very carefully. Unless you do, by Monday morning, you might just be out of a job."

* * *

Hale stood between two men in business suits, staring up at the picture of Piero della Francesca on the mantel. "Actually," he continued, sucking in his stomach, "very little is known about the man's life. He was born about seventy miles southeast of Florence. Worked mainly for the monasteries, confraternities, and country lords."

"No Medici?" asked one of the men.

"Not as far as we know. Surprisingly, after his death he was revered less as a painter than as a mathematician. He was very interested in solid geometry. Even wrote a treatise on perspective."

"Fascinating," muttered the other man. "Has much of his work survived?"

"A few paintings. Religious themes, of course. Mostly in Tuscany, Umbria, and the Marches. Ivy and I made a special Piero Pilgrimage about ten years ago. It was absolutely marvelous."

"Did you use a travel agent?" asked the second man.

"We did. There's a woman in town who specializes in art tours. Here—I'll write down her name for you." He spotted his copy of the most recent IAI catalogue resting on the coffee table. He'd been carrying it around all evening. As he picked it up, a piece of paper slipped out from between the pages and fell to the floor. Hale put his foot over it as he wrote down the information on the cover flap. Then, tearing it off, he handed it over.

"Well," said the first man, "I think I'd better go find my wife. We've got to be up early tomorrow morning."

"Same here," said the second man. "Hale, this was a wonderful party, as always. Thanks again."

They all shook hands.

Hale watched their backs disappear into the crowd and then bent down to retrieve the piece of paper. As he turned it over he noticed it was a drawing. Instantly his body froze.

"Something wrong?" asked Louie, walking up to him

from behind. He was holding a plateful of food. "Ivy asked me to find you and tell you she needs a word right away. It sounded important."

Hale ignored him, his eyes transfixed by the image on the paper. "He's here," he whispered under his breath.

"I beg your pardon?"

"Hawks!"

"Hawks who?"

"Oh, shut up. I've got to think." He looked up and saw John Jacobi standing near the front windows talking to that son of Sophie Greenway's. Who invited them? He felt the back of his neck break out in a cold sweat.

"Hale, old boy, you don't look so hot."

"Just leave me alone!" He started to back away.

"Where are you going?"

"To the gate house."

"Are you all right?"

"Mind your own business."

Louie took a few steps toward him. "But what should I tell Ivy?"

"You're a pathetic excuse for a man, do you know that?" He cast his eyes furtively to the front door. "Tell her and that musclebound doctor of hers to go to hell!"

He bumped past Kate, who was standing just a few feet away, and stumbled into the kitchen. It felt as if all the air had been crushed out of his chest. He had to get outside. Clear his head. Once he was alone in his office, he could think. He knew he had to formulate a plan, and for that he needed quiet. His one trump card—the gun—was going to tip the balance in his favor. If tonight was really going to be the final confrontation, as the words under the drawing implied, let the bastard come! Whoever he was, Hale knew he was ready.

# 19

Rudy burst through the kitchen door and into the dining room, his eyes desperately searching the crowd for his mother. Spotting Bram sitting in one of the wing chairs in the living room, he let his gaze wash over the faces near the fireplace. There she was. Talking with a group of women. In an instant he was next to her.

"Rudy!" she said, giving him a hug. "John said you were here. I've been looking all over for you."

"We've got to talk."

She could see he was breathing hard. "What's wrong?"

He pulled her off to one side. "Something's happened. You've got to come with me."

"Why?"

"It's . . . Just come, okay?"

She could tell he was upset. "What is it? What's going on?"

He looked around the room, making sure their conversation wasn't being overheard. "It's Hale. He's been shot. I think he may even be . . . dead."

Her hand flew to her mouth. "How on earth did *you* find him?"

"I'll tell you later. Right now, you've got to come out to the gate house! That's where he is. We have to do something! Call the police—get a doctor." His eyes pleaded.

"Are you sure he's dead?"

"I didn't touch him, if that's what you mean. But he looked . . . *still.* I couldn't see him breathing."

Sophie knew they didn't have a minute to lose. She crossed to Bram and whispered in his ear, "Call 911 right away. Hale's been shot." She saw the shock in his eyes, but put a finger to her lips. "Don't make a scene. Just tell the dispatcher to send a paramedic and the police right away. Then go find Ivy."

He gave her a cautious nod, rising immediately and retreating into the far hallway.

"Come on," said Sophie, returning to Rudy and grabbing him by the arm.

"But what about the police?"

"Bram's taking care of it. Our job right now is to see if there's anything we can do for Hale."

"What's this?" asked Sophie, noticing a piece of crumpled paper near the Micklenbergs' back door. She picked it up.

"Mom, hurry!"

"Right." She stuffed it into her purse and scurried after him. A wide path had been shoveled in the snow between the main house and the gate house. "How did you get in?"

"The front door was open."

They dashed up the steps and into the first-floor gallery. The only light came from the door at the top of the stairs.

"Is he up there?"

Rudy nodded.

Sophie led the way. As they entered the room, she saw Hale's body on the floor next to the desk. He was lying on his back, one arm flung to the side, the other on his stomach. "He's been shot in the head," she said, bending down.

"What should we do?" asked Rudy, fidgeting with the zipper on his jacket. He stood next to the door, unwilling or unable to come any closer.

Sophie tried to get a pulse. "I'm afraid," she said, holding her fingers to the side of his neck, "he's beyond help." Slowly she stood, taking a moment to examine the scene. The murder weapon was nowhere in sight. The desk was empty of papers. A bottle of Scotch and a half-filled glass sat next to the computer. A cigar had been crushed in the ashtray and then broken in half. Nothing gave any clue as to what had just happened.

"How did you find him?" asked Sophie, turning to her son. He looked so terrified, she wanted to take him in her arms and comfort him like a little child—tell him everything was going to be all right. Except everything wasn't all right.

"Well," he began, his voice just above a whisper, "I'd gone outside for some air and I heard this shot. I looked up and saw the light and knew immediately it'd been fired from up here. So I tried the front door."

"Did you see anyone?"

He shook his head. "When I got inside, the gallery was dark. I ran up the stairs and found . . . I mean, when I saw his body . . . I couldn't move!"

She stepped toward him. "That's fine. You were right to come for me. Now listen for a minute. We have to go back to the main house and talk to the police. Since you found the body, they'll almost certainly ask you some questions. Do you think you can handle that?"

He swallowed hard. "Yes."

"Good. I know how awful this feels. I feel the same way. But you've got to recall everything you saw or heard. It could be terribly important."

He nodded.

"You didn't touch anything did you?"

"No," he whispered. "I don't think so."

Even through his hunting jacket, she could feel him tremble.

# 20

Rudy was led through the crowd to a study on the second floor of the Micklenbergs' home. After taking a chair by the only window, a detective named Cross entered, instructing a uniformed officer to stand by the door and prevent anyone else from entering. Another uniformed officer sat behind the desk with a pad and pencil, ready to take notes. Rudy was nervous, but since he'd had some time for reflection, he felt a bit more confident.

Detective Cross pulled up a chair and sat down. "Now, Rudy"—he glanced at his notes—"will you tell us what happened?"

Rudy took a deep breath. "Well," he began, "I'd gone outside to get some air. The party was pretty smoky."

"What time was this?"

"I don't know. Probably close to eleven."

"What time had you arrived at the party?"

"About ten-fifteen."

"Alone?"

He hesitated. "No. I'd driven over with a friend."

"What's the friend's name?"

"John Jacobi."

The detective nodded. "Go on."

"Well, I was standing out in the back, looking up at the sky, when I heard this gunshot."

"How did you know it was a gunshot?"

Rudy stopped. "I don't know. I guess I just assumed

it. My father owns lots of guns. I'm familiar with the sound."

"All right. Continue."

Rudy didn't care for the man's abrupt manner. He reminded him of the vice principal of his high school in Montana. Crew cut, brown hair. Thick body. Military bearing. "As I was about to say, I was pretty sure it came from the gate house. I looked up at the second floor and saw a light, so I ran around to the front and tried the door. It was ajar."

"You didn't see anyone?"

"No. I heard a dog barking, but that was all. When I got inside, I stopped by the stairs and listened. When I didn't hear anything, I climbed to the top. That's when I found Hale's body."

"Was he still breathing?"

"I don't think so. I didn't actually touch him."

"And you saw and heard nothing?"

"Well . . . as I was coming up the stairs, I thought I heard a sound—like someone closing a door."

"Inside the gate house?"

Rudy nodded. "After I realized what had happened, I stepped over to the window—the one next to the filing cabinets. I saw a figure enter the back door of the Micklenbergs' house."

The detective's head jerked up, like an animal picking up a scent. "Could you tell who it was?"

Rudy shook his head. "No. But it was a woman."

The detective scratched something in his notes. "What was she wearing?"

"A dress. A bright color. Pink maybe. Or red. And a short, dark coat. I don't remember the color. And she was thin. Not large."

"Blonde? Brunet?"

"Sorry. I can't say for sure."

The detective fixed him with a hard stare. "How well did you know Mr. Micklenberg?"

"Not well. I'd met him a few times at the Chappeldine Gallery. That's where I work part-time. I'm a freshman at the University of Minnesota."

"Did you know he was having . . . marital problems?"

Rudy gave him a blank stare. "No."

"Did you two get along?"

Rudy could feel the acid in his stomach begin to churn. "If you mean did I like him, the answer is no."

"Why not?"

"He was . . . a jerk."

"Be more specific."

"He liked to torture people—especially artists. He'd give them a bad review even when they didn't deserve one."

"Sounds like you know what you're talking about."

"I do."

"Who, for instance?"

Again, Rudy shrugged. "Just artists. Kate Chappeldine, the owner of the gallery, spoke about him. Nobody liked him."

"You don't know anyone personally who got one of these bad reviews?"

His eyes fell to the floor.

"Answer the question, Rudy."

"Well . . . yes and no."

"You have to be more specific."

"It's just . . . see, John—"

"John who?"

"Jacobi."

"The same one you came with tonight?"

"Yeah."

"Is he a good friend of yours?"

Rudy nodded. This conversational turn was precisely what he was trying to avoid. He was making a mess of things.

"How long have you known him?"

"About two months."

"Would you say he held a grudge against Hale?"

"No. Absolutely not. See, it's kind of a long story. John's got a show at the gallery right now. Hale came by one afternoon to look at his work. He told several people that he thought it was amateurish, that it lacked depth, among other things. But the review he published in the paper was a good one. Hale wouldn't explain it, even when John called him on the phone to thank him." Rudy had the sinking sense that he was babbling. He'd already said too much.

The detective leaned forward in his chair. "Did Hale ever do anything to you?"

"To me? What do you mean?"

"Anything that might have made you angry with him?"

He shook his head. "Nah. He was just mean."

The detective studied him for a long moment and then turned a page in his notes. "When you entered the second floor of the gate house, did you touch anything?"

"No!"

"Did you notice anything unusual? Anything that didn't look right?"

Rudy scrunched up his face in thought. "Not really."

"Describe the scene for us."

"Well, Hale was lying on the floor in back of his desk."

"Did you see a weapon?"

Rudy shook his head.

"Describe the desk."

"I think it was pretty cleared of papers. There was a bottle of Scotch. And an ashtray. Kind of a funny-looking one. Painted brass."

"Anything else?"

"Maybe some crumbs. And when I walked in back of the computer monitor, my hand brushed against it. It felt warm. Like it had just been turned off."

The detective nodded. "Good. That's good. What else do you remember?"

Rudy closed his eyes. "I just don't see anything else."

"Nothing?" He let the word hang in the air.

"No."

"What about the positioning of the chairs in the room?"

"I think one of them was pulled up to the desk. Like maybe he'd been talking to someone?"

"Is that your conclusion?"

"I don't know. I wasn't there." He glanced at the policeman taking notes. "I don't suppose—?"

"What?" asked Detective Cross.

"Well, I mean . . . I don't suppose it could be a suicide?"

"We found no weapon."

Rudy could feel his stomach turn over.

"What did you do after you discovered the body?"

"I went back to the party and tried to find my mother. I thought I should tell her first, since she knows the Micklenbergs better than I do. Her husband called 911 while we went back to the gate house to see if Hale was still breathing."

"You didn't tell anyone else?"

He shook his head. "Not until my mother had determined he was dead. She tried to get a pulse, but there wasn't one. Then we came back to the main house and she found Ivy—that's Hale's wife. She broke the news to her privately. A few minutes later you guys arrived."

The detective finished writing and then looked up. "What kind of coat did you wear tonight, Rudy?"

"My coat? It's a hunting jacket. Red-and-black plaid."

"We'll need to see it."

"Why?"

"There was a nail sticking out of the rear door. A piece of fabric was caught on it. It may or may not belong to the murderer."

Rudy's hand shook as he passed it over his mouth. "You think it was mine?"

"That's what we need to find out." The detective stood. "That's all for now. But we'll need you to come down to the station sometime tomorrow and sign your statement. Most likely we'll want to talk to you again. You weren't planning to leave town, were you?"

"No."

"Good." He motioned for the officer to follow him out.

# 21

John turned his Blazer into a scenic overlook and stopped. The Mississippi River Valley lay in front of them, vast and black in the weak moonlight. Rudy had said very little after the police finished with him. Sensing his need to get away from everyone who might want to ask more questions, John poured Rudy a stiff brandy and waited while he drank it. Then, explaining to Sophie that he'd make sure Rudy got home safely, he'd stuffed his sullen friend into the front seat of his truck and headed across town to 494, then south to Bob Dylan's famous Highway 61. The lights of Red Wing shimmered in the distance.

"Quite a view," said Rudy, turning down the radio. "I'd like to come back here sometime when it's daylight."

John pointed to the sky. "What do you think of that?"

Rudy leaned forward to get a better look. "The northern lights! I've seen them once before, but they weren't this bright."

"You have to leave the city to get the full effect."

Rudy leaned back in his seat. "Thanks."

"For what?"

"For kidnapping me."

John laughed.

"What an evening."

"Yeah. You don't have to talk about it. We can just sit here and watch the show." He could tell Rudy was a little high.

They were both silent for several minutes.

Finally Rudy said, "Did I ever tell you I used to believe Christ was going to return on the Feast of Trumpets, 1989?"

"Pardon me?"

"Yup. I was going to be whisked away into the heavens with the rest of God's elite. I guess God's apostle got the date wrong."

"Who's God's apostle?"

"The head of our church. Howell A. Purdis."

"I see. Well, that's too bad—for him, I mean."

"And for everybody who sold their houses and businesses and gave the money to the church in anticipation of the great event."

"Well, didn't the church just give it back? I mean, it was their error."

"No way. I guess you could say that was the first time I had a real argument with my father. I told him I thought it was wrong."

"What did he say?"

"He told me the people that did it were following their own conscience. God would bless them in the end."

"In the meantime, they could always go on welfare?"

"I guess."

John unzipped his leather jacket. "Rudy?"

"What?"

"Well, I mean you sound pretty bitter."

He shrugged.

"Do you still believe all the stuff you were taught as a kid?"

Another shrug. "Did you know the first time I was ever around a Christmas tree was this winter? Bram and my mother bought a big Norway pine. I felt kind of funny having Christmas dinner with them. It's a pagan day, you know. Nothing Christian about it."

"Really?"

"And doctors. We never went to doctors, except once when I was little. I've never even taken an aspirin. That is, until last fall. I had to get all these shots before I could attend the university. My dad would have pitched a fit."

"What did you do when you got ill?"

"We sent for the elders of the church to pray."

"And if that didn't work?"

Rudy stretched his arms over his head. "Well, that meant you didn't have enough faith. If you did, God would heal you. Except, I found out from a friend that some of the top ministers were going to doctors. But the people in the local church areas were still forbidden."

John shook his head. "You're lucky you never got sick."

"I know," said Rudy. "I had a good friend die of skin cancer. I didn't realize at the time how treatable it was. She was an older woman. I'd known her since I was little."

"I'm sorry," said John.

"Yeah. Such a waste." He wiped a hand across his eyes. "I used to have to study the Bible an hour every night. And pray two hours a day. We even had a prayer closet. That way Dad could monitor me and Arlene—the woman he married after he divorced Mom."

"What did you pray about for two whole hours?"

"Oh, sometimes I'd go into the closet and sleep. Other times I'd think about . . . you know. Sex."

John grinned. "I did most of my daydreaming in the woods."

"The thing is, in our church, no one could have sex before marriage. Sometimes I nearly went crazy thinking about it."

"Did you have a girlfriend in high school?"

He rubbed his hands along the tops of his jeans. "No. Dad wouldn't have allowed it. We couldn't be unequally yoked together with unbelievers. I could have dated someone in the church, but . . . I don't know. I never did."

John watched him.

"I really want to have kids," continued Rudy. "That would be the greatest. How about you?"

"I haven't given it much thought."

"I'd make sure they grew up being able to make their own decisions about . . . life. About God. Not that my father is a bad man. I know he loves me."

"Do you still believe in God?"

"Yeah. Absolutely. I've just got a lot of sorting out to do. I have to make my peace with certain things. It's hard to explain." He shifted in his seat. "What about you? Do you believe in God?"

"I'm not sure God means to me what he does to you. Fundamentalists have always seemed like a lot of emotional bullies to me. And these TV evangelists . . . I can't stand to watch them. They're so smug about their ignorance." He shook his head. "I hope that doesn't hurt your feelings."

"No," said Rudy, looking up again at the sky. "You know, I used to be so sure about everything, about where I fit. My entire life was mapped out for me. I'd go to Purdis Bible College. Graduate and become a minister like my father. I'd marry, have children, preach sermons every Sabbath, attend ministerial conferences, anoint the sick. Everything was decided. I knew with absolute certainty what was right and what was wrong. All I had to do was believe what I was told and my life would be great. But somewhere along the line, things changed."

"You grew up."

"Maybe. But it's more than that. It's like I hit a wall. Nothing's been the same since." He pressed his fists hard against his temples. "Sometimes, my mind just aches from thinking."

John started the motor and turned up the heat. It was beginning to get cold inside the truck.

"You know, Hale was a terrible man." Rudy leaned his head against the glass.

"I agree," said John. "Was the police questioning pretty bad?"

"Not really. I just told them what I saw."

"And that was?" John knew he shouldn't press him, but he had to know.

"I told them I'd heard someone close the back door while I was coming up the front stairs. By the time I'd recovered from the shock of finding Hale dead on the floor and I'd walked over to the window, all I could see was a form entering the main house."

"Could you describe the person?"

"No, other than to say it was a woman. That's all I know for sure."

John nodded. "I see." He stared straight ahead. "Why did you go outside in the first place?"

"To look for you. I couldn't find you anywhere. Where'd you go?"

"Upstairs."

"I thought that was off-limits."

John shrugged. "I didn't see a sign. Anyway, Bram was introducing you around. I thought I'd take the chance to check out the second floor. See how rich people really live."

"And?"

"There were lots of bedrooms. Oh, and there's a great library filled with old art books."

Rudy nodded. After a minute, he said, "Hey, I've got an idea. Let's drive into Red Wing. See if we can find a Burger King or something."

"All right." John slipped the truck into reverse and pulled back out onto the highway. It was best to let the rest of his questions drop. For now. "That's a good sign, you know."

"What is?"

"You've got your appetite for junk food back."

"After eighteen years of brown rice and vegetables, what do you expect?"

"Perfect arteries?"

"And perfect boredom."

# 22

Late Monday afternoon, Bram stood in front of the window in Sophie's office and watched the traffic move silently along Kellogg Avenue, twelve stories below. Rush hour was always a snarl in downtown St. Paul. The light snow, which had been falling since noon, didn't help. "I can't believe the police suspect that Rudy had anything to do with Hale's murder. Unless there's something we're not being told."

Sophie leaned her elbows on top of the massive oak drafting table, which had served as her desk for the past twelve years. She preferred it to a regular desk. The space available for layout was much greater, but most of all, being of diminutive size, she liked the sense of height and power it gave her. "Then why do they want to talk to him again?"

Bram glanced over his shoulder, but said nothing.

"I just wish . . ." Her voice trailed off.

"Wish what?"

"Oh, you know. What I always wish—that I knew him better."

"Come on now, Soph. Don't tell me *you* think he's involved?"

"No. Of course not." She straightened a stack of papers and looked glum. "But that doesn't mean he's telling us the entire truth. Something's going on with that kid."

"Maybe John knows what it is. They spend enough time together."

"You mean, when he's not working or reading." She dropped her chin on her hands. "He invited me into his room the other night. I couldn't believe my eyes. He must have had two hundred plays up there. He said he'd read every one."

"He burns the midnight oil."

She shook her head. "Why won't he open up to me?"

Bram walked over and stood behind her, putting his hands on her shoulders. "Maybe you want it too much. He senses that and it puts him off."

"Do you think so?"

"I think," he said, nuzzling her hair, "that this has been a bad couple of days. What say I take you out to dinner?"

"I've already made reservations."

He swiveled her chair around, keeping his face very close to hers. "Where?"

"You'll see." She flapped her eyelashes.

"I was thinking maybe a burger and a brew."

"Is that what you were thinking?"

"The oyster bar at the Maxfield?"

"You're getting warmer." All day she'd been fantasizing about the lemongrass beef, heavy on the garlic, served at their favorite Vietnamese restaurant. And, of course, a plateful of delicate spring rolls with vinegar and anchovy sauce.

He straightened up, folding his arms over his chest. "You know"—he walked back to the window—"I've given Hale's murder a good deal of thought. Somebody at that party the other night was undoubtedly responsible. All we have to do is determine the motive."

"I suppose wanting to rid the world of an arrogant ass isn't enough."

He raised an eyebrow. "Not usually."

"A week ago, I would have said Ivy was the one whose life was in danger. First someone takes a shot at her. And then the day she was on your show, she nearly collapsed. I know everyone thought it was just a drug mix-up, but Kate thought otherwise."

"What do you mean?"

"She suggested that Hale was responsible for both."

"Attempted murder?"

Sophie nodded.

Bram shook his head. "What a mess."

"I agree. And now we're involved, whether we want to be or not." She reached for her shoulder bag, the one Bram lovingly referred to as the potato sack. "It's all such a muddle."

Instead of continuing to brood, Sophie decided to take a quick look at her makeup before they headed down to the parking garage. Inside her bag was the small, beaded purse she'd worn to the Micklenbergs' party. With all the commotion yesterday, she hadn't thought to empty it. This morning, she'd simply tossed it into her bag, knowing she could sort out the contents later. As she opened the clasp, she saw the piece of crumpled paper she'd found two nights ago at the party.

"What's that?" asked Bram, seeing her face flush with interest.

She smoothed it flat against the drafting table. "I

found it on Saturday night. Since I was in a hurry, I just stuffed it into my purse."

"And forgot about it?"

"Don't be tedious."

It was a drawing. A sphinx with fire between its paws. A picture of Hale had been pasted in the flames. Underneath someone had printed:

> I'm here and I'm watching. I want you to call the police and tell them the truth. Tell them what you did. Nothing less will be acceptable. *Do it now.* If you refuse, you'll pay the price. Remember: "For every evil under the sun, there is a remedy . . ." *Make that call!*
>
> Ezmer Hawks

Bram moved up next to her. "Who the hell is Ezmer Hawks?"

Sophie was bewildered. "He's an artist. One of Hale's favorites." She tapped a pencil against the top of the desk. "But if he was at the party Saturday night, why didn't he introduce himself? Kate never mentioned seeing him. Neither did anyone else. He's doing a show at the Chappeldine next month."

Bram picked up the note and studied it. "I think the answer is pretty obvious."

Sophie's eyes rose to his face.

"Don't you see? This note makes everything clear. It's not only given us the motive for his murder, but the name of the murderer! Hale was threatened. That's why he went out to the gate house. He must have been waiting there for—"

"Ezmer Hawks," whispered Sophie. "Of course. But what did this Hawks fellow want Hale to tell the police?"

Bram shrugged. "That's just a detail. Maybe Hale did something illegal. Something he got away with. This guy knew about it and wanted him to fess up."

"But why should he care? Hale didn't even know the man."

"He didn't?" Bram scratched his head. "But that's impossible. He must have."

Sophie had to agree. The note sounded too familiar. And come to think of it, it wasn't the first note he'd received from the artist. That day she'd run into Hale at the gallery he'd received one in the mail. She tried to remember his face, his demeanor, after he'd read it. Something had clearly upset him.

"You better show this to the police right away," said Bram. "It's just what they're looking for."

She nodded. "Right."

He put his hands on his hips. "Sophie? What's going on inside that head of yours?"

She looked up, realizing he'd caught the hesitation in her voice.

"Come on. Out with it."

"Well, I mean, Rudy . . . is my son. And right now, he seems to be a suspect."

"So?"

"It's just . . . maybe the police will think I'm trying to manufacture evidence to get him off the hook."

Bram stared at her. "Nonsense."

"Is it? Think about it. My fingerprints are all over the note. If Hawks was careful at all, his won't be."

"But we can't withhold evidence."

Her shoulders sank. "I know. I just think giving it to Detective Cross right now might make matters worse."

Bram brushed a golden hair away from her face. "It's a risk," he said, his voice gentle, "you have to take. In the long run, it's going to be best for everyone if the police can find out the truth."

"Right," said Sophie, though she knew her voice held little conviction.

# 23

"When do the lawyers read the will?" asked Max, his feet propped up on the glass coffee table in his office. He and Ivy were both reclining on the sofa, his arm around her shoulders.

"On Wednesday morning. Everyone named in the document has been summoned to the offices of Weise and Crawford." She closed her eyes and let her head sink back against the cushions.

He leaned over and gave her a kiss. "It'll be over soon."

"Not soon enough."

"Come on, Ivy. Don't get impatient. In a matter of days we'll have everything we want, even *more* than we dreamed."

She loved the look of his strong, doctor's hands. God, how was it possible she'd lived for so many years without passion? What a waste. "I know. You're right."

"Black suits you," he said, tracing the curve of her jaw with his fingers. "When is the funeral?"

"Tomorrow afternoon. It seems like this is my week for funerals."

"Mmm. Right." His mood changed almost instantly as he reached for his glass of mineral water. "How did your lawyer friend do this morning?"

She knew he didn't like Louie. Well, he could just deal with it. Louie was her friend. She wasn't about to send him packing just because Max didn't want him around. "It was hard for him. His wife wanted to be buried at Lakewood, so he made all the arrangements. There were lots of relatives and friends—people he hasn't seen in years. I sat with him in the front row."

"Did you?" He took a sip, making a sour face. "I hate funerals."

"Why? Because they remind you you're mortal?" She squeezed a particularly hard muscle in his arm.

He brushed her hand away. "Is Louie still staying with you?"

She shook her head.

"Good. I don't like competition."

"Oh, get real. You don't seriously think Louie is a threat?"

"He cares a great deal for you."

"The feeling is mutual."

Max downed the rest of his water, setting the empty glass back on the coffee table with a crack. "Wonderful."

Ivy watched him and then got up and moved to the desk, sitting down in his chair. A little space between their bodies felt necessary right now. "Max, you're the man I love. Not Louie. Not Jack Moline. Not Bruce Holland. Not any of the men you've periodically accused me of lusting after."

"And not Hale?"

"Of course not!"

"But you did love him. Once."

She leaned forward, resting her arms on the desktop. "Why do you do this to yourself? Yes. I loved him. A long time ago."

"But it was over?"

"Yes."

"And even if he'd changed his mind, insisted he wanted to work out the problems in your marriage, you would never have gone back to him?"

"Max—"

"Answer the question."

She was surprised by the coldness in his voice. "No. I'm committed to you now. Completely and forever."

His eyes held hers for a long moment before looking away.

"What are you trying to suggest? I hated him! You know that."

"Did you?"

"Yes!"

"As much as I did?"

"More!"

"Enough to kill him?"

Her eyes opened wide. "What?"

He got up and walked to a filing cabinet, lifting out one of the folders. "Have the police questioned you?"

She felt a small spasm in her cheek. "Of course they have."

"And what did you tell them—about us?"

"Nothing!"

He slipped the folder into his briefcase.

"Where is this coming from?" Her mind struggled to understand his sudden anger. "Is it Louie? You can't really be worried about our relationship. We're friends, Max. Nothing more." She'd seen his jealousy before, but it had never been this strong.

He grabbed his suit coat and yanked it on. "I'd never let anything or anyone come between us, do you understand that?"

"Of course."

"Hale deserved what he got."

"Max, you're frightening me."

"Am I?" His eyes flashed.

"Yes!"

His face looked as if it had been carved from a block of granite. Slowly his smile returned. "You're right. After all we've done to achieve this moment, I'm not going to think another negative thought. Negative programming leads nowhere. I know you love me. Come here." He held his arms open wide.

Something about his demeanor continued to frighten her. Still, as he stood there, his handsome face lit up just for her, she couldn't resist.

He folded his arms around her body, whispering very softly, "We both know what happened to Hale. And that secret will bind us together. Forever."

# 24

Bright and early Tuesday morning, Sophie was shown into Detective Cross's office and asked to wait. She was clad in a comfortable pair of old jeans and, compliments of her husband, a WMST sweatshirt. She'd taken the day off. Too much was happening and she needed some time to sort everything out. She felt apprehensive as she took a seat, fidgeting with the note she'd reluctantly brought with her. No matter how sure Bram was, she still wasn't certain this was the best thing to do.

Cross entered a few minutes later, stuffing the remains of a doughnut into his mouth. "Ms. Greenway. I didn't expect to see you today." He sat down behind the desk.

"I didn't expect to be here," she said, pushing the piece of crumpled paper toward him. "I thought you should see this right away."

He picked it up, taking a moment to study the contents. "Where'd you get it?"

"I found it the night Hale died. I was hurrying over to the gate house with my son when I spotted it on the floor next to the back door. Since I didn't have time to look at it right then, I put it in my purse. I forgot about it until yesterday when I was looking for my lipstick."

He studied her carefully. "You think someone gave this to Hale?"

She nodded.

"Who is"—he looked down—"Ezmer Hawks?"

"An artist. A favorite of Hale's. Next month, the Chappeldine Gallery is having an opening for his new work."

"He doesn't sound like much of a friend to me."

"I agree."

"Did anyone see you pick this up?"

She knew what he was thinking. "Just my son. Look," she said, attempting to control her frustration at being doubted, "I'm not lying. I don't presume to know what everything in that note means, but I can't help but believe it's important. My husband feels it's nothing less than a death threat—with the signature of the man who murdered Hale at the bottom."

"And what do you think?"

"I agree with him."

"Because it would get your son off the hook?"

She uncrossed her legs and sat forward in her chair, giving herself a moment to regroup. "I was afraid you'd think that. And you're right—I'd do anything to help my son."

"Even manufacture evidence?"

"No! Of course not. I *found* the note Saturday night. My husband thought you had a right to see it. It might help you solve the crime, and ultimately, that would benefit Rudy."

He nodded. "All right."

Sophie knew he wasn't convinced, but he also couldn't afford to ignore the letter. "Actually, while I'm here, maybe you'd like to explain something to *me*."

"Like what?"

"Well, for one thing, just because my son found Hale's body doesn't mean he . . . shot him."

"That's true."

"So why have you called him down here twice since Saturday night?"

"He hasn't told you?"

"Told me what?"

Cross leaned back in his chair, making a bridge of his fingers. "We found jacket fibers on a nail near the back door of the gate house. We've determined that this was how Mr. Micklenberg's killer exited the building."

"So?"

"The fibers were from your son's coat."

Sophie let out an involuntary gasp. "What are you saying?"

"He lied to us about the chain of events that night, Ms. Greenway. When we talked to him, he never once said anything about going down the back steps. Yet, those fibers tell us very clearly that he did. Also, he said he saw a woman going into the back door of Micklenberg's house. The problem is, you can't see the back door of the main house from the gate house's second-floor window. He may have seen someone go in all right, but he saw it from the back door—or outside. Either way, he's not telling us the truth. We want to know why."

Sophie had never even considered that Rudy might have lied. "I—I don't understand."

"I can see this comes as a shock, and I'm sorry. But until Rudy decides to talk, he's going to remain a prime suspect."

"I see," she whispered.

"We'll check out the note. And I'll send someone over to the Chappeldine Gallery today. Maybe the owner can shed some light on it."

"Maybe," said Sophie. Her mind felt dazed, unable to focus on what he was saying.

Cross looked at his watch. "I'm afraid I can't give you any more time this morning. I have a meeting."

"Of course." She stood. "Thanks for seeing me."

"No problem." He moved around the desk and walked over to the door, opening it for her as she passed in front of him. "Oh, and Ms. Greenway?"

"Yes?" She stopped, meeting his eyes again with some difficulty.

"Try to convince your son to level with us. In the long run, it'll be best for him."

She nodded and then silently left the office.

Since the Chappeldine Gallery was on her way home, Sophie decided to stop and see if Kate had a few minutes to talk. She needed a friend right now. A ton of bricks had just been dropped on her head. Even though deep inside she knew Rudy couldn't have had anything to do with Hale's murder, she was at a complete loss to explain why he'd lied. Still, she had one advantage over the police. She knew the note she'd found was genuine. And it meant something important. Perhaps it was the key that would unlock the truth behind Hale's death. Or maybe it was just a dead end. Either way, she knew she couldn't rest until she found out.

From comments Rudy had made, Sophie knew Hale had visited the gallery several times recently to view Ezmer Hawks's new works. Not only did she want to take a look at them for herself, but she had some specific questions she wanted Kate to answer.

On Tuesday mornings, the gallery was closed to the public. Kate usually worked on the computer in her small office in the back. Sophie knocked loudly, hoping she would hear. In a matter of seconds, the young woman emerged from the hallway, waving a greeting as she trotted to the door. "Hi," she said brightly. "What brings you here so early?"

"Offer me a cup of coffee and I'll tell you." She moved into the darkened gallery.

Kate seemed a bit puzzled by her unexpected appearance. "I've already got the pot on. Come on back." She led the way to the storage room.

Once seated comfortably on a stool, Sophie watched Kate pour fresh coffee into two red and white mugs. She looked unusually pale today. The events of the other evening had no doubt taken their toll on her as well.

"So?" said Kate, wiping up a spill on the counter. She kept her back to Sophie. "What's up?"

"Well, I was hoping you'd have a few minutes to chat."

"About what?"

No use beating around the bush. "Ezmer Hawks."

Kate straightened her shoulders, but didn't turn around. She folded the washcloth very carefully and placed it next to the sink. "What about him?"

"I thought maybe you could give me some background. I'd be interested in anything you know about the man."

"Why?"

Sophie was getting the distinct impression Kate was stalling. She wondered why. "I think he may have had something to do with Hale's murder."

Very deliberately, Kate turned, crossing her arms over her chest. "Who told you that?"

"Nobody."

"Then how can you make such an accusation?"

"That's what I came to tell you. Last Saturday night, as I was following Rudy over to the gate house to see if we could help Hale, I noticed this piece of paper on the floor next to the back door. I picked it up, but I was in such a hurry, I just stuffed it in my purse. I found it again last night." She hesitated, wishing Kate would hand her the mug. She'd only had one cup of coffee at breakfast. Normally she didn't feel human until her third. "It was a note written by Ezmer Hawks to Hale."

"Do you still have it?"

"No. I gave it to the police."

Her eyes searched Sophie's face. "When?"

"This morning. Anyway, it was a drawing. A sphinx with fire between its paws. A picture of Hale was in the fire."

"Really?" Kate handed her the mug. She took a sip from her own as she leaned against the counter. "I think I may have something you'll be interested in seeing. But finish your story first."

"Well," said Sophie, holding the hot mug in her hands, "the thing is, it wasn't just a drawing. There was a note as well. It said"—she reached into the pocket of her jeans and retrieved the piece of paper onto which she'd copied the words:

> "I'm here and I'm watching. I want you to call the police and tell them the truth. Tell them what you did. Nothing less will be acceptable. *Do it now.* If you refuse, you'll pay the price. Remember: 'For every evil under the sun, there is a remedy . . .' *Make that call!*
>
> Signed, 'Ezmer Hawks.' "

Kate held the mug to her lips and peered over it. "What do you make of it?"

"It's pretty clear. Hawks wanted Hale to make some sort of confession. If he didn't, he'd *pay the price.*"

Kate looked surprised. "You think Ezmer Hawks murdered Hale?"

"Don't you? It's an obvious threat."

"I suppose."

Sophie didn't understand her lack of excitement. After all, she knew Rudy had been interrogated the night of Hale's murder. And he'd been called away from the gallery on Sunday afternoon for more questioning. The sooner the murderer was caught, the sooner Rudy could get back to his normal life.

Kate pulled up another stool and sat down. "So. What do you want to know from me?"

"Well, first, was Hawks at the party Saturday night?"

"No. Not that I was aware of. But I'm at a disadvantage. I've never actually met the man."

"You're kidding!"

"We do all our business by mail. He lives somewhere near Soldiers Grove in northern Minnesota. When I offered him the chance to have a show here this spring, he jumped at it. He's been sending me his work little by little. I have seven of his most recent pastels."

"Was he going to come down for the opening?"

"He hasn't said."

Sophie found her answers frustrating. How could she know so little? "Is that normal? Don't you usually go to someone's studio to judge their work before you offer them a show?"

Kate shrugged. "He's eccentric. It wasn't an option."

Sophie wasn't satisfied, yet there wasn't much she could say in response. Kate had the right to run her business any way she saw fit. "I understand that Hale came here several times to see the new work."

"That's right."

"Did he always have such a violent reaction?"

"Violent reaction?"

"Well, the day I was here, he no sooner looked at the drawing than he started to sweat."

Kate turned the mug around in her hand. "Yes, I remember that, too. Actually, the first pieces Ezmer sent down really delighted him. But the next time he came, he did act kind of weird. Almost like he was frightened."

That was it, thought Sophie. Fear. "And you know nothing else about Ezmer Hawks? His age? His background?"

"All I have is a box number, which, by the way, I gave to Hale that morning. That's it."

"You don't have a short biography? A résumé of some kind?"

Kate stood, once again turning her back to Sophie. "Well," she said, drifting over to a pile of papers on top of a low file, "yes, I think he sent me something once. I don't remember where I put it. It was before I had my file system in order. I should ask him about sending another." She turned around, giving Sophie a sheepish smile. "I look a lot more organized than I am."

Sophie found that hard to believe. "Could I see the drawings?"

"Sure. Just wait a sec." She left her mug sitting on the counter and crossed to the back. After rummaging through a group of portfolios, she found the one she wanted. "Okay. Stand over by this easel and I'll go through them with you."

Sophie quickly obliged.

Kate lifted the first one up.

Just as Sophie had suspected, the pastel drawing was rather innocent, almost childlike. Nothing very exceptional. The gesture was kind of nice. "Let's see the next one."

Kate placed it on the easel.

Again, just a simple, rather silly drawing. After a respectful pause, Sophie said, "Next," attempting to keep the impatience out of her voice. This time, the picture was definitely an outdoor scene. A vast blue sky above logs and a flame. "Do you really like these?" she asked, trying not to sound judgmental.

"Yes. I think they're wonderful."

Well, no accounting for taste.

Kate placed the fourth drawing on the easel.

Another outdoor scene. Lots of pinks and violets. Sophie motioned for her to move on.

"This is the drawing I think you might find interesting." Kate lifted up the largest one so far.

Sophie's eyes opened wide. "It's that sphinx with the fire between its paws!" She stepped closer, unable to take her eyes off it. "How did Hale react when he saw this?"

"The same way he acted the day you were here. And

when he saw this one"—she held up an even larger drawing—"he got even more upset."

"I can see why." This time the flames held a face. The likeness of a boy. Sophie stared at it for almost a minute before speaking. "You have no idea what it means?"

Kate shook her head.

"Well, the police can't imagine I made up the note after they see these."

"Excuse me," said Kate. "They think you made it up?"

Sophie sipped her coffee. It was almost too cold now to enjoy. "I was afraid they might assume I'd concocted it as a way of taking some of the heat off Rudy. There's no question now. I've never even seen these before. You can swear to that."

Kate massaged her forehead, a scowl forming.

"What's wrong?"

"Oh . . . nothing."

"Come on. Give."

Kate set the portfolio down, leaning it against a table. "Well, maybe it was a mistake to give that note to the police."

"Why?"

"Don't take this wrong, Sophie—and I'll do anything in my power to make sure nothing comes of it—but even though you haven't seen these before, I know someone else who has. Someone who's shown a great deal of interest in them."

"Who?"

Kate swallowed hard. "Rudy."

# 25

On Wednesday morning, Ivy and Max were shown into a conference room at the offices of Weise & Crawford in downtown Minneapolis. At one end of the long table sat Charles Squire, a tissue held to his nose. He sniffed them a greeting and then blew hard.

"Bad cold?" inquired Ivy, waiting while Max pulled out a chair for her.

"Yes."

"Pity." There was no love lost between them, so why pretend now? Max sat next to her, nodding to a man in a postal uniform. "Don," whispered Ivy, laying her purse on the table. "How . . . nice to see you . . . again." Don Micklenberg was Hale's only living relative. A nephew by his now-deceased brother. She'd spoken with him briefly at the funeral the day before.

"Good to see you, too," said Don, his tone hushed. His gaze returned to Max, eyeing his expensive suit.

Ivy could tell he was curious. "This is Max Steinhardt," she said, deciding it was best not to keep him in suspense. Not that she didn't enjoy keeping people like Don in suspense. She just didn't have the energy today. "My doctor."

Don grunted. "You not feeling well?"

"I've had a few problems lately." She hoped he'd leave it at that. The last thing she needed was his interest in her personal life. It was complicated enough without adding Don, his wife, and his three kids.

"Anything I can do?"

Ivy knew he thought of himself as irresistible to the op posite sex. He'd even made a pass at her once—in the bathroom of his mobile home in Coon Rapids. She banished the repulsive memory from her overburdened mind. "No. That's why Max is here."

His head snapped back. Good. She'd put him off. Her eyes traveled down the table to an elderly woman. "Mrs. Malmquist!" she said, unable to hide her surprise. "I didn't expect—"

"I didn't, either," came the gentle reply. "A lawyer called me Monday afternoon and asked me to be present." Her eyes were puffy and red, a linen handkerchief clasped tightly in one hand.

Ivy continued to stare.

"It's hard for me to get around these days." She nodded to the walker standing next to her chair. "My grandson brought me. He's out in the waiting room." She hesitated. "I'm so sorry about what happened, Ivy. I hope you'll . . . be . . . all right. I wish I could have made it to the funeral yesterday, but . . . it was a bad day for me."

Ivy remembered Betty from years ago when she used to walk her miniature schnauzer in front of their house. She lived in the same neighborhood, though in a much poorer section. She often stopped to talk. Ivy had been fond of the woman. So had Hale. But what the hell was she doing *here*?

"And to think I just saw your husband not two weeks ago."

Ivy cocked her head. "You did? When was that?"

Betty patted the back of her white hair and looked down at the table. "Oh, he came by quite often. Last time he stopped, he had an entire sackful of presents with him. He was such a kind man. So generous."

Generous? thought Ivy. Had the old woman had a stroke?

At that moment, Robert Weise entered the room, a portfolio tucked under one arm. "Good morning," he said, striding to the head of the table and making himself comfortable in one of the chairs. "Everyone is here I see. Good. I think we can begin."

Charles Squire folded his hands over the table. He stared straight ahead.

Betty placed her hands in her lap and leaned forward ever so slightly.

Don fidgeted with his cap.

Max gave Ivy a knowing nod. Together they sat quietly, calmly, their eyes locked on the lawyer.

Robert Weise pulled out the will and adjusted his glasses. "This shouldn't take long. I would ask that each of you refrain from talking until I've finished. There will be plenty of time once we're done to explain anything you don't understand. Are we ready?"

Ivy nodded.

"All right." He began to read. " 'Article One. I, Hale R. Micklenberg, a resident of the City of St. Paul, County of Ramsey, State of Minnesota, being of sound mind and memory and not acting under duress, menace, fraud, or influence by any person whomsoever, do hereby make, publish, and declare this to be my Last Will and Testament, and do hereby revoke all former Wills and Codicils of Wills made by me at any time.' "

Robert Weise peered over his glasses to verify everyone was listening. Assuring himself of rapt attention, he went on. " 'Article Two. I nominate and appoint my assistant, Charles Squire, to be my personal representative, and to act without bond. I direct my personal representative to pay from the residue of my probate estate all of my just debts allowed in the course of administration of my estate, the funeral and burial costs, the expenses of administering my estate, and all estate, inheritance, transfer, succession and legacy taxes and duties occasioned by my death. I further direct that Charles Squire be appointed chairman of the board of International Art Investments, and that he manage this corporation for a period of one year, at a salary of four hundred thousand dollars plus benefits and options. At the end of that year, a vote shall be taken by the stockholders. He may continue or not continue as board chairman at their request.' "

Ivy gave Max a questioning glance. He shook his head and returned his attention to the lawyer.

" 'Article Three. To Don Micklenberg I leave the sum of twenty thousand dollars. If he precedes me in death, the money shall be distributed equally among his heirs.' "

Don bristled, hitting the table with his fist. "Twenty thousand fucking dollars. Is that all I was worth to the old fart?"

"Shh," said Charles, giving him a withering stare. "I'd say you did rather well," adding somewhat snidely, "under the circumstances." He glanced at the man's uniform, his eyes lingering on the soiled red, white, and blue shirt.

Betty peered at the interaction from her perch near the front of the room.

"Please," said Robert Weise, laying his hand flat on the table. "May we continue?" He waited until the room was silent and then went on.

" 'Article Four. To Ivy Micklenberg I leave the sum of one dollar.' "

Ivy gasped!

" 'If she precedes me in death, the money shall be divided equally among her heirs.' "

The edges of Charles's lips curled into a smile.

Ivy grabbed for Max's hand. "He can't do that! I'm his wife!"

"Please," said Robert Weise, looking to Max to quiet her down. "May I continue?"

Max put his arm around Ivy. Since she could feel his body shaking with rage, he was little comfort. She turned and looked him square in the face. His color was ashen.

" 'Article Five. I give and devise all the rest, residue, and remainder of my estate, whether real or personal, of whatever nature and wherever situated, to Betty Malmquist. If she does not survive me, I leave such interest to her surviving grandchildren in equal shares.' "

Betty blinked, glancing at Ivy, and then at each succeeding face.

" 'This instrument, consisting of three typewritten pages, each of which has been signed by Hale R. Micklenberg, was on the date thereof signed, published, and declared by said person to be his Last Will and Testament, in our presence, who at his request have subscribed our names as witnesses, in this presence and in the presence of each other.' Signed, 'Robert L. Weise and John B. Crawford, attorneys-at-law.' "

The room was deathly still.

"What does it mean?" asked Betty, her voice like the tinkling of a tiny bell.

"It means, my dear woman," said Robert Weise, taking off his glasses and laying them on top of the portfolio, "that you have just inherited International Art Investments. In other words, you are now a multimillionaire. Congratulations."

Betty continued to blink.

# 26

"So what do you think?" asked Bram, setting a plate of hummus on the kitchen table. It was Wednesday evening, and he'd promised to prepare dinner. He beamed proudly, pushing a basket of warm pita toward Rudy.

"You made it yourself?" asked Sophie, eyeing it a bit uncertainly.

"Absolutely! I had a woman on my program this morning who had just written a vegetarian cookbook. She gave me the recipe before she left the station."

"May I see it?"

Bram waved the question away. "It's all right here," he said, tapping his forehead.

"You memorized it?"

"Well," he muttered a bit belligerently, "what's so hard about hummus? It's garbonzo beans, tahini, garlic, salt, and olive oil."

Rudy selected a pita wedge and poked at the edge of the mass with the tip of the bread. "It looks kind of . . . thick."

Bram glowered.

"What about the lemon juice?" asked Sophie. She tried to keep her voice neutral.

"What about it? I added several tablespoons, just like the woman said."

"And how did you thin the mixture down?"

"Thin it? Well, I just kept adding olive oil." A hand rose to his hip. "What's wrong with it?"

"Didn't you use any water?"

"No one said anything about water."

"Mmm," said Sophie, giving him a cheerful smile.

"That *mmm* is pregnant with meaning."

"No, it isn't."

"Yes, it is," said Rudy, backing away from the table.

"You stay here," ordered Bram, turning to glare at him. "I want your honest opinion before you leave."

Rudy glanced at the oily heap. "Well, it's . . . ah . . . good. Very . . . unusual. I'm sorry I can't stay and have dinner with you, but I've got some studying to do. Besides, I stopped at Wasserman's Deli on the way home from school for a cornbeef sandwich."

"Heavy on the mustard," added Sophie.

"That's right."

Bram looked from face to face. Finally he erupted: "I'm being humored!"

"No, you're not, darling," said Sophie, putting her arm around him and walking him toward the living room. She motioned for Rudy to take off. He gladly obliged, heading for the stairs. "I appreciate it very much when you want to try new recipes, Bram dear."

"Don't call me *dear*. You're not the only cook in this family."

"You're absolutely right. You're a fine cook."

Bram grunted, stomping to the sofa and throwing himself down.

Sophie sat down next to him, returning her arm to his shoulder. "Have I told you lately what a sweet man you are?"

Bram grimaced.

"Oh, come on." She gave him a kiss.

"Can't you pick another adjective?"

She nuzzled his neck. "How about sexy?"

"You're getting warmer." He kissed her cheek. "Oh, well. You can't hit a home run every time. Maybe we can give the stuff to Ethel."

At the sound of her name being called, Ethel poked her head out of Bram's study and began a slow lurch into the living room. She stopped just short of the sofa and slouched to the floor, heaving a deep sigh.

"Hard day," said Bram, watching her lick her paw. "Her tennis ball got stuck under one of the living room chairs. She was standing—or I should say *sitting*—guard beside it when I got home. Probably never had a moment's peace all day. I mean, you never know what kind of dastardly trick a tennis ball is going to pull."

"Poor thing."

"Yeah."

The front doorbell sounded.

"Bram, tell me the truth," said Sophie. "You didn't invite anyone over for—?"

"Hummus and pita? No. I thought I should try it out once before I went public."

"Good thinking. I wonder who it could be."

"One way to find out." Bram stood and walked directly to the front door, peeking through the peephole. "Oh, shit," he said, clenching his fist. "This is going to be our lucky night. I can just feel it."

"What's wrong?" called Sophie, following him into the hall.

Bram opened the door, nodding to Detective Cross and a uniformed policeman.

"Good evening, Mr. Baldric," said the detective. His eyes traveled over Bram's shoulder to the interior of the home. "I'd like to talk to you and your wife for a moment if I could."

Bram stepped back and allowed them to enter.

"Detective Cross," said Sophie, trying to cover the annoyance in her voice. What was he up to now? He had no business bothering them at home. She hadn't found out anything from Rudy that he didn't already know. "This is a surprise. Won't you come into the living room?"

"No, thanks." He opened his topcoat and lifted out a piece of paper. "I have a warrant here. We'd like to search your son's room."

Sophie was stunned. She'd never anticipated something like this happening.

"Is he here?" asked Cross.

"Yes," said Bram, moving closer to his wife. "What's this all about?"

"May we see the room?" asked the detective. He was polite, but just barely.

"All right." Bram led the way to the stairs, with Sophie bringing up the rear.

Rudy had been given the bedroom at the opposite end of the second-floor hall. It overlooked the backyard, and had a nice view of the Washburn water tower. Up until last fall, it had belonged to Bram's daughter, Margie. In September, she'd moved to St. Cloud with her boyfriend. It was a relatively small room, with a single bed, a desk, and a highboy dresser. In the months since his arrival, Rudy had added his own touches. Several theatre posters, a small stereo with a growing CD collection, and a brick and cedar bookcase.

Sophie knocked on the door. An Eric Clapton song was quickly turned down. "Rudy?" She paused. "There's someone here who wants to see you."

"Just a sec," he called. A moment later the door opened. Rudy's smile faded when he saw who it was. "Oh," he mumbled, squaring his shoulders. "What do you want?"

Sophie touched his arm. "Detective Cross would like to examine your room. He has a warrant."

"No!" Rudy moved to block his entrance. "Don't I have a right to some privacy?"

Sophie took the words like a blow. She saw the frightened look in his eyes. But what could she do?

Detective Cross pushed roughly past them into the room. The uniformed officer followed. "You can all stay if you want, but I must ask you to remain out of the way."

Rudy squirmed away from Sophie and threw himself onto the bed.

The detective gave him a hard look. "Did you hear what I said?"

"I'm not in your way. I'm just sitting here. It *is* my room."

The two policemen exchanged glances.

Sophie wished she knew what to do. She watched helplessly as they began their search. First the closet. Then the bookcase. Minutes passed. Everyone remained silent as the room was pulled apart.

"What are all those?" asked Cross, pointing to several stacks of books under the bedroom window.

"They're plays," said Rudy.

"He's interested in the theatre," offered Sophie, trying to be helpful. For some reason, even that small explanation made her feel like a traitor.

Rudy gave her a sullen look.

Finally, after everything had been thoroughly ransacked, the detective stood in front of Rudy and said, "Get up."

"Why?"

"I want to check under the bed."

"There's nothing under there you'd be interested in."

Why was Rudy doing this? thought Sophie. He was only making things worse.

"If you don't get up on your own, I'm going to have Patrolman Peters here physically remove you. It's your call."

Rudy eyed the man who outweighed him by a good hundred pounds. Pressing his lips together angrily, he rose and stood next to the dresser. He kept his eyes on the floor.

Cross got down on his hands and knees and lifted up the bedspread. Carefully he pulled out a suitcase, and then a cardboard box, about a foot long by two feet wide. First he opened the suitcase. It was filled with religious material. A King James Version of the Bible. A Moffat version. The Greek New Testament. A thick concordance. A Harmony of the Gospels. A Bible dictionary. Two Bible commentaries. And several stacks of pamphlets. The one on top said, *The Book of Revelation Revealed.* Cross paged through a few of them. When he finally glanced up, he gave Rudy a long, measuring stare.

Rudy said nothing.

Sophie couldn't stand the silence—or the misunderstanding that was no doubt forming in the detective's mind. She knew how Cross must see this. Right now her son was being pegged as a crackpot, a religious nut. "Rudy comes from a very religious family. His father is a minister."

"You read the Bible a lot, son?" asked the detective.

Rudy shrugged.

The detective lifted up a volume entitled, *Bible Archeology*. A bookmark stuck out of one end. As he opened it, he nodded, handing it to the patrolman. "Interested in ancient Egypt, are you?"

"I haven't looked at that book since I did a paper in ninth grade."

"Really?" Cross returned it to the suitcase.

Sophie wondered if Rudy could hear the condescension in the detective's voice. For his sake, she hoped he couldn't.

As the detective turned his attention to the cardboard box, Rudy made a move to stop him.

"Hold the kid," ordered Cross, shooting a nasty look at the patrolman.

"Let's just be cool now," said the patrolman calmly. He gripped Rudy's shoulder. "This will be over in a minute."

Cross held up a series of black-and-white photos. "Did you take these?" he asked.

Rudy chewed his lower lip. "I did."

"Who developed them?"

"I have a friend taking a photography class at school. He blew them up for me." The way Rudy was fidgeting, he looked like a caged animal. Sophie felt terrible for him—not that she entirely understood. Why was he so nervous?

Cross paged through them. "Where were they taken?"

"At the Chappeldine Gallery."

"And the man in the photos?"

"He's a friend."

"What's his name?"

Rudy hesitated, but only for a moment. "John Jacobi."

"Why'd you take pictures of this artwork?" He continued to leaf through the stack.

"I like them. They're John's mostly. I got a camera for Christmas. I was just trying it out." He attempted to give the impression that it was no big deal, but Sophie could tell Cross wasn't buying.

The detective stopped when he came to one particular photo. As he held it up, Sophie's heart leapt inside her chest. It was a picture of one of the pastels by Ezmer Hawks. The sphinx with fire between its paws. "What's this?" asked Cross.

Rudy's eyes bounced off it briefly. "A pastel drawing. The artist is going to have a show at the gallery next month."

"And why did you take this picture?"

"I don't know. It interested me. What's the difference?"

Cross returned it to the stack.

"Stop now, okay?" said Rudy, his voice almost desperate. "There's nothing more in there that could possibly interest you."

Sophie watched in frustration as Cross ignored him, flipping through the rest of the contents.

"Come on, now," said Rudy, rubbing his hands against the sides of his jeans. "If you've got any more questions, just take me down to the station. I'll answer anything you want."

Slowly the detective's eyes rose to Rudy's face.

"Please!" he pleaded. "Just let's go."

"Take it easy, son," said the patrolman. He tightened his grip on Rudy's shoulder.

The detective glanced at Sophie, then at Bram. Finally he placed everything back in the box and closed it up. "We'll need to take this downtown." As he stood, he came eye-to-eye with Rudy. He stared at him for a long moment, saying nothing. Then, taking one last look around the room, he said, "We'll show ourselves out."

Bram followed them down the stairs.

After they were gone, Sophie leaned against the doorframe and closed her eyes. Her own tension had been so great, it was all she could do now to remain standing. She felt drained. Confused. Angry. How could they just barge in here and riffle through someone's belongings? She knew it was the law, but it was a horrible violation. She had to say something to Rudy. Comfort him in some way. When she opened her eyes, she saw that he'd put on his jacket.

"Where are you going?"

"Out." He bumped past her.

"But we've got to talk."

"Not now," he said as he rushed down the hall.

"But, Rudy! I have to know what's going on!"

"Later, Mom. I love you. Don't wait up."

# 27

Bram sat behind the desk in his study, intently folding a paper airplane. He knew he should be working on the rewrites of a science fiction thriller he'd started several years ago, but his mind was elsewhere. When it came to disciplined writing, his mind was often elsewhere. Tonight, however, he had a legitimate reason. Sophie was in the kitchen, banging away at the pots and pans, attempting to make a chocolate cake. It was her way of releasing tension. After Rudy had bolted from the house, she'd seemed lost. Bram tried his best to comfort her, but what could he say? He didn't understand the kid's behavior any better than she did. How could he explain that photograph? Or the fact that Rudy had lied to the police?

He glanced up as he saw a movement in the doorway. Sophie was leaning against the doorframe, a spatula in one hand, a ticking timer in the other. She was watching him. She'd changed out of her green wool suit and heels, and was now wearing jeans, a red flannel shirt tucked in at the waist, and soft, brown suede boots.

"I heard the engine noise," she said, nodding to the folded piece of paper on the desk. "I thought you might need a copilot."

His smile was tender. "Always."

"I've been thinking."

"That can be dangerous."

She sat down in his favorite comfy chair. "I can't roll over and play dead just because Rudy won't talk to me. I've got to do something."

"Like what?"

"Well, here's what I think." She licked the spatula. "Hale's past might just be the key. Since I know very little about the man, I've got to do a little research."

"Meaning?"

"Talk to some of his friends and past acquaintances. For instance, who do we know who knew Hale years ago?"

Bram shrugged. "Ivy?"

"True. And I may want to speak with her. But I was thinking of someone else—someone we met at the party the other night. Someone who was very angry at Hale because of a current business deal."

"That photographer?"

"Exactly. Ben Kiran." She hesitated. "So I called him."

"You did *what*?"

"He lives in West St. Paul. It's a listed number; it wasn't hard to find."

Bram was amazed. When Sophie got a bee in her bonnet, there was no stopping her. Sometimes that was good; sometimes not. Whatever the case, this whole situation made him uneasy. "And?"

"I asked if I could come over and talk to him."

"Now?"

Sophie jumped up. "I can't just sit around the house and do nothing!"

Bram watched her begin to pace.

"I know it's a long shot, but I've got to start somewhere. Maybe Ben has some idea who this Ezmer Hawks is—or where I can find him. Or maybe he knows something he doesn't realize is important."

"Are you going over there *now*?"

Sophie looked at her watch. "Yes. I said I'd arrive around eight. So"—she plunked the timer down on the desk—"you're in charge of seeing that our cake comes out on time." She handed him the spatula.

He took it and stared at it as if she'd handed him a scepter of office. "I'm not so sure this is a good idea."

"Why? All you have to do is take a toothpick and poke—"

"No! I'm not talking about the cake."

"Then what?"

He rose and stepped around to the front of the desk. "I'm not sure you should get involved in this, Soph. The police are professionals. Let them handle it."

"Oh, the police are doing just a *fine* job. I especially liked the way they barged in here tonight and terrorized my son."

Bram shook his head. He knew trying to change her mind was useless. "Okay," he said, taking her in his arms. "But you'll call me if you need me?"

"Of course I will. I've left his phone number on the fridge." She pressed her head tightly to his chest. "You just stay here and keep the home fires burning, the paper airplanes flying, Ethel's tennis balls in plain sight, and that cake from turning into a piece of charcoal." She smiled up at him, kissing the bottom of his deeply cleft chin.

* * *

Ben wiped the sweat from his face with a thick white towel as he ushered Sophie into the living room of his town home. It was a spacious, sparsely decorated room dominated by a tan-and-white-striped futon couch and two leather chairs. He was wearing navy blue sweats and a red bandanna around his head. He'd obviously been exercising before she arrived. A Nordic Track sat in one corner of the room.

"Is Rhea here?" she asked, making herself comfortable on the couch.

He shook his head. "She's stopping by a little later. Her dance group is in rehearsals for another show they're doing next month in Madison. At the university," he added, disappearing into the kitchen and reappearing a moment later with a pitcher of orange juice and two glasses. "Can I offer you some?" he asked.

"That would be nice." She waited while he poured.

He handed her the glass and said, "I'm not exactly clear on why you wanted to talk to me tonight. I really don't know that much about Hale Micklenberg."

She took a sip. "But you said something interesting the other evening. You mentioned you knew him years ago. He was working as a counselor in a summer arts camp?"

"That's right." He sat down in one of the leather chairs and tossed the towel over his shoulder. "I was eleven. My parents had always encouraged me to take an interest in drawing and painting. My father was an illustrator, mostly of children's books. When Mom and Dad heard about the arts camp, they thought it would be fun for me. My sister was going to go the next year, but as it turned out, there wasn't a next year."

"Really? Why?"

"A kid was lost."

"What do you mean? In the woods?"

He shrugged. "Maybe. I don't think anyone knows for sure."

"He was never found?"

"He just disappeared."

"That's awful!"

"Yeah." He removed the sweatband from around his head. "That's why they shut the place down. I heard the people who ran it lost their insurance. Nobody would cover them anymore."

"How did it happen?" Sophie leaned back against a pillow and sipped her juice.

"Nobody knows. We used to line up before dinner so that the counselors could count heads. Eric—his name was Eric Hauley—simply didn't show up one evening, so they went looking for him. They searched his cabin. Nothing was missing, except for the clothes he had on that day."

"How old was he?"

"I don't know exactly. About the same age as me I think."

"How well did you know him?"

"We took a canoe out together a couple of times. I liked him. He had a lot of guts. When one of the counselors would piss him off, he sometimes walked into Bright Water. That was the nearest town." He shook his head and looked out the window. "Camp Bright Water. What a crock."

"Was that allowed? Leaving the campsite, I mean?"

"No way. But Eric didn't care. He was kind of independent. Headstrong. He and Hale really rubbed each other the wrong way. Hale liked to needle him. Nothing Eric did—especially artistically—was ever right. Even some of the other counselors noticed the antagonism . . . and I think the head of the camp talked to Hale about cooling it. But the needling didn't stop. It was almost like they were locked in some kind of competition. I never got it. I mean, Hale was a grown man. But then again, he liked to set himself up as the final word on all things artistic. It didn't surprise me to find that, years later, he'd actually become an art critic. Eric thought he was a nerd. So did most of the other kids." He paused to wipe his arm across his forehead. "I remember Eric worked for almost a week with some ferroconcrete and bricks. He was building a barbecue pit. It was really a great idea. He had this picture of an Egyptian sphinx up on the mirror in his room—"

Sophie nearly choked on her orange juice. "A what?"

"Yeah." Ben smiled. "Great idea, huh? He built the thing to look just like a sphinx. Between the paws he'd made a deep pit for the logs. The first night we used it for roasting hot dogs, the entire camp cheered. I think we all felt like we were ancient Egyptians—not that they had hot dogs back then, but you know what I mean. We were kids and we were having a ball. Eric was the center of attention. He really did have a great deal of artistic talent. He just wouldn't kiss Hale's ass." He grimaced, as if the idea turned his stomach.

Sophie was almost too stunned to speak. Here was a connection to the paintings at the Chappeldine Gallery. To Ezmer Hawks. But what did it mean?

Ben threw back his head and chugged the juice until he'd drained the glass. Then he poured himself some more. "The funny thing was, there was an old woman who lived on a farm about a mile outside of Bright Water. She said she often saw Eric walking into town. She was sure she'd seen him the day he disappeared."

"So the authorities thought he might have run away?"

"I guess. They ruled it a disappearance. No foul play was ever established. What I can't understand is: if he was going to hit the road, why didn't he take any of his things?"

"I'm sure the police and the camp officials wondered that as well."

He nodded.

"But no one ever found out?"

"Sorry. That's all I know."

"How did Hale take the disappearance?"

He shrugged. "I guess he was upset. I don't actually remember him saying anything. An assembly was called the next day. The camp director explained what had happened. Some police came and asked questions. The counselors wanted to make sure we weren't traumatized or anything, so we talked about it afterward. The day after that my parents came to get me. That's it. End of CBW."

"CBW?"

"That's what we all called camp. The brochures my dad showed me had this very outdoorsy logo. A bunch of logs with a flame above it, and CBW stamped across the top. Nice place, really, except for the occasional asshole like Hale."

Again, Sophie thought of the pastel drawings at the gallery. One of them looked very much like the description of that logo. This was too incredible to be a coincidence. "I don't suppose you know someone named Ezmer Hawks?"

"Who?"

"He's an artist."

"Never heard of him." He drained half the glass. "Why do you ask?"

"He was at the party the other night. Hale got a note from him. And a drawing—a sphinx with fire between its paws. Hale's face was in the fire. The note demanded that Hale tell the police about something that happened in his past. After what you've told me, I think it may be related to this incident at Camp Bright Water."

Ben whistled. "Unreal!"

"Maybe Hale had something to do with Eric Hauley's disappearance."

"You mean like he . . . caused it?"

Sophie was silent as she considered the question. Finally she said, "Maybe."

"As in . . . *killed him*?"

"I suppose we can't rule it out."

"But who's Ezmer Hawks? How did he know about any of this?"

Sophie tugged on the strawberry blonde wisps of hair around her ears as she thought it through. "There wasn't a kid at the camp with that name?"

Ben shook his head. "No, I'd remember. It's not a name you'd forget."

Sophie had to agree.

"Wait a minute."

"What?"

Ben pointed a finger at her. "Eric Hauley? Get it? E. H. Ezmer Hawks. They have the same initials."

Sophie felt as if she'd been struck by a bolt of lightning. "Of course!"

"Maybe they're one in the same person. Eric didn't die. Maybe he really did run away. And he came back to . . ." He let the sentence trail off.

Sophie's eyes held his.

"Eric hated Hale. I know that for a fact." He sat forward eagerly in his chair. "This is incredible. Is it possible we're onto something here?"

"If what you're telling me is true, then yes. But . . ."

"What?"

"Well, someone made an attempt on Ivy's life a couple of weeks ago, too. At least it looked that way. As I think about it, there might even have been two attempts." She paused. "Didn't you say that Ivy was at the camp that same summer?"

"Sure! She was there. Maybe she's part of it!"

Sophie was somewhat repelled by his enthusiasm. Perhaps it was his normal style, but it seemed excessive.

"Are you going to talk to her?" he asked. "I think we should. She might know more than she's told the police."

At the sound of the doorbell, he rose and sprinted

into the front hall. "Be just a minute," he called over his shoulder. "Hi!" he said, opening the door for Rhea and lifting several paper sacks out of her arms. "You got Chinese. Great!" He gave her a kiss on the cheek.

As Rhea stepped into the living room, she saw Sophie sitting on the couch. "You have company," she said, glancing at Ben.

"Yeah. You remember Sophie Greenway. From the party the other night?"

Sophie stood.

"Please, don't get up on my account," said Rhea, giving her a thin smile. She took off her coat and hung it in the coat closet.

"No, really. I have to go. It's getting late." All Sophie wanted to do right now was ruminate. If she took the parkway back to Minneapolis, she'd have plenty of time to herself.

"We've been having a great talk," said Ben.

Sophie was curious about one more topic. "I was wondering: did you ever figure out who was going to photograph the new IAI spring catalogue?"

Ben gave her his best Cheshire cat smile. "I am. Of course."

"Really?"

"No question about it. Chuck Squire's a good buddy of mine."

"Chuck?" Sophie repeated the name with undisguised amusement. Nobody called Charles Squire *Chuck*. At least, nobody who'd lived to tell the tale. "That's wonderful. Congratulations."

He grinned. "Thanks. We're going to finalize the deal tomorrow. Did you know Chuck's the new president of IAI? Lucky for me."

Sophie was surprised. She'd assumed Ivy would take over that position. "Well, then, give *Chuck* my best."

"Will do. But wait. We haven't finished talking about Hale yet." He seemed disappointed by her departure.

"Hale?" said Rhea, giving him a puzzled look.

"Yeah! Wait until I tell you the whole story. It will blow your mind!"

"Ben," said Sophie, her voice taking on a cautionary tone, "right now I'd like to keep this just between us, at least for a few more days. There are some facts I need to check out before this gets around. I'd like to handle it myself."

"Oh." Again, he seemed disappointed. "Sure. I suppose."

"Thanks. Good to see you again, Rhea." She wondered what two newly divorced people were doing spending so much time together. Well, to each his and her own.

"You're sure you won't stay and have some dinner with us?" asked Rhea. She grabbed the sacks from Ben's arms and headed into the kitchen.

"No, thanks. Another time perhaps."

"Sure thing," said Ben, walking her to the door. "You let me know if there's any way I can help. This is all pretty incredible. I feel like Sam Spade!"

He looked more like Alec Baldwin. She couldn't help but sigh. Oh, well. Bram wasn't exactly chopped liver.

Ben entered the kitchen and got down two plates and two wineglasses from the cupboard. Rhea was already sitting at the kitchen table, unwrapping the cartons of food. "Did you get the shrimp toast?"

"Would I forget your shrimp toast?"

He grabbed the bottle of chardonnay off the kitchen counter and sat down. "No." He grinned. "Not if you know what's good for you."

"I'm not sure I do," she said, her eyes grazing his.

"Oh, come on. Like I said, one day at a time." He handed her a plate and then poured the wine. "To us," he said, holding the glass high.

"To . . ." She stopped.

". . . us," he said, completing her sentence.

Reluctantly she nodded, clinking her glass against his.

"I assume that you've heard about the reading of Hale's will this morning." He selected the carton of chicken and pea pods and dumped some onto his plate.

"No," she said, continuing to sip her wine. "Other than what you just said. About Mr. Squire."

"Hale left Ivy one dollar." He laughed.

"You're kidding!"

He shook his head. "That bastard. That stinking, slimy, arrogant bastard! He left everything to some old woman. Ivy didn't inherit a penny."

Rhea stared at him. "Why do you hate him so much?"

"Me? Who said I hated him?"

"It's the way you look every time his name is mentioned."

"You're crazy. I just don't like to be shafted in a business deal."

"No, it started before that."

"Eat your pepper steak." He popped a piece of the shrimp toast into his mouth.

After a few minutes of total silence, he said, "Now who's acting funny?"

She felt a chill in the room. "I'm just not very talkative tonight."

"Well, then I'll do the talking. First order of business is"—he made a trumpeting sound—"I may have a solution to all your financial problems."

"What do you mean?"

"I know a way to get my hands on the money you need to sponsor a tour for your dance company."

"Ben—"

"Now," he said, holding up his hand, "don't worry. It's all legit."

"I doubt it."

"You wound me when you say things like that, Rhea. Sometimes business . . . has rough edges. But we can't let that stop us. It never stops the big boys. Just wait and see."

Ben had always wanted to play in the big leagues, as he called it. One day she hoped he'd finally grow up and realize that wheeling and dealing weren't going to get him anywhere. It was his talent he needed to rely on. Maybe she was naïve, but that's what she believed. "Are you going to tell me what you and Sophie Greenway were talking about?"

"Eventually."

"But it has to do with Hale's death?"

He nodded, his mouth too full of food to talk.

She stared off into space.

"Say, what *is* wrong with you tonight? You're a million miles away."

"Maybe so."

"Care to talk about it?"

"Not really. Except—"

"What? You can tell me anything."

She finished her glass of wine. She was beginning to feel a slight buzz. "Well . . ."

He poured her more wine.

"To be honest, I know something about the night Hale died."

He stopped chewing. "Like what?"

"It's a secret."

He became instantly angry. "No secrets, Rhea. That's what got us in trouble last time."

"What are you talking about? Secrets had nothing to do with our breakup. Why are you getting so hostile?"

"Just tell me!"

She finished the second glass of chardonnay. God, she loathed white wine. She wished he'd opened a bottle of cabernet. "If you must know, I saw someone."

He stared at her. "Define *saw someone*."

"I saw someone outside the night of Hale's party."

"Who?"

"No, you don't."

"This isn't a game!"

"I know that!"

"Then tell me."

"I won't."

"Why?"

"Because I promised this person I wouldn't say anything until we had a chance to talk."

"You've already talked to . . . *someone*?"

"Briefly."

He raised an eyebrow. "What are you up to?"

As she picked up her chopsticks, she realized that she'd completely lost her appetite. "I want some information."

"About what?"

"Look," she said, leaning back in her chair, "I'm simply not going to talk about this anymore. I should never have brought it up. It's just, you were being so smug about that conversation you had with Sophie."

"And you're too damn competitive to ever give me an edge." His smile returned.

"I hate it when you wax psychological."

He slipped his hand over hers. "All right. I'll stop." His expression turned serious. "Want to see my new rubber ducky?"

"Huh?"

He wiggled an eyebrow.

"You mean a bath?"

"If you'll join me."

She hesitated. She'd never felt so torn in her entire life.

"I've got the music all selected. The sandalwood incense is waiting to be lit. And I have a bottle of merlot and two glasses waiting for us tubside."

"You're incorrigible."

"I know."

"I should go home, take a quick shower, and hit the sack."

"Oh, no," he said, beating his chest and shrieking, "another attack of the *shoulds*!"

She started to laugh.

"Come on," he said, pulling her to her feet. He put his mouth next to her ear and whispered, "I love you, you know? I never stopped."

She felt his arms slip around her body. There was no use arguing. She didn't want to leave. She simply had to put all her questions on hold. If everything went as she hoped, in a matter of days she'd know the truth.

# 28

Ivy dialed Louie's home number. It was nearly midnight. Thankfully he rarely went to bed before one. As she switched off the sound on the TV with the remote, she heard him answer, "Hello? State your name, rank, and serial number."

"Hi. It's Ivy."

"Hey, kiddo! Good to hear from you. I called your house earlier today, but you must have been out. Since I didn't feel like shooting the breeze with the machine, I hung up."

She could hear him crunch something. "What are you eating?"

"None of your business. I will say, since I've withdrawn my membership from teetotalers of America, I have developed quite a penchant for junk food. But, disciplined man that I am, I'm limiting my intake. Only so much a night."

He sounded high. "If you won't tell me what you're eating, then what have you been drinking?"

He laughed. "Well, let's see here. Ah, yes. The label on the bottle says rye whiskey. It's quite good—at least, it has the desired effect."

Ivy wondered if she should be worried about him. Alcohol and grief were often a potent combination. "How are you . . . feeling?"

"I'm holding up. But my stomach has been acting funny. I talked to my doctor and he said to try an antacid. To be honest, I was a little embarrassed when I bought the bottle. I've never had trouble with my digestion before."

"Age gets us all in the end." She could hear him crunching again.

"Hey, where's my mind?" he exclaimed. "What happened this morning at the lawyer's office? Am I now speaking to a genuine heiress?"

Ivy could feel her stomach tighten. "Oh, Hale was very generous."

"Really? What's the bottom line?"

She closed her eyes. "One dollar."

The line was silent. "Pardon me?" he said after a long pause. He started to laugh. "This connection is bad. I thought you said one dollar."

"I did."

Again, silence. "How—how is that possible? You'd seen his will, hadn't you? I remember years ago you mentioned he'd shown it to you."

"He must have changed it."

A more thoughtful crunch this time. "But he can't do that. This is a community property state. You're entitled to half his estate."

"Max is checking into that with his lawyer, but it doesn't look promising."

"Why? I don't understand."

"It's that prenuptial agreement we signed."

"But that was in case of divorce."

"Not according to Hale's lawyers."

"God, I suppose that does muddy the waters. Ivy, I'm so sorry. I really am. This is terrible. I should have seen it coming. I should have found a way to protect you!"

"It's not your fault."

"But it is. I helped write that damn thing!" More silence. "Maybe there's something I can still do—legally."

"I don't think so."

"But I have to try!"

"Max wants to handle it."

"But if there are loopholes, I'm best qualified to find them."

How was she supposed to tell him that Max had insisted she find herself a new lawyer? No, not insisted, *demanded*. She was squarely in the middle—between the two men she loved most in the world—though she cared about them very differently. Max was her passion. But Louie had been a friend and ally since her youth. How could Max place her in such an unconscionable position? It was so callous of him.

"Ivy? Are you still there?"

"Yes."

"I'll start tomorrow, then. I'll force the court to see it our way, don't worry. I'm every bit as good an attorney as those jackasses Hale hired. You'll see."

"Louie?"

"What?"

She had to stall. She couldn't deal with this tonight. She got an idea. "Listen, tomorrow morning I was going to visit the *Times Register* offices and talk to Hale's editor."

"Why?"

"Well, to be honest, Hale never actually wrote that column in the paper. I did."

"You're kidding."

"Afraid not."

"Ivy, that's incredible. That guy was a phony from the word go. Does anyone else know?"

"No. I promised to keep it a secret. But now that he's dead, I want the paper to recognize me. I think once they understand, they'll offer to let me continue the column. I can use the money."

"Don't worry about finances, kiddo. I'll break that will if it's the last thing I do."

She felt warmed by his concern. "Maybe you'd like to drive over to the paper with me. I could use the moral support. Are you free tomorrow morning?"

"Completely. I've taken a leave of absence from the firm. Shall I pick you up?"

She smiled. "That would be great."

"How does ten sound?"

"Perfect. And Louie?"

"What?"

"Thanks for always being on my side."

"Always, Ivy. Always."

By morning, after a long, sleepless night, Ivy had made a decision. When it came to Louie, Max was simply going to have to stuff his jealousy. She would not find another lawyer. She would not dump him as a friend. And that was all there was to it.

Louie arrived promptly at ten. By ten-thirty, they were seated outside the office of Aaron Johanssen, arts editor for the *Minneapolis Times Register*. Ivy had known Aaron for many years. She found him to be fair and generally quite pleasant. Ever since she'd made up her mind to tell the truth about Hale, and about her own complicity in his lie, she'd felt a sense of relief. She also relished the idea of exposing her husband as the fraud he was. It was like that fairy tale: *The Emperor's New Clothes*. She couldn't wait to show the world how naked Hale had been all these years.

As she waited, she glanced at Louie. He didn't look

good. She wondered if he had a hangover. "How are you feeling?" she asked softly.

"So-so." He placed a hand over his stomach.

"It's not a hangover?"

"Who made you my mother?" His frown turned immediately into a smile. "No, Ivy. It's not a hangover. The night after your party, to be honest, I did have a doozer."

"I wondered where you'd gone that night. I didn't see you for such a long time. Then, when the police were searching the house, there you were, upstairs in your room."

"And until I was so rudely interrupted, I was sleeping like a baby."

"More like a drunken sailor."

He sniffed, raising an eyebrow. "I decided next day that I was never going to do that again. Champagne can sneak up on you." He reached into his pocket and took out several antacid tablets, popping them into his mouth.

"Your digestion is still giving you problems?"

"It's nothing," he said, squeezing her hand. "But thanks for worrying." He chewed for a moment and then said, "How's Max?"

Not the topic she would have picked, but she knew she had to say something. "Fine. He's in surgery all day today."

Louie winced. "What a profession."

"Yeah." The truth was, Max was beginning to worry her. He seemed to think, now that Hale was out of her life for good, that he had a right to make demands—unreasonable demands from her standpoint. After all, as he'd begun to point out almost hourly, he'd risked everything for her. That kind of talk made her uneasy. She'd risked every bit as much—even more. And his jealousy was beginning to frighten her.

The secretary at the desk put down the phone and said, "Mrs. Micklenberg? You can go in now."

She looked at Louie. "Wish me luck."

"You don't need it. Just tell them the truth, kiddo."

She hoped it would be that easy.

"Ivy," said Aaron, rising and motioning her to the chair across from him. "How nice to see you. I was so terribly sorry to hear about Hale. I'm sure the police will find out who did it. It's not much of a consolation, but it's something."

She nodded and sat down.

"How are you doing?"

"It's been hard."

"I don't doubt that." He dropped a file into a wire basket on his desk and leaned forward, studying her. He was a small man in his mid-forties. Mousy brown hair and eyes. "Well. So. What can I do for you?"

She decided to make this encounter as brief as possible. No extraneous details. Nothing but the facts. "I need to tell you something. Something important."

"Yes?"

"Hale never wrote the column that appeared in your paper. I did."

He stared at her.

"My husband and I made a pact years ago. I would write the column in an effort to further his career. In return, I would reap the benefits as his wife. Not a very liberated arrangement, I grant you, but then, I was quite young at the time. I also promised total secrecy."

"I . . . don't know what to say."

She held up her hand. "Let me finish. I've come to ask you to put an end to this charade. Hale's column will be up for grabs now. I'd like you to know that it can continue as it always has, but I want my name on it. I am a tenured professor of art history at Morton, so I bring my own credentials to the job. You can tell the truth about this matter—or not—however you want to play it. But I want to be free to discuss it with the art community. I think, after all these years, I deserve that much."

Aaron picked up a pencil and began to twist it between his fingers. "Ivy, I—"

"You believe me, don't you?" She watched him fidget. His body language told her he didn't.

"To be honest, I don't know what to think."

"I wouldn't make something like that up!"

He sighed. "We . . . I don't know that. And, well, I did hear that Hale was not very . . . liberal in his bequest toward you."

Her mouth set angrily. So. The gossip mills were already grinding their venom.

"I can see why you'd be angry," continued Aaron. "Don't get me wrong. But . . . as far as your taking over the column, I don't think that's possible."

"Why?" She perched on the edge of her seat. "Tell me *why*, Aaron. I'm the best qualified! I've been doing it for years!"

"That remains to be seen." He leaned back in his chair. "Even so, the fact is we've already offered the job to someone else."

"What? Who?"

"Charles Squire."

She felt as if he'd slapped her across the face. "Tell me this is a joke. You can't be serious."

"Indeed we are. We felt he was perfect for the job. When he came to us yesterday afternoon—"

"He came to you?"

Aaron nodded. "He explained that he'd been the managing editor of *Squires Magazine* for several years before Sophie Greenway took it over. He left to pursue other interests."

"He left because his father realized he was an inept idiot and fired him!"

Aaron gave her an indulgent smile. "He's now the CEO of IAI. As I see it, he has ample qualifications."

He rested his hands on the desk, palms up. "I think, in a more sane moment, you would agree."

"Never!" she said, rising from her chair. "Not in a million years."

Charles Squire—everywhere she went, he was there supplanting her. If anyone had benefited by the death of her husband, it was Charles Squire.

"I'm sorry I couldn't be of more help," said Aaron, touching the tips of his fingers together.

Ivy started for the door.

"Do keep in touch."

"Go to hell," she said, slamming it behind her.

# 29

The gate house door creaked open.

"Oh," said Charles, standing behind it, the edges of his mouth turning down in disappointment, "it's you." He gave a weary sigh, adjusting the flower in his lapel. "I thought you might be Mrs. Malmquist and her grandson."

"You should oil those hinges." Ben smiled. "Well," he said, rubbing his hands together, "I'm right on time. May I"—he twirled his finger—"come in?" He'd always been amused by people like Charles, men and women who wore their ennui like a fashion statement. He moved silently into the first-floor gallery.

"Come with me," said Charles, switching on the track lighting. Mozart's *Requiem* played from two speakers at the far end of the room.

Ben decided *Mrs. Malmquist and grandson* must be

potential clients. The gallery was being readied for a showing.

Once upstairs, Charles took a seat behind the desk and waved Ben to a chair. He looked perfectly at home in Hale's old office. He'd even made a few changes. Gone was the gaudy brass ashtray. In it's place was a cut-crystal bowl filled with miniature chocolates. And the modern leather chairs had also been replaced, this time by two elegant antique wing backs covered in a subtle, mauve silk.

"Nice touch," said Ben, sitting down on one of them.

Charles nodded, eyeing Ben's plaid shirt.

Ben took off his bombardier jacket. That way, Charles could get a better look at the fascinating contrast between plaid and brocade.

"So," said Charles, unwrapping a chocolate, "I assume you've come to talk about the photographs for the spring catalogue."

"Among other things."

They stared at each other, both understanding the implication.

"As I said to you on the phone," continued Charles, slipping the contract folder out of the bottom desk drawer, "I am prepared to offer you the job."

"Good."

"I do need to have some estimate of the cost."

"Of course." Ben leaned forward and wrote a figure on a notepad. He shoved it toward Charles and then leaned back, waiting.

Charles stared at it. "Is this a joke?"

"No joke."

"You've got to be out of your mind."

"Afraid not." He folded his arms over his chest. "See, I'm planning to use the extra cash to finance a national tour for my ex-wife and her dance company. What's a couple hundred thousand, give or take, to you now that you've become president of IAI? Besides, you needn't worry. Your capital will be put to good artistic use."

Charles was silent. After eating another chocolate, he asked, "Did you bring the disks?"

"They're right here." Ben tapped his pocket.

"How do I know you haven't made copies?"

"You don't."

He drummed his fingers on the desktop. "I need some time to consider this."

"You've got one minute."

Charles's eyes flashed angrily. "Who do you think you're talking to?"

"Well, for starters," said Ben, "I'd say I'm talking to the man who helped falsify Hale's 1994 tax return. Second, I believe that same man participated in helping Hale to hide money in several Swiss—"

"You can't prove any of this!"

"But, Chuck, you know I can."

"Those disks are merely records."

"Do you really want to chance it? Maybe I should drop them off at the nearest IRS office and see what *they* think?"

Charles sat forward in his chair, folding his hands over the contract file. "What if I called your bluff? I didn't even start working for Hale until six weeks ago."

"Plenty of time."

"Most of the information recorded on those disks happened years ago."

"A minor point. Come on, Chuckie. We both know one of those foreign accounts has your name on it. What was it? A bribe? You discovered the extent of Hale's illegal dealings—and to keep you quiet, he gave you a . . . small gift? Unless you're smarter than I thought, the information I have will nail you, as well as your ex-boss."

Slowly Charles rose from his chair. "I believe our meeting is over, Mr. Kiran. I want you to leave."

Ben was stunned. He hadn't expected this. "But—"

"I don't care if you mail those disks directly to the White House! Publish them in the Congressional Record for all I care. That was Hale's business, not mine. I was merely an assistant with no knowledge of any untoward business activity. Neither you nor anyone else can prove otherwise. Believe me when I tell you, Mr. Kiran, I *am* smarter than you think. Smarter than anybody's ever given me credit for. With the money I have at my disposal now, I could tie up any potential litigation in court until hell freezes over." He leaned forward, pressing his hands on the desktop. "And I can eat someone like you for breakfast."

Ben was speechless.

"Now, get out!" roared Charles.

"But . . . the shoot?"

"Didn't you hear me? I thought I'd made myself perfectly clear." He yanked on his pin-striped suit. "If you're too thick to get it, I'll say it again. You and that ex-wife of yours can rot! I will not be issued an ultimatum. Not by you. Not by Hale. Not by anyone!"

Ben took a moment to get his bearings. Charles did seem to have the upper hand. Slowly he rose and dropped the disks on the desk. It didn't matter. He had several copies at home. "You know what, Chuckie? You've turned beet red."

Charles glared at him.

"You clash with your chairs."

"Get out!"

"I'm going." As he got to the door, he had the urge to turn. He wanted to say *you haven't seen the last of me, buddy*. But not only did that sound trite, unless he could come up with another plan, Charles may indeed have seen the last of him.

# 30

"Can I help you, sir?" asked the hostess, walking up to Sophie with several menus tucked under her arm. It was Thursday evening, and the dining room of the new Mediterranean Winds restaurant was packed.

"Why, yes," said Sophie, using her deepest voice. Once again, in order to write a completely honest restaurant review—a review she'd promised her paper *last* week—she'd donned a disguise. If she didn't, people were immediately on their best behavior. Staff would fuss and fawn. The management would make sure that every plate that reached her table was meticulous. She was sure all the restaurateurs in town had a picture of her face—perhaps in combination with a dart board—in their kitchens. But she'd found a foolproof way to thwart all this. Tonight she had on a tweed sport coat, one of Bram's best ties, and a black wig and beard. And she was smoking a pipe. Bram said the pipe was too much. He had *no* drama in his soul.

The first time she'd visited the restaurant was two weeks ago. She and Bram had been searching for a spot to have a leisurely Sunday morning brunch. The buffet looked so enticing, they decided to give it a try. Lovely cold salads. Marinated eggplant and red onion. Cucumber and tomato in a lightly minted yogurt dressing. Small, crispy phyllo pillows of spinach, Boursin cheese, feta, parsley, and fresh dill. And the main dish, a rich moussaka. The béchamel sauce on the top was perfection. Thick and creamy, scented with nutmeg. She wondered if it was still on the menu. The only disappointment was the dessert. A cloyingly sweet rice pudding that tasted more like her grandmother's cold cream. A little too much rose water for her palate. But the rest of the meal was so good, she was able to overlook it.

"We don't have any tables right now," said the hostess. "But I can put your name down on the list. It shouldn't be more than fifteen minutes."

Sophie was surprised to see the dining room so crowded. It was less than two blocks from the Chappeldine Gallery, not the busiest section of south Minneapolis. "That would be fine," she said, biting down authoritatively on the pipe stem.

"Name?"

"Clinton." She smiled. "No relation."

The woman looked down at her, unsmiling.

Sophie decided she must be a Republican. She wished she were a few inches taller. It would make this disguise business considerably easier.

"The bar is right through there." The woman pointed.

As Sophie stood in the doorway and searched the smoky room for a table, her eyes fell to a booth in the back. There in the dim light sat John and Kate, deep in conversation. John looked upset.

Sophie inched her way to a table directly across from them and sat down. Thankfully she was far enough away from the main action to be able to hear. After ordering a gin and tonic, she sat back and listened. Normally she wouldn't eavesdrop on a private conversation, but with everything that had happened recently, she couldn't contain herself.

Kate was speaking: "You had no right to go into my desk!"

"I was looking for some strapping tape," said John. "I wasn't snooping. I'd already noticed those postmarks on Hawks's packages. I knew they were phony. There is no such thing as a Soldiers Grove postmark, Kate. All the mail from the town goes through Duluth. I can't believe you went to all the trouble of getting a stamp made."

"You don't know that! You don't know anything."

"I know what Rudy told me. His mother found a note Hawks had written to Hale the night he was murdered. It threatened him. I also know Hale received mail at the gallery from Hawks. Was it all a fraud, Kate? Tell me what's going on!"

"It's none of your business." She pushed her beer away.

"How do you figure that? Rudy is one of my best friends. He's in trouble. Since the police think he may have had something to do with Hale's death, it affects him, which affects me. And it should affect you!"

Sophie thanked the waitress for her drink and sipped it as she watched Kate give John a long, hard look.

"A friend, huh?" She raised a suggestive eyebrow.

John gave her a disgusted look. "Stuff it."

"Now who's getting defensive?"

"It was a cheap shot. Besides, you're trying to change the subject."

"So what if I am? I didn't want to meet you here tonight. You forced me."

"You're right. I said I'd take what I know to the police, and I will." He paused, looking directly at Sophie.

She quickly turned away, shielding her face with her hand. Damn. She'd forgotten to take off her diamond. She slipped it off and put it in her pocket. When she glanced at him again, he was staring into his beer. She heaved a sigh of relief.

"Come on, who is this Ezmer Hawks anyway?" he demanded. "Hale was as tight as a drum before he died. What were you doing? Helping someone terrorize him?"

"None of your business."

"I think the police will look at it differently."

"You wouldn't do that!"

"I would. I *will*. Unless—"

"What?" She twisted her thin blonde hair behind her ears.

"Unless you tell me the whole truth."

"If I do, will you promise not to go to the police?"

"I can't do that. Don't you feel guilty? Rudy is taking the heat and you might be able to help him!"

She covered her face with her hands.

"Look, Kate. I just want to understand."

"No, you don't. You want to put me in jail!"

"How can you say that?"

"Because . . . I'm in too deep." She stopped. "John, I've never told anyone about . . . any of this."

"Any of what?"

She shook her head.

"You'll have to. Sooner or later."

She wiped a hand across her face and squared her shoulders. For several seconds she let her eyes wash over the crowd. Finally they came to rest on Sophie. Again, Sophie turned away, pretending to look for someone at the front entrance.

"I can't," said Kate, her voice full of defeat. "You have to trust me. I had nothing to do with Hale's murder, unless wishing a person dead means anything."

"You hated him that much?"

"I . . . can't talk about it. Not tonight. If that means you take the fake postmark to the police, then so be it."

"You admit you had it made?"

"I admit nothing." She sat up straight. "Look, if you could just see your way to giving me even a couple of days, I promise—" Again, she stopped. "No! That would be a lie. I can't promise anything. I'm scared, John. I've never been so scared in my life. If I told you the truth, if the police knew what was going on, I'm afraid they might think I killed him."

"Did you?"

Again, their eyes locked. "No! I've got to go now."

As Sophie watched her bolt from the room, she had the urge to run after her, but knew it would be useless. She couldn't believe what she'd just overheard. Kate had been keeping something important from her—maybe even something that could prove Rudy's innocence. In Sophie's mind, that was unforgivable.

"May I sit down?" asked John. He was standing over her, his half-empty glass of beer held in one hand.

She stuffed the pipe into her mouth. "Well—"

"Thanks." He pulled up a chair. "So." He smiled. "You come here often?"

Oh, God. She cleared her throat. "I . . . ah . . ."

"Me, neither. Are you meeting someone?"

She swallowed hard.

"Say, when did you start smoking a pipe, Ms. Greenway? It's an unusual touch. But then, so is the beard."

# 31

"Won't you come in?" asked Louie, moving back and allowing Rhea to enter.

She stepped into the large foyer, her eyes taking in the messy living room. A large NO SMOKING sign hung above the couch. This wasn't what she'd expected at all. A lawyer's house should look polished, professionally decorated. This place was cluttered and musty, with the distinct air of neglect. As she turned to

Louie, she realized he looked exactly the same way. His sweater was old, in need of repair. And, if it was actually possible for a human being to look dusty, Louie did. Nevertheless, he excuded a kind of benevolent warmth. And his eyes were intelligent, if a little distracted.

"Please," he said, taking her coat, "come on back to the study. It's the most comfortable spot in the house."

Rhea noticed a wedding band on his finger, though as they moved through the darkened rooms, she had the sense they were alone.

"Can I offer you anything to drink?" he asked. He picked up his bottle of beer and took a sip. "This is . . . Oh, what do they call it? Pale ale, I believe. It's quite good." A half-eaten bag of pretzels lay on the coffee table. "I also have wine, whiskey—" He stopped. "Oh, just listen to me, will you? I sound like the neighborhood bar. Would you like some coffee?"

"No, thanks." It was best to get this over with as quickly as possible. She thought of Ben. Louie might be the only man who could help.

He sat down across from her and grabbed the bag of pretzels, selecting one and then offering her the sack.

She shook her head.

"So," he began, munching thoughtfully, "on the phone you said you wanted to talk to me about something personal. I can't imagine what that would be, since we met only briefly at Hale and Ivy's party. But I am curious." He reached for a bottle of Maalox and took a swig. "Sorry. My digestion's been kind of poor lately." He picked up the beer to wash it down.

Rhea glanced at the doorway. "Is someone here?" she asked. She thought she heard a noise. "I was hoping to speak to you privately."

His hand trembled slightly as he set the bottle back on the table. "My wife died a little over a week ago."

"Oh . . . I didn't know." She'd really put her foot in it this time. Out of the corner of her eye, she saw a cat slink into the room and jump up on the desk chair. "I'm sorry."

"She'd been sick for a long time." He made a move to get up. "Will you excuse me for a minute?" He rushed into the kitchen, closing the door behind him.

Rhea waited, watching the cat lick its paws. In the quiet of the old house, she could hear him vomiting. She felt like a criminal. No wonder his digestion was so bad. Grief did awful things to people. She tried not to stare at him when he returned. Even so, she couldn't help but notice that his skin was even more sallow now than before. Poor man.

"I'm sorry," he said, resuming his position on the couch. He put a hand gingerly over his stomach. "Where were we?"

Even though he was in obvious distress and probably shouldn't be bothered, she knew it was now or never. She had to know the truth. "You brought up Hale and Ivy's party a moment ago. That's what I came to talk to you about. That night, I'd gone out for a walk about eleven. I couldn't stand the smoke and the noise. Parties often affect me that way."

"Really? I find the mindless uproar soothing. But go on."

"Well, about half a block away from the house, I heard this noise—like the backfire of a car. I realized later that it must have been the shot that killed Hale."

"I expect you're correct. That would have been the right time."

She looked down at her hands. If only she could bury her doubts. Nothing was stopping her from getting up right now and leaving. No one would ever know the difference. Except she'd never lived her life that way. And she wasn't going to start now. If she and Ben were ever going to have a chance at a new life together, she had to know the truth. Then, one way or another, she'd deal with it. "As I was coming around the side of the house, I saw someone go in through the back door. I looked up and saw a shadow move across the window in Hale's office."

"How terrifying for you."

"At the time, it didn't mean anything. Looking back, I'm sure I was seeing his murderer."

"I suppose that's possible."

"It was you I saw go into the house, Mr. Sigerson."

Very calmly, he picked a piece of lint off his slacks. "Yes."

"I want to know what you saw."

He waited for almost a minute before answering. When he did, his voice had grown hoarse. "Very little."

"Did you see someone go into the gate house?"

He shook his head. "I'm sorry to disappoint you, but my attention was elsewhere. There was a magnificent display of northern lights that night, and—"

"But you must have seen something!"

His smile was sad. "The window was open slightly in Hale's office. I heard . . . arguing. That's all. I don't know who he was talking to. And I don't care."

"How can you say that!"

"Very easily." He attempted to cross his legs, but the pain in his stomach seemed to prevent any change in position. "Look, are you familiar with the nursery rhyme—?"

"Nursery rhyme?" Had he lost his mind? They were discussing a murder!

Patiently, he continued, "The one that begins: 'For every evil under the sun—' "

She shook her head. She was more than annoyed at the digression.

"I'm not saying we should take our moral cues from Mother Goose, but in this case, I think she was on the right track."

"What do you mean?"

"Well, I guess . . . Very simply put, I believe in fate. It gives a kind of symmetry to our existence. I don't need certainty, but I do need closure—no matter how unfair or quirky. 'For every evil under the sun, there is a remedy or there is none. If there be one, seek till you find it. If there be none, never mind it.' We're all pawns, Rhea. To a certain extent, I suppose I believe what goes around comes around. If there ever was a man who deserved what he got, it was Hale Micklenberg."

Was she hearing him right? "You're saying he deserved to die?"

He nodded.

She was aghast. "Murder is always wrong, Mr. Sigerson. Always."

"I don't disagree."

"But?" He was confusing her. Besides, she didn't want to argue a moral point with him right now, she wanted *answers*. "Then who did it?"

He shrugged.

"For God's sake, you're a lawyer! You can't let a criminal go free."

He simply stared at her.

"You saw who did it, didn't you? You're protecting someone."

He sighed. "We just have to wait and see."

"What do you mean by that?"

"Rhea, what I saw or didn't see is nobody's business but mine. You mustn't worry." His tired blue eyes studied her, a perplexed look on his face. Finally his confusion melted into understanding. "Oh . . . I see, now. Of course. That answer isn't good enough for you, is it? Sometimes I'm as thick as a brick when it comes to human emotions. I'll tell you what you've come to know." With some effort, he leaned forward. "Listen to me very carefully. Your boyfriend had nothing to do with it."

Her mouth dropped open. How could he know she was worried about Ben—about his anger, his penchant for doing the wrong thing at the wrong time?

"I watched the two of you together that night. I know

how much you love him, though it was clear to me you were holding back. My advice to you is, don't. Live your life, don't analyze it. Take what's good and hold on to it. And don't be afraid."

She felt tears well up behind her eyes. "I love him so much, but sometimes he doesn't think before he acts."

"He's young. He'll learn."

"But he's got himself into terrible financial trouble. Hale promised him he would be the one to photograph the IAI spring catalogue. And then, for some stupid reason, Hale rescinded the offer. In the meantime, Ben went out and bought all this new equipment. He's in debt up to his ears! He'll have to file for bankruptcy if he doesn't get another big job. This morning, he went to talk to Charles Squire. I thought for sure Mr. Squire would see what a swine Hale had been. I was positive Ben would leave with a signed contract. At first, I think their talk went pretty well. Then, out of the blue, Mr. Squire changed his mind and threw Ben out. I don't know what's going to happen now."

Louie sat quietly, staring up at a small painting above his desk. "I agree. That's pretty bad news."

"I don't suppose you have any pull with Mr. Squire?" Rhea wiped her nose with a tissue she'd fished out of her pocket.

"You never know."

"Oh, would you try? It would mean so much."

"Of course, but I can't promise anything."

"I understand. Really, I do."

He tapped a pensive finger against his chin and then smiled. "I'll call you if I have any news."

She stood.

"If you don't mind," he said, stretching out on the couch, "I'll let you show yourself out. I'm not feeling very well tonight."

She didn't want to seem nosy, but she had to ask. "Have you seen a doctor?"

Wearily he nodded. "They're all quacks."

"But you've seen one?"

"Yes, briefly. Several days ago. He just said to try antacids. What does he know?"

"Maybe you should go in for some tests?"

His face turned stony. "No! None of their snake oil and endless poking. I'll never subject myself to that."

She was surprised by his vehemence. Then again, it was his business. "Well, I hope you're feeling better soon. Come to think of it, my aunt had poor digestion. She always took a little honey and vinegar before bed."

He grimaced. "Thanks, but I've found a better solution."

"What's that?"

"Well, do you remember what the apostle Paul said in the New Testament? 'A little wine for thy stomach's sake'? I've taken a few liberties with the type of alcohol, and I added the pretzels, but all in all, I think I've captured the spirit." He held up his beer bottle. "Have a wonderful life, Rhea. And give my best to Ben."

# 32

Shortly after Bram left for the station on Friday morning, Sophie picked up the phone and called Kate Chappeldine's home. There was no answer. After the conversation she'd overheard last night, she was convinced they had to talk. John may not have been able to get any explanations out of her, but one way or another, Sophie was determined to be more successful. When she called the gallery, she got a recording that said the business would be closed on Friday due to illness. So, at least for now, Kate had effectively thwarted any attempt at communication.

As Sophie sat at the kitchen table, picking in frustration at a bran muffin, she wondered if it would do any good to go over to Kate's house. If she was there, all she had to do was not come to the door and that was that. Sophie couldn't exactly break it down. Or stand outside and shout accusations through the mail vent.

After having some time to think things through, Sophie realized her first response had been the most accurate. She felt deeply betrayed. It was apparent Kate had information she knew could help Rudy, and, still, she was keeping it from the police. The reason for her silence was also painfully apparent. She feared she would incriminate herself if she told them the truth. But what specifically had she done?

John's concerns centered on a rubber stamp—a phony Soldiers Grove postmark. Did it mean the letters and drawings from Ezmer Hawks were all fakes? Why would Kate tamper with a postmark, if indeed that's what she'd done? And who the hell was this Ezmer Hawks in the first place? Did he have some connection with the disappearance of Eric Hauley from that arts camp so many years ago? Were he and Eric Hauley one in the same person? It seemed clear that the drawings at the gallery had frightened Hale. And the night of his murder, Hawks had sent him a note threatening his life if he didn't tell the police the truth about some past transgression. But what transgression? It was a good bet it had to do with Camp Bright Water, perhaps even the disappearance of Eric Hauley, but what had Hale done? And where was this Ezmer Hawks now? Was he someone she knew? Sophie could sit and theorize until the proverbial cows came home, but the only one who could shed light on the subject was Kate Chappeldine. And Kate wasn't talking.

If John had any further information, he wasn't saying anything, either. After Kate had left the bar last night and John had come over to her table, Sophie tried to get him to open up. All he would say was that he was sure Rudy had nothing to do with Hale's murder. Period. End of story. Except, both of them knew it wasn't the end of the story. Ultimately, John's reassurances only made her angry. It upset her terribly that he had a better idea of what was going on in Rudy's life than she did.

After the police had searched Rudy's room two nights ago, John mentioned that Rudy had come to his apartment in St. Paul. Even more infuriating, he was as tight-lipped about Rudy's behavior that night as Rudy had been. For the past couple of days, Rudy had been getting up before daylight and leaving the house. He didn't return until well after midnight. Sophie hadn't waited up for him because she felt the message was clear. He wanted his privacy. But that understanding didn't make life any easier.

Rising from the table, she dragged herself over to the counter and poured herself another cup of French roast. As she stirred some cream into it, she tried to clear her mind. Even though Rudy preferred to shut her out right now, she would just have to understand, and have faith that their relationship would continue to grow. But if she was going to get to the bottom of Hale's murder, there were other aspects of the whole affair she needed to consider.

Yesterday, via the office grapevine, she'd found out that Hale had apparently left Ivy only one dollar in his will. The bulk of the estate had gone to an elderly woman, a Mrs. Betty Malmquist. Sophie was more than curious about why Hale would choose to leave everything he'd worked his entire life for to someone other than his wife. Ivy was no doubt furious. Sophie knew she should make a trip over to her house just to check in, see how she was doing, but this morning, she had another plan in mind. She'd found Betty Malmquist's address in the St. Paul phone book. Perhaps she could persuade the woman to talk to her. It might lead nowhere, but then again, anything about Hale's life might prove important.

Switching on Bram's morning radio program, and being warmed by the sound of his voice, she dumped the breakfast dishes into the sink and began cleaning up. Within the hour, she would be standing in front of Betty Malmquist's front door, hat in hand, and hoping for the light of revelation to dawn.

Betty led the way into her tiny living room and made herself comfortable in the recliner rocker. Sophie took a seat in a wooden captain's chair directly across from her. She was amazed at the amount of artwork filling the walls. The hallway, the dining room, the living room, everywhere she looked she saw framed oil paintings. Many were portraits of Betty. Some were of a garden. And still others were portraits of people Sophie didn't recognize. "Did you do these?" she asked, gazing at them with undisguised admiration.

"No," said Betty, though her voice carried a note of pride. "I suppose there's no reason to keep the secret any longer. Hale was the artist."

Sophie didn't even try to hide her surprise. "I had no idea."

"No one did. He wanted it that way. He's used one of my second-floor bedrooms as a studio for many years. At first, he rented the space, but after we became such good friends, it seemed kind of silly. I loved having him in the house. I couldn't imagine living here without his visits. So, I refused to take any more money. That's when he started buying me all sorts of things. A new TV set—anything he saw I needed. He's been like a second son."

Sophie was beginning to understand. "But why didn't

he want anyone to see his paintings? They're wonderful."

"I know." She sighed. "I always encouraged him to take them over to one of those galleries he talked about and have a show. But he wouldn't hear of it. I don't think he thought his work was good enough. He was embarrassed to show it to people. He didn't even want my grandkids to know who did them. It was like—" She shook her head. "If he couldn't be the king of the hill, he didn't want to play the game. He was a terribly competitive man."

Sophie knew from firsthand experience that Betty was right. "And yet he spent all these years secretly painting. He must have gotten something from it."

"Oh, he did. He found a great deal of peace. I don't think he had much of that in the rest of his life. You know, I told him once that all he needed was a little more confidence. Do you know what he said to me? He said, 'Betty, I've got plenty of confidence. What I don't have is courage.' " She shook her head. "I never understood what he meant."

Sophie was at a loss. "I'd have to think about it."

"Were you two pretty good friends?" Her voice was tinged with sadness. She held out a bowl of lemon drops.

Sophie took one and smiled. It took her back to her childhood. "We'd known each other for many years." She thought it best not to add what she really thought of him. "And I went to grade school with Ivy."

"Such a small world." Betty leaned her cane against the arm of the chair and then retrieved a handkerchief from her apron pocket and pressed it to her eyes. "Hale was such a dear boy. So many of the things in this room he brought me. But most of all, he brought me his love. Would you like to see the postcards?"

"Postcards?"

"From all over Europe. He made sure I got at least one every time he went abroad."

"Maybe another time." Sophie was surprised to find that Hale had such a soft side. In everyday life, he'd hidden it well.

"But you know, it wasn't the presents that were important," continued Betty, patting her lap and waiting while her little schnauzer jumped up and made himself comfortable, "though they *were* a delight. No, it was knowing he was happy here. Sometimes I'd fix us dinner. He'd stay downstairs afterward and we'd play Scrabble. Do you play Scrabble, Mrs.—? I'm sorry. I've already forgotten your name."

"Greenway. Sophie Greenway. Please, call me Sophie. And yes, I love Scrabble."

"Well, then, you'll have to come over sometime for a game. I may be moving soon, though I'm not sure where. My eldest grandson says I need to get out of here before the house crumbles around my ears. It's funny. I've lived all my life without much money. It feels silly to make all this fuss now. My needs are small. But, of course, I'm glad for my grandchildren. My son and his wife were killed in a plane crash many years ago. It was a hard road for the kids, growing up."

"I'm sorry," said Sophie.

She nodded. "At my age, death is no stranger. But when someone young dies, like Hale, it seems a terrible tragedy. He was such a talented man." She looked down at her dog, patting his head lovingly. "Oh, I know he was full of the devil, too. I'm not blind. But underneath, he was kind."

Sophie couldn't believe they were talking about the same man. Yet, even though Betty's views weren't those generally held, it didn't make them any less valid. "When did you see him last?"

She tugged on her handkerchief. "It was just a week or so before he died. He brought me a shopping bag full of presents. He told me to open one every day—just to keep my spirits up until spring. He knew how much the winter weather gets me down. It's hard to get out when you're old, but in the winter, it's even harder." She stopped and shook her head, a look of puzzlement crossing her plump face as she glanced at a small cabinet that sat against the wall, just a few feet from her chair.

"Is anything wrong?"

Betty took her cane and pushed the rubber tip against the front panel. The door sprang open. "Take out that brown paper box. I want to show you something."

Sophie knelt down and removed it, closing the door behind her. She handed it to Betty.

"I want you to look at this and tell me what you think." Betty lifted off the cover. Inside was a small container of rifle shells, a white plastic bottle labeled LASIX, and another small glass bottle of a white powder. ARSENIC was written in red ink on the cover. "What do you make of it? It was at the bottom of the sack of presents, only it wasn't wrapped in fancy paper like the rest. Why would Hale give me something like that? The more I think about it, the more upset I get."

Sophie didn't know how to respond.

"I thought I'd have an opportunity to talk to him about it, but he . . . died before I had the chance."

"Have the police been here to see you?"

"Yes. Yesterday. But I didn't show it to them. I didn't think it was any of their business. Now, I'm not so sure I did the right thing. You were Hale's friend. What do you think it means? Did I make a mistake not telling them?"

"I don't know," said Sophie, struggling to make sense of it. As she leaned forward in her chair, she remembered something Kate had said. Lasix was the drug that was mistakenly put into Ivy's pillbox several weeks ago. She could have died if it hadn't been discovered. Kate thought it was a clear attempt on Ivy's life, just like the shots that were fired. She was sure the two events were connected. And, more to the point, she thought Hale was responsible. If she was right, perhaps Betty's discovery was proof of Hale's involvement. He had been trying to murder his wife—and here was the evidence. But why would he hide something so incriminating in a sack and then give it away? It didn't make sense. It seemed even less likely he'd forget where he'd stashed the evidence. And why would he save it in the first place? Unless . . . Sophie looked up and saw Betty watching her. She knew she had to say something.

"What are you thinking?" asked the elderly woman.

Sophie shook her head. What if Hale hadn't known what was in the bottom of that sack? Maybe someone had planted it there to incriminate him, not knowing he was about to give it away. If that was true, then the next logical question was, who did it? It seemed likely it was the same person who'd made two unsuccessful attempts on Ivy's life. And that person had to have access to Hale's and Ivy's personal belongings—even if only briefly. But who? As she mulled it over, the name Charles Squire came to mind. He certainly had access to the gate house. Depending on where Hale had stored the shopping bag, he might well have had plenty of opportunity. But what was his motive? Why would he want to incriminate Hale for the attempted murder of his wife? Or worse, why would he want to murder Ivy?

"I think you should put this box away for now," said Sophie, trying not to upset her any further. "I have some ideas, but I'm not sure where they lead. I'll have to do some checking. In the meantime, you should keep it safe."

"All right," said Betty, placing the box on the table and pushing it away with obvious distaste. "I was thinking of just dumping it in the trash."

"No, don't do that. It may be important."

"I suppose you're right." She glanced at the clock on the wall. "Oh, look at the time! My youngest grandson should be here any minute. He's taking me to lunch."

Sophie felt it was her cue to leave. Still, she had one last question that hadn't been answered. Before rising from her chair, she asked, "Betty, I'm curious. Were you surprised by what Hale did—leaving you the majority of his estate?"

"Surprised? I was shocked! I realize Ivy must be awfully upset, but I assume Hale left her well provided for in other ways. I don't have any idea why he did it. Perhaps she does."

Sophie assumed Ivy had a pretty good idea.

"I hope she doesn't . . . think ill of me."

Before Sophie could reassure her, the phone on the end table began to ring.

"Will you excuse me for a moment?" asked Betty, picking it up. "Hello?" she said, patting her dog's head absently as she listened. "Oh, hello, Ivy! Yes . . . yes, I recognize your voice. This *is* a surprise. When? Why, yes. That would be lovely. Seven o'clock." She paused. "Oh, I'm sure I could get one of my grandsons to bring me." Another pause. "I see. What was that name again?" She listened more carefully, closing her eyes. "I have it. Dr. Steinhardt. Yes, I remember him. He was the man you were with at the lawyer's office. Well, that would be wonderful if it wouldn't be too much trouble." She nodded. "Good, then I'll look forward to it. Thank you for the invitation. I'll see you tomorrow evening." She placed the receiver back on the hook.

"I take it you're being invited to dinner."

Betty nodded, looking a bit perplexed. "I never expected something like that."

For a fleeting second, Sophie had the urge to tell her not to go.

"You know," said Betty, "for a woman who's spent so many years living alone, ignored for the most part by the rest of the world, this is all beginning to feel like, well, like an adventure." She winked, her eyes taking on a mischievous twinkle.

Sophie couldn't help but laugh. She was beginning to get an idea why Hale had loved this woman so much.

"I wonder why that Dr. Steinhardt is with Ivy all the time. He came to the reading of the will on Wednesday, and he's picking me up tomorrow night. I hope she isn't sick."

"I hope so, too," said Sophie. At Hale's funeral, Ivy had looked remarkably well. Better than she'd looked in years. None of this was adding up. Perhaps it was time to pay Ivy a visit. Since Sophie didn't have to be to the office until after lunch, and Ivy's home was only a few blocks away, now was the perfect opportunity. "Well," she said, with one last glance at the paintings, "this has been enlightening. You saw a part of Hale he rarely showed to the world."

"I know," said Betty, her voice once again sad. "He was a complex man. I may not have understood him, but I loved him. And for me, that was enough."

# 33

"Sophie!" said Ivy, a look of surprise on her face as she opened the front door. She glanced a bit anxiously over her shoulder. "How . . . nice to see you." Her smile was something less than sincere.

"May I come in?" asked Sophie, wondering at Ivy's hesitation. "If this is a bad time—"

"No." She said the word much too quickly. "Of course not. I was just . . . I mean . . ." Again, she attempted a smile. "Please." She held the door open wide. "Actually, there's someone here I'd like you to meet."

Sophie had a good idea who that might be. She stepped into the foyer and waited while Ivy closed and locked the door behind them. Then she followed her back to the atrium. The glass-enclosed space contained at least twenty huge cactus plants in bright Mexican pots. Near the rear of the room, a man was standing with his back to her. He was reading a newspaper, one hand massaging the back of his neck. As they entered, he turned. His hair was gray, his face angular. He wasn't exactly handsome, though the quality of health he projected was very attractive. He had on a suit, but had taken off the jacket and rolled up the cuffs of his light blue, Oxford cloth shirt.

"Sophie," said Ivy, "I'd like you to meet Dr. Max Steinhardt."

Max moved toward her, his hand extended. "Very nice to meet you," he said, his voice full of enthusiasm.

For some reason, Sophie felt as if she were being ushered into *The Price Is Right*. Max had the distinct air of a game show host.

"Ivy's told me a bit about you and your husband," he continued, pumping her arm. "And of course, I've been reading your restaurant reviews in the *Times Register* for as long as you've been writing them. Very commendable job. Very commendable, indeed. And even though I rarely get time to listen to morning radio, I've also enjoyed your husband's show on occasion."

"Thanks," said Sophie, glancing at their locked hands.

Instantly, he let go.

"Max has been a friend as well as my personal physician for several years," said Ivy, as if answering an unasked question. "Since Hale's death, he's been a dear. I'm afraid he comes whenever I call."

Really? thought Sophie. That *was* a good friend. "Are you feeling all right?"

"Tired," said Ivy, "though Max says that's to be expected."

"A death in the family isn't the easiest of times," he replied, giving Sophie a doctorly frown. He folded the paper and sat down on the white wicker sofa.

Sophie made herself comfortable in one of the matching wicker chairs. So much for introductions.

"To what do we owe this unexpected visit?" asked Ivy. She slid down next to him, making sure their bodies weren't too close. But close enough.

No matter. Sophie had already caught the scent. The vibes were unmistakable. Ivy and Max were lovers. This put everything in a very different light. She wondered how long the affair had been going on—and if Hale had known. "Well," she began, "I was visiting someone else in your neighborhood." She paused for effect. "Betty Malmquist."

First Ivy responded. "Betty Malmquist, you say?"

Next Max. "How interesting."

Again, Ivy. "I suppose you've . . . heard about, well, about what Hale did? Leaving his entire estate to her?"

Max patted Ivy's hand. "Wills can be broken. Don't worry."

Sophie wondered if the faint sound she was hearing was teeth grinding.

"So," said Ivy, her voice taking on a fake lightness, "how is Betty?"

"She's fine."

"Have you known each other long?" asked Max.

"No. We'd never met before today."

"Really?" He glanced questioningly at Ivy. "Was it . . . a social call then?"

"I suppose you could say that. I don't know if you two are aware of this, but the police seem to think my son had something to do with Hale's murder. I'm positive that's not the case, but since I'm not entirely impressed with the direction of their investigation, I've decided to do a bit of checking on my own."

"You think Betty had something to do with Hale's death?" asked Max.

"No, of course not. But I've been trying to talk with people who knew Hale. I thought I might get a better idea of who might want to . . . see him harmed."

"Have you found out anything?" asked Ivy. This time, her manner seemed more sincere. She sat forward, waiting for a response.

"I have some ideas," said Sophie, "but I'm not sure where they lead."

"Like what?"

"Well, for one thing, I was talking with Ben Kiran the other evening. He was at the party the night Hale died. It seems he first met Hale—as well as you, Ivy—at a summer camp many years ago. It was the same summer a boy disappeared. Eric Hauley. Do you remember him?"

The corners of Ivy's mouth turned down. "Why . . . yes. A very sad time. Why do you bring it up?"

"Hale received a note at the party from a man named Ezmer Hawks."

"The artist?"

Sophie nodded. "It directed him to call the police and confess to something he'd done—something in his past. Hawks was at the party that night, Ivy. And the note was a clear threat."

"You think he killed my husband?"

"It's possible."

"But . . . how did you know about the note?"

"I found it by the back door of your house. The police have it now."

Her eyes flicked to Max. "What's this got to do with Camp Bright Water?"

"I was hoping you could tell me."

"I—" She pulled nervously on her pearl necklace. "I can't imagine."

Sophie was sure Ivy knew more than she was letting on. "Perhaps I should tell you that Mr. Hawks has been sending some of his new work to the Chappeldine Gallery. Hale had stopped by to see it several times. One of the drawings is a sphinx with fire between its paws. A boy's face appears in the fire."

Ivy's entire body stiffened. "A . . . sphinx you say?"

"Sounds like a load of nonsense to me," muttered Max. "Don't worry. The police will make sense of it—if there's any sense to be made."

Sophie kept her eyes on Ivy. "The note also contained part of a nursery rhyme. 'For every evil under the sun—' "

Ivy's hand flew to her mouth.

Max put his arm around her, patting her shoulder. "Sophie, I think this is too upsetting right now. Perhaps we could change the subject."

"Of course."

"No, I'm fine," said Ivy, brushing a tentative hand over her face. "Really."

"What else did you and Betty talk about?" asked Max, resuming a more casual tone.

"Well, did you know Hale was saving up presents to give to Betty? He'd been storing them in a shopping bag."

Ivy and Max exchanged glances.

"What's your point?" asked Max, a bit of the warmth leaving his voice.

"After Betty received them, she noticed that at the bottom of the sack was a small brown box. It wasn't wrapped like the rest. Inside she found rifle shells, Lasix, and arsenic."

Ivy sat up very straight. "I don't understand."

"Betty doesn't, either," said Sophie.

As if picking up a cue, Max said, "The police were right! They thought Hale was responsible for those attempts on Ivy's life. As far as I'm concerned, we now have proof!"

"I'm not so sure," said Sophie, sensing she was about to make an enemy of the good doctor. "I mean, just think about it. Why would he hide incriminating evidence in a sack and then give it away? And why would he save it in the first place?"

"How should I know?" barked Max.

Ivy took hold of his hand. "If Hale wasn't responsible, then who was?"

Sophie shook her head. "It would have to be someone with access to your house."

"Like?"

"Well, I don't want to accuse anyone, but what about Charles Squire?"

Ivy's expression turned hard. "That little rodent used to come and go in here as if he owned the place. Well, he doesn't! It's the one thing he couldn't get his sticky little fingers on. I'm evicting him *and* IAI from the gate house at the end of the month."

So much for a synopsis of her feelings toward Charles, thought Sophie. "Do you know where Hale was storing the shopping bag before he gave it to Betty?"

Ivy shrugged. "No idea. I never saw it."

"This is pointless," said Max. "You're both ignoring the obvious. Betty must simply turn this evidence over to the police and let them take it from there. Don't you see, Ivy? This could be the lever we've been looking for to break that will!"

Their eyes locked. When Ivy returned her gaze to Sophie, something had changed. Ivy now seemed ill at ease. She fidgeted with her watch and the buttons on her blouse. Max had silenced her. Why? "I think Max's right," said Ivy. "Let's let the police handle it. I just want this to be over."

"That's the point," said Sophie. "I think we're all overlooking something vitally important. It may *not* be over. Your life may still be in danger. There were *three* methods of murder found in that box, Ivy. Only two attempts were made on your life. If Hale wasn't responsible, then that means another attempt may be made."

A muscle in Ivy's face twitched.

Max seemed annoyed that his opinion was being challenged. "But if it was Hale, as I maintain this evidence *proves* beyond the shadow of a doubt, then you have nothing to worry about. Besides, I'm not going to let anyone poison you." His disgust at such an idea bordered on the heroic.

"I don't like any of this," mumbled Ivy.

"Well, like it or not," said Max coldly, "those are the cards we've been dealt and we have to play them."

It felt almost as if he were blaming her for something. There were emotions at work here Sophie knew nothing about. Max was being entirely too controlling, and Ivy just seemed lost.

"Has that woman informed the police about what she found?" asked Max.

"I don't believe so."

"Then it's fortunate you invited her to dinner tomorrow night," he said, turning again to Ivy. "We'll have to insist she do so. Immediately."

Ivy nodded.

"Well," said Sophie, realizing the conversation was going nowhere—and wasn't going to go anywhere with Max calling all the shots—"I suppose I better hit the road. That magazine I work for doesn't run itself."

"Of course," said Ivy. "I'll walk you to the door."

"It was nice meeting you," said Sophie, standing and smiling down at Max. It was an effort.

"Same here." He didn't stand. "Perhaps we'll run into each other again."

Right. You in a minivan and me in a cement truck. "I'm sure we will." She followed Ivy out of the room.

As they got to the door, Ivy turned and whispered, "Max doesn't understand my . . . fears sometimes. I know he's trying to be helpful, but I *am* concerned about the arsenic, Sophie. Very concerned."

The vehemence in her voice caught Sophie off-guard. She decided to ask a leading question. "Do you think Hale tried to murder you?"

"Without a doubt."

"Why?"

"Oh, that's simple. He had someone else. You didn't have to live with him, Sophie, but he was cruel. And he was never home. He was gone almost every weekend and lots of evenings each week. I never knew where to reach him. I'm sure he had more than one woman on the side, but he must have found somebody he wanted to marry. He knew I'd fight him on the divorce. Tie him up for years."

"I'm . . . not so sure."

"What do you mean?"

Sophie didn't know if she could tell Ivy about what she'd found at Betty's house. Yet, as his wife, didn't she have a right to know? "Hale spent most of his free time at Betty Malmquist's home. He'd rented a room there."

"He what?"

"He used the space as a studio—for his painting. Betty has hundreds of canvases he's worked on over the years. I'm sure she'd let you see them."

Ivy was almost speechless. "I don't believe you!"

"Go see for yourself." She watched as the ramifications of her words slowly sunk in. "If he didn't have another woman, Ivy, why would he want you out of the way so *badly* that he'd try to murder you?"

"He *was* sleeping around. I know he was! He hated me! He knew I saw right through him—saw him for the phony he was."

"Ivy," called Max from the other room, "is that woman gone yet?"

"Yes," she shouted back. "She's just leaving." She held the door open.

"Are you all right?" asked Sophie. Ivy looked terrible. Her face had lost all its color and her hands were shaking.

"I'm fine. Just fine. Give my love to Bram."

"I will."

"And Sophie? Forget what I said about the arsenic. It's not important. Just chalk it up to the stress I've been under lately. Everything's under control now. I've got nothing to worry about. Nothing in the world."

"Right," said Sophie as the door was slammed in her face.

# 34

"Arsenic," whispered Sophie as she bent over the reference book on her desk. It was late. Nearly nine-thirty. Most everyone had left the magazine offices hours ago. Around six, she'd phoned Bram and told him she needed to work late. He'd be on his own for dinner. She suggested he finish the cold pizza in the fridge, or, if he was feeling particularly brave, he could always whip up another batch of hummus. After sputtering for a good minute and a half about how his culinary talents were not being appreciated, he said he had to go. The beef Wellington he'd prepared for dinner was done and he had to take it out of the oven before it burned. He announced that he was going to invite their neighbor, the one who looked like Ingrid Bergman, to eat with him. After all, she'd been a costar of his years ago. They had a lot of catching up to do. After wishing her a positively *swell* evening, he hung up.

A little after nine, she finally put the project she'd been working on all afternoon to bed. As she stepped into the meeting room, the only place where the coffeepot was still on, she picked up the book she'd asked her secretary to find for her earlier in the day. *Classic Poisons*, by Arnold Pim Monroe. Pouring herself another cup of sludge, she returned to her desk. Arsenic was so important it had its own chapter. She sipped as she read:

> Arsenic is a metal which cannot be broken down further into other chemicals. Since it is found in the manufacture of many common products, it is one of the most accessible toxins.

Wonderful, thought Sophie. It was so nice to know all the potential poisoners out there had such an easy time of it. She continued:

> Down through history, arsenic has been the most popular of poisons. Traces of the element are found in all human tissues. In its most common form, *arsenic trioxide*, it appears as a white powder. Although generally swallowed, arsenic can also be inhaled as a dust or a gas.

She turned the page, hoping for a few more specifics. She pressed her finger against the type and slid her hand down until she came to the heading *Symptoms*.

> The classic symptoms of arsenic poisoning are generally seen to be gastric in nature, although arsenic can also be carcinogenic. Misdiagnosis as gastroenteritis is common. After long periods of exposure, an individual can develop a rash, called exfoliative dermatitis. Often, in cases of immediate death, only an inflamed stomach can be determined. If death is de-

layed, arsenic will appear in the kidneys and the liver. Death occurs generally after bouts of dizziness, headaches, vomiting, diarrhea, and an inability to void. There may even be periods of paralysis. Convulsions and coma generally come toward the end, with death a result of circulatory failure.

Under the heading *Treatment*, Sophie read:

The first measure a physician will generally take is to pump the stomach and give dimercaprol for several days. In addition, penicillamine is often prescribed until the arsenic level in the urine goes down. Shock, dehydration, pulmonary edema, and liver damage must also be addressed. However, if caught in time, many victims do survive.

Sophie shivered as she thought of someone being subjected to such a death. She leaned back wearily in her chair and took off her reading glasses. It had been a long day. She couldn't help but worry about Ivy. What if another attempt was being planned on her life? Max insisted she had nothing to fear, but how could he be so sure? The more Sophie thought about the conversation she'd had with the two of them, the more she realized Ivy was in trouble. Max was a stifling presence. If only she could get Ivy alone, she might find some real answers—not the polite playacting she'd been subjected to earlier in the day.

As she sat sipping her coffee, thinking how much Ivy needed a friend right now, the name Louie Sigerson popped into her head. Louie was one of Ivy's best friends. He'd been at the party the night Hale died. He had even stayed at the Micklenberg mansion for a few days after the death of his wife. Sophie wondered what he had to say about all of this.

Even though it was late, she felt a telephone call was worth a try. If he was in bed, she'd be suitably apologetic and attempt to set up a time to see him tomorrow. But, with any luck at all, he might still be up. Perhaps he'd even see her tonight. She grabbed the phone book and began the search for his number.

"When you called," said Louie, nodding to a stack of papers and law books on his desk, "I was trying to read through Hale's will. Ivy got me a copy. I'm hoping there's something we can do about breaking it." His eyes fell to the glass of brandy in his hand. "I feel partially responsible for the trouble she's having."

"Why?" asked Sophie. She was seated in an ancient leather chair in Louie's study. Unfortunately, upon arriving, she'd found not only the house, but Louie himself, in a rather acute state of disrepair. She'd followed him into the kitchen to help make a pot of tea and was surprised to find the sink and counters littered with dirty dishes and half-eaten meals. The chaos was everywhere. Bags of garbage were piled haphazardly in the back hall. As Louie sat and talked to her now, unshaven, his hair uncombed, she noticed the bathrobe he wore was badly in need of washing. And, as much as she hated to admit it, he seemed like a man who had had entirely too much to drink.

"Because," he said, taking a sip from his glass, "I was the one who helped draw up a prenuptial agreement between them. It separated their assets in case of divorce. Unfortunately, that precedent will make breaking this will difficult. I should have done something about that prenup years ago. I just wasn't thinking."

Sophie didn't feel much like drinking the tea. Normally she wasn't all that fastidious, but this place was such a pit, not even a simple cup of Earl Grey appealed. She felt terribly sorry for Louie, for what he must be going through after the death of his wife, but she also thought it best to limit the conversation to Ivy tonight. She set her cup down on the coffee table, next to a bag of pretzels. "Look, Louie, we know each other only socially, but I've always been aware that you and Ivy were close."

He nodded, putting a hand over his stomach. He seemed to be in some pain. From the looks of his refrigerator, it was probably food poisoning.

"I hope you won't think I'm prying," continued Sophie, "but I went to see her this morning hoping she could clear up a few things for me. When I left, I had more questions than when I arrived."

"Questions about what?" He reached for a pretzel.

"Well, for one thing, are she and Max Steinhardt . . . well, I mean, are they—?"

"Having an affair?" He smiled at her discomfort. "I suppose I'm guilty of being kind of nosy myself. Yes, I believe they are. I think they've been involved for some months."

"Did Hale know?"

"I'm afraid so. Why do you ask?"

"Were you aware of the two attempts made on Ivy's life?"

Louie nodded. "I was with her both times."

"Do you think it's possible Hale had anything to do with them?"

His expression turned dark. "I'm almost sure of it. He wanted out of that marriage, Sophie. I heard him say so myself."

"But that's no reason to kill her."

"I don't know. Maybe not. But he was furious. I think he wanted to get back at her because she'd found someone else. Maybe he just wanted to scare her. He was doing a pretty good job of that, if you ask me. The night he took those shots at her, the main house got a strange phone call. I answered it. It was a kid's voice repeating that nursery rhyme: 'For every evil under the sun, there is a remedy or there is none.' "

Sophie's breath caught in her throat. There it was again! That rhyme! "A child's voice?"

"Yes. A young boy."

Very slowly, she repeated, "A *boy* called the house?" She couldn't believe her ears.

He nodded. "Although, I'm pretty sure it was a recording."

Sophie felt a cold shiver run down her back. She thought of Eric Hauley. "Did he give a name?"

"No."

"Louie, I don't think Hale made that call."

"Well, of course I can't prove it."

"No, it's more complicated." She watched as he rummaged in the magazine rack for a bottle of Maalox. "Are you feeling all right?" she asked. She had noticed his skin was kind of yellow.

"Indigestion. Or maybe it's stomach flu. I don't know. My doctor said to try antacids." He glanced at her cup of tea, giving a rueful smile. "It's probably best you don't drink that. Believe me, you wouldn't want to come down with this. My stomach has never felt so awful."

"I'm really sorry."

"Yeah. Thanks."

Sophie decided to forge on. "You know, I spent part of the morning visiting with Betty Malmquist. Several weeks ago, Hale brought a shopping bag full of presents to her. She was supposed to open one every day, just to keep up her spirits. But when she got to the bottom of the sack, she found something odd. An unwrapped box containing rifle shells, Lasix, and arsenic."

Louie whistled. "Quite a present. The meaning is pretty clear, don't you think?"

"I'm not so sure. Hale wasn't stupid. He'd never incriminate himself so blithely."

"Maybe he forgot he put it in the sack."

"Would you?"

"I see your point."

"I don't think Hale had anything to do with those two attempts on Ivy's life. I think someone else was behind it."

"Like who?"

"I don't know. I'm still working on it." She paused. "How well do you know Max?"

"You think *he* was responsible?"

She shrugged. "Something was going on between him and Ivy this afternoon. It was like . . . I don't know . . . like she wanted to talk, but was afraid to. Ivy may be having an affair, but I don't think she's very happy."

Louie shook his head. "My wife always did tell me I was kind of thick when it came to things like that. The problem is, I've rarely seen them together, but I can't see why he'd want to hurt her."

Sophie had to agree. "You were there the night Hale died. Did you see anything?"

Louie selected another pretzel and chewed it thoughtfully. "I know Hale got some sort of note late in the evening that upset him. He found it in a catalogue that was on the coffee table. After he read it, he went out to the gate house."

"Did he say anything about the contents?"

"Honestly, I don't remember. I think he just growled his usual abuse and then took off through the kitchen. Ivy was looking for him, so I went and told her where he'd gone."

"I don't know if you've heard this, but the police seem to think my son had something to do with Hale's murder."

Louie raised his eyebrows in surprise. "They should have more sense!"

"Do you know Rudy?"

"Yes. We met at the party. Handsome young man. He looks a bit like you."

"Thanks." Her smile quickly faded. "The police searched his room several nights ago. We're all terribly upset."

"I don't doubt it." Louie was clearly indignant. "Well, don't worry. Nothing will happen to your son."

"I wish I could believe that. Innocent people have gone to jail before."

Louie shook his head. "Not in this case."

"What do you mean?"

He looked away, finishing his brandy and then taking another sip of Maalox.

"Who do you think murdered Hale?"

His eyes rose to a painting above his desk. It was placed in between a NO SMOKING sign and another sign that said IF WE SEE YOU SMOKING, WE WILL ASSUME YOU ARE ON FIRE AND DOUSE YOU WITH WATER. "Did you know that was an original de Kooning?" he asked, scratching the stubble on his chin. "Ivy gave it to me for my thirty-fifth birthday."

"You didn't answer my question."

"No, I suppose I didn't. Hale was a swine, Sophie. When the police finally get tired of trying to pin it on your son, they'll find a veritable battleship of potential suspects. All with admirable motives, I might add. And most all of them at the party that night. But that's the problem. We mustn't let someone innocent be blamed." He hunched over, hugging his arms tightly around his waist. "I'm afraid I'm going to have to excuse myself. I'm not feeling very well tonight."

She had noticed that in the last few minutes, his face had gone white as a sheet. "Is there anything I can do?"

"No. Just make sure the door is locked behind you when you leave."

"Of course."

"And Sophie. I'll talk to Ivy tomorrow. If I find out anything important, I'll let you know. If Max is creating problems for her, she'll tell me. I'm confident of that. Thanks for caring. Ivy needs all the friends she can get right now." He put his hand over his mouth and raced from the room.

# 35

Rudy followed John into the living room of his apartment carrying a tray full of cheese, dark rye bread, and thick slices of summer sausage. John carried two beer steins filled with his favorite brew. They made themselves comfortable on the floor in front of the couch, their toes almost reaching the fireplace. Before Rudy's arrival, John had built a fire with some apple wood he'd been drying.

"I tried calling you several times today," said Rudy, unscrewing a bottle of German-style mustard. "Friday's your day off, right?"

John nodded, taking a deep sip of beer. "I took a short trip."

"Really? Where?"

"Well"—he paused, making himself a bit more comfortable by stuffing a couch pillow behind his back—"I haven't said anything to you about this, but I'm almost positive Kate Chappeldine is involved in something pretty strange, maybe even illegal. It has to do with Hale and that artist she's featuring next month, Ezmer Hawks." John took a newspaper clipping out of his pocket and handed it to Rudy. "I want the police to know about this. I mean, I can't just sit around and watch Cross harass you. It's ludicrous to think you had anything to do with Hale's murder."

Rudy unfolded the clipping. The paper was old and yellowed, with tape in several places to prevent total disintegration. The words "*Bright Water Sentinel*, August 10, 1971" had been written in black ink across the top.

"So, what is it?" asked Rudy.

"It's an article about the disappearance of a boy from a summer arts camp up near Bright Water, Minnesota. The kid, Eric Hauley, was from Duluth. He was eleven. It seems, one day, he just walked away from the camp and never came back. No one knows why. A woman who lived near Bright Water said she used to see him walking into town occasionally. She was pretty sure she saw him the day of his disappearance."

"So," said Rudy, reading through it. "I don't see what this has to do—" He stopped. "Oh, it says here Hale Micklenberg was one of the counselors."

"Right. Interesting, don't you think?"

"But what's it got to do with his death?"

"That's what I'd like to know. I found the clipping in Kate's desk drawer several days ago, along with a rubber stamp—a fake Soldiers Grove postmark. At the time, I was helping her pack one of my drawings—she'd sold it to a woman in Minnetonka. I went back to her desk looking for some strapping tape and there they were. She knows I found the stamp, but I never said anything about the clipping. My guess is that the pastels from this Hawks guy are either fakes, or he's doing them, but concealing his address. Either way, Kate's in on it."

Rudy continued to stare at the clipping. "I don't get it."

"I don't, either. That's why I drove up to Bright Water this afternoon."

"*That's* where you were?"

John nodded, reaching for a slice of cheese and nibbling the end. "I thought I'd check the place out. The campsite doesn't exist anymore. It's been turned into a fishing resort."

"How did you know where to look?"

John stopped chewing. "Well, I . . . asked several

people in town. I went to the newspaper office first and looked through their back issues. I found this." He drew out several Xeroxed sheets of paper from his back pocket. He handed one to Rudy. "Look at that."

It was a series of camp pictures taken the same year as Eric Hauley's disappearance. It had apparently been a feature article in the paper. One photo was a group shot. Unfortunately the right side of the photo was rather badly developed. It was too dark to see any of the faces. But the left side was clear.

Rudy held it closer to the firelight.

"Look at the kid, front row, third from the end," said John. "Who does that look like to you?"

Rudy squinted, smoothing the paper against his knee. "I don't know."

"Sure you do." John moved a bit closer. "Look at the shape of the face. The smile."

The light of recognition dawned. "Kate!"

"Exactly."

"But I thought she grew up in New York City."

"So did I."

"But . . . why would she lie?"

"Good question."

Rudy scratched his head.

"Think about it," said John. "If we're to believe this photo, she's known Hale a lot longer than she's let on. She was there the summer Eric Hauley disappeared. You know, your mother told me something interesting. The night Hale was murdered, he got a note from Ezmer Hawks demanding he tell the truth about some event in his past."

"This kid's disappearance?"

"I don't know. But I'll bet Kate does."

"What are you saying? You think Kate knows who killed Hale?"

John shrugged. "Maybe, although it's what the *police* think that's important." He took another bite of cheese. "I called the gallery as soon as I got back to town. I wanted to tell Kate I intend to talk to Cross first thing tomorrow morning. If she's been withholding evidence, it's going to look pretty bad. But I never got to talk to her. There was a message on the machine that said the gallery was closed due to illness."

Rudy shook his head. "I wonder if my mother knows about any of this?"

"Probably. She's been nosing around ever since Hale's death. If I were the murderer, I'd watch my back."

"Yeah, well you're not. So you've got nothing to worry about." He took an indignant bite of summer sausage.

"She's pretty upset with the way the police are handling the investigation."

"So am I," said Rudy, tipping his beer back and taking several hefty swallows. "If they can't nail me for one thing, they're going to nail me for another."

"What do you mean?"

He shook his head, switching his attention to the piano. "Say, who *is* that guy's picture you've got up there? The one that looks like a high school photo."

"He was a friend. His name's Ted Fielding."

"How come you've still got it?"

"Are you sure you want to know?"

Rudy took another sip of beer. "Sure."

"Well, he was my first lover. I cared about him a lot. Still do. He's living in Michigan now." John could sense Rudy's body stiffen and pull away.

"You're gay?" asked Rudy.

"I can't believe someone didn't say something to you. Like Kate. I don't keep it a secret."

"But *you* never said anything!"

"Is it important?"

"You're damn right it is!"

"Why?"

Rudy crawled over to the fire, keeping his back to

John. "Because . . . it is." He tightened his grip on the beer stein.

When John couldn't stand the silence any longer, he asked, "Tell me something. You *really* never had any idea I was gay?"

Rudy turned and gave him a hostile stare. "Well, maybe I did."

"But you found it a hard subject to bring up."

"Wouldn't you?"

Another long silence. "You know, your mother cares a great deal about you."

"So? What's that got to do with anything?" He lifted the beer to his lips.

"When are you going to tell her the truth?"

Rudy's hand froze. "The truth about what?"

"About you."

"I don't know what you're talking about."

"I think you do." John knew he was taking a risk, but since he'd started the conversation, he couldn't stop now. Drawing his legs up to his chest, he wrapped his arms around them and said, "It took me a long time to figure you out. I don't think your mother has quite the edge I do, so, unless you give her a break, it's going to take her longer. The thing is—and please don't take this wrong—but I've never known an ex-religious nut before."

Rudy didn't smile. "Meaning?"

"Look, you have to understand one thing. You're like someone from another planet. That's what threw me at first. Every time I assumed I knew what was going on with us, I'd change my mind. You had me completely confused, and *that* doesn't happen very often. I realize, because of your background, you've got lots of spiritual questions to come to terms with, but I also know it's more than that." He hesitated. "Come on, Rudy. Tell me I'm wrong."

Abruptly, Rudy began making himself a sandwich. His movements were jerky, his face tense.

"You can't hide forever. Your will to experience life on your own terms is too great. We're a lot alike. You don't want to live someone else's dream. You want your own. It's what made you leave your home in Montana and come here. You broke with everything you've ever known, Rudy. That took a great deal of courage. You may not believe this, but I know what that feels like. Not the religious part. I was never religious. But I left home, too. Many years ago. I know what you're going through."

Rudy's face flushed. "You couldn't possibly," he said, slapping the top piece of bread over the cheese.

"But I do," said John, taking hold of Rudy's arm. "When are you going to say it out loud? After the first time, it gets easier." He paused, waiting. Finally he said, "You're gay, Rudy. So am I. It's nothing to be ashamed of."

Carefully, Rudy placed the sandwich on the side of the tray and pushed it away. "I—I don't understand how you knew."

John smiled. "Radar."

"Huh?"

"I thought I knew the first time we met. Normally, I'm not so shy about introducing the subject, but I guess I was afraid. I wasn't completely sure, and I didn't want to scare you off. I enjoyed talking to you when I'd come to the gallery, liked the way our friendship was developing. Later, even though I still didn't understand how your background fit into your life now, I did see what was happening between us. That was unmistakable. *Have* I scared you off?"

Rudy stared into the fire, his body trembling. "No." Tentatively he reached for John's hand.

John held on tightly. "Good," he said, his voice gentle.

"But . . . I mean . . ." He let his head sink forward. "How am I ever going to tell my mother? The night the police searched my room, I was terrified they were going to find those . . . magazines."

"Gay magazines?"

Rudy nodded. "And then, of course, they did. Cross thought it was hilarious. Thank God he didn't say anything."

John had suspected it was something like that. Rudy had been so upset that night, almost beside himself with worry. "Rudy?"

"What?"

"Maybe it's none of my business, but I know you can trust Sophie and Bram. As a matter of fact, I think you're pretty lucky. They both have gay and lesbian friends. I asked Kate and she confirmed it. They're not remotely homophobic."

Rudy raised an eyebrow. "It's one thing having *friends* who are gay. It's another having a gay son."

"Maybe. But in this case, I think you're wrong. You have to realize, you're not home in Montana anymore. You don't have to hide what you're thinking and feeling. There are people here you can talk to—people who won't condemn you. But," he added, "I do think you may have a harder time with your father."

"Lord!" whooped Rudy. "Don't I know that. I had to get away from him just to get my head straight. I don't believe the same things he does anymore, but even so, I can't chuck every moral precept I've ever been taught. I don't know how I'm going to defend my sexuality—biblically, I mean. I've been reading everything I can get my hands on about what the Bible has to say about homosexuality. It doesn't look good."

John nodded. "I'm sorry. It's not a problem for me, so I don't know much about it."

"Well, it is for me." His jaw set angrily. "But at least I don't think it's a sin anymore. I never really could bring myself to believe that. In some very fundamental way, I'm much more afraid of my father than I am of God. Afraid of his anger, of disappointing him. I just wish there was a place for me somewhere within Christianity. If there is, I haven't found it."

"I think you should keep looking," said John, squeezing his hand. "I'll help all I can."

Rudy's eyes filled with tears. "John, I—you're so important to me."

"I know," said John, smiling tenderly. "You are to me, too."

"Promise you won't give up on me just because I'm weird."

"I happen to like weird." He glanced at the jawbone of a moose and two rabbit skulls resting against the side of the fireplace. "Don't worry. I'll be the solid, sensible one in this relationship."

Rudy followed his gaze. "Right," he said, shaking his head and smiling.

# 36

It was nearly midnight by the time Sophie arrived home. As she pulled her car into the drive, she noticed the lights were off in the upstairs bedroom. The study was also dark. Bram must have finished his evening with Ingrid Bergman and hit the sack. Drat. She needed to talk, to unwind and process what had happened today. Oh, well. It could wait until morning. She switched off the motor, climbed out of the front seat, and headed for the back door.

Dragging herself up the steps, she realized she was beat. Even the prospect of a good night's sleep wasn't enough to put the events of the last few days into perspective. On that depressing note, she turned the key in the lock and entered the kitchen.

"Hi," said Rudy, holding up his mug in greeting. "I thought I heard your car."

Sophie nearly dropped her briefcase. He'd been avoiding her for so many days, seeing him now, sitting so casually at the kitchen table, she was at a complete loss.

"Care for a drink?" he asked, nodding to the carton of chocolate milk next to him.

"Don't mind if I do," she answered, without missing a beat. She couldn't let on how surprised she was. Quickly she removed her coat, grabbed another mug from the cupboard, and sat down. The room was dark, except for the small hood light above the stove. She assumed he was waiting for her. No other explanation seemed reasonable. "So," she said, making herself comfortable, "did you just get home?"

"About half an hour ago. John and I had dinner together over at his apartment."

He *had* been waiting for her! She poured herself some milk. "I haven't . . . seen you in a while. How is everything?"

He stretched, leaning back in his chair. "School's fine. I've got a paper due next Monday. And I've been pretty busy at the gallery. Kate's been too occupied with other things to get much framing done, so she asked me if I'd put in some extra time. She even gave me a key so I could work after hours."

Sophie nodded. "And how about *you*?"

He took a sip from his mug, turning it around several times in his hands. "Okay, I guess. Actually, John and I had a long talk tonight. He helped me make a decision."

She could feel the muscles in her neck tighten in anticipation. "About what?"

Rudy looked down. "He told me I should trust you."

Sophie's heart beat faster. She knew this might be the

breakthrough she'd been waiting for. It was terribly important how she responded. But how *should* she respond? "You *can* trust me, Rudy. John was right."

His set his mug down. "I hope so."

"What's this decision you came to?"

"I want to tell you . . . something important."

She waited, her fingers knotting together under the table.

"See . . . Mom, the thing is—"

"Yes?" she said, sensing he needed her reassurance before he could continue.

"I guess there's no easy way to do this other than to come right out and say it."

Why was this so hard for him? Did it have something to do with Hale's murder? Was it possible—could he know more than he was telling?

"What I want to say is . . . I'm gay."

She blinked. "What?"

"I've known ever since I can remember. Dad would never have understood. That's why I left."

Instinctively she reached for his hand. In the brief moment their eyes met, she saw what his life must have been like during the years of their separation. All the anger and sadness she'd ever felt came rushing back to her. "Oh, sweetheart," she whispered, her eyes brimming with tears, "surely you know that's not a problem for me. I'm sorry this was so hard for you."

"You really don't care?" he said, his eyes opening wide.

"Why should I care? I want you to be happy! If that happiness comes from loving a man, that's fine."

He shook his head in disbelief. "John said you'd say something like that."

"Rudy, listen to me. I don't believe being gay is wrong, or sinful, or evil. I don't even think in those terms anymore." She could feel him pull away. What had she said?

"That's exactly what you don't understand," he said

angrily. "I can't ever turn my back on God the way you have. I can't just chuck it all."

"Is that what you think I've done?"

"Haven't you?"

"And you think I expect you to make the same choices?"

He nodded. "More or less."

How did these things become so confused? "I suppose, in your eyes, it might look like that. You're right. I'm not a Christian. And I'm not going to apologize for that, any more than I'd ask you to apologize for being gay."

He looked down at his hands. "You tossed your religion out the window, Mom. I'm . . . relieved that you don't have a problem with my sexuality, but the *reason* you don't *is* a problem for me. I can't do what you've done. I have to understand my life within the context of my beliefs."

"So do I!" She paused for a moment to regroup. Losing her cool now wasn't going to get them anywhere. "Look, this isn't going to be a one-time conversation. For each of us to understand where the other person is—how we reached the point we're at—is very complex. But rest assured, my spiritual life is every bit as important to me as yours is to you. I don't expect you to be a mirror image of me, of my values and beliefs, just because you're my son, and I hope you don't expect me to mirror you. We're separate people, Rudy. We get to live our own lives. But we're also a family. As a parent, I want to support you. I want to be there for you when you need my help. And most of all, I want to love you. I haven't had the chance to be a mother since you were *six*. From my standpoint, that religion you're so quick to defend has caused a great deal of pain."

"I know," he said softly. "I don't really understand that. It's not the way it should be."

"No, it's not. And I'll be damned if I let any religious

dogma divide us now that we're so close to having the relationship I've wanted for so long. Of course you have to be free to believe what you want, Rudy. Just don't shut me out."

He stood and moved to the counter. "I never wanted to shut you out. It's just . . . I've had so much to think about since I moved here. I don't know where things fit anymore. Sometimes I feel like my head is going to explode."

Her heart went out to him. She knew what he was going through, even though he would never concede that she understood. She'd gone through a similar process herself many years ago.

"And with this murder investigation," he continued, "I wasn't sure what you thought of me. I didn't kill Hale, Mom. I have no idea who did."

"I know that!"

"Do you? Do you really believe me? After all, we hardly know each other. I wouldn't blame you if—"

"Stop it," she insisted. "I've never doubted your innocence."

He slumped back into the chair. "I just wish the police would find out the truth. Then my life could get back to its normal chaos." The edges of his lips curled into a slight smile.

Sophie smiled back. "We'll figure it out. It's just going to take some time."

"Yeah. John said you'd been doing some snooping." His expression relaxed. "Thanks."

"Don't mention it." She paused, not sure how he'd take the next question. "Rudy? Why did you lie to the police?"

He hung his head. "This is such a mess."

"Explain it to me."

"Well," he said, folding his arms over his chest, "the night of the party, Bram was introducing me around to a bunch of your friends. When I looked up, John was gone. I searched, but I couldn't find him anywhere.

That's when I got the idea to look outside. I stepped out the back door and almost immediately heard what I thought was a gunshot. It seemed like it had come from the gate house, so I took off running. The front door was unlocked."

"Unlocked or ajar?"

He thought for a minute. "It was open slightly. Like it hadn't been shut all the way."

"Good. Go on."

"I raced up the stairs and that's when I found Hale's body. He was completely still. Somewhere in there I heard a door slam. I looked up and saw the back stairs. Mom, you have to understand. I was terrified John had done it. I know it didn't make any sense, but that's the first thing that came into my mind. I was paralyzed with fear. Then, without thinking, I just bolted down the back stairs. I kept calling John's name. When I got to the bottom, I looked outside and saw a woman going in the back door of the house. I wasn't lying about that. Maybe she was the murderer!"

"But you don't know who it was."

"It was too dark."

"What did you do then?"

"I stood there several seconds longer trying to figure out what my next move should be. Then, I came to find you. If I caught my jacket on something, I never noticed it."

"Why didn't you tell the police the truth about running down the back steps."

He shook his head. "All I could think about that night was protecting John. How could I tell them what I really feared? I wasn't thinking clearly. After I was on record and they knew I wasn't telling the truth, I didn't know how to get out of it."

Sophie was beginning to understand. "Why did you take those pictures of Ezmer Hawks's drawings?"

He shrugged. "I liked them. I didn't have any particular reason. I just thought they were cool. And I wanted to try out my camera. That's all."

She believed him. "Did you ever find out where John was at the party that night?"

"He said he'd gone upstairs. He wanted to see how rich folks lived. He found a library of art books."

"Did anyone see him upstairs?"

"What are you implying?" He sat up very straight. "He didn't kill Hale, Mom. He's no more guilty than I am!"

She decided it was best to back off the subject of John Jacobi. At least for now.

"Come to think of it," said Rudy, his voice growing excited, "John discovered something really interesting. When I was having dinner with him tonight, he mentioned that he'd driven up to Bright Water this afternoon. He found a clipping in Kate's desk drawer at the gallery—something about the disappearance of a boy from an arts camp up near there. Hale was a counselor the year it happened."

"You said he found it in *Kate's* drawer?"

Rudy nodded. "And look at this." He withdrew the Xeroxed copy of the camp photograph John had given him and handed it to her. "It's a picture of the kids at the camp. John's pretty sure the girl, third from the end in the front row, is Kate Chappeldine. Apparently, she was there that summer, too."

Even in the semidarkness, Sophie couldn't miss the likeness. "I though Kate grew up in New York."

"Maybe not."

An idea began forming in her mind. "Did I hear you say you had a key to the gallery?"

"Yup. Why?"

"I want to go over there and take a look at her office."

"You mean now?"

"You've got other plans?" She stood. "I've been trying to get in touch with her all day. If we could just talk, I'm sure she could clear everything up. But since she refuses to come out of hiding, maybe I can at least get a look at her office. Who knows what I might find!"

"That's breaking and entering, Mom."

"Not if you have a key."

"Well, just entering then."

"Not if you spend a few minutes framing. Then it's just a . . . motherly visit."

He grinned. "All right. You're on."

"Good!"

"You think she had something to do with Hale's murder?"

Sophie shook her head. "My gut tells me no. But I can't conclude anything final until we talk."

He nodded. "My mother, the sleuth."

"Among other things."

"I'm glad you're on my side."

"Don't ever doubt it," she said, giving him a hug and holding him tight. "One other thing," she whispered.

"What?"

"Finish your milk."

# 37

Rudy peeked inside the back door of the gallery and listened. After a moment, he whispered, "I don't hear anything, but there's a light on in the storage room."

"So?" said Sophie. She stood directly behind him, looking both ways down the deserted alley. The last thing she wanted was to run into a police car. "Is that a problem?"

"Usually Kate turns all the lights off back here before she leaves. But she wasn't in today."

"Well, then consider this a mission to help her save a few bucks on her electric bill."

Rudy seemed uneasy. "I don't know."

"Come on. Let's get this over with." She nudged him with both hands.

Taking one last look around, he held the door open while she entered. The hallway was dark, except for a high window that allowed the streetlight to stream in from outside. Sophie could see into Kate's tiny office. It was empty.

"Wait," he whispered, grabbing her arm as soon as the door closed behind them. "I think I heard something."

"What?"

"I don't know. Just listen."

They both stood very still. From across the hall came the unmistakable sound of footsteps.

"I was right," whispered Rudy. "Someone's here! Let's get out while we still can."

"Wait a minute," she whispered, moving a few feet closer to the storage room door.

"No, Mom! Leave it, okay? I'm already in enough trouble."

"I want to see who's here. If it's Kate, this may be my only chance to talk to her."

Rudy rubbed his palms anxiously against the sides of his jeans. "You're making me a nervous wreck!"

"Just stay put. I'll be right back." She stepped cautiously to the edge of the door and peeked inside.

There, in the rear of the room, almost hidden by a large canvas propped against a table, stood Kate. She had her back to Sophie, hands on her hips. A single light burned, casting deep shadows against the bare concrete walls. In front of her on the easel was one of the pastels. Even at this distance, Sophie easily recognized the sphinx with fire between its paws. Suddenly Kate grabbed the picture and began to shred it, angrily crushing the pieces against her chest. As they fell to the floor, she muttered, "Damn you! Damn you! I hope you burn in hell!"

Sophie was stunned.

Without warning, Kate whirled around. She started for the door—but stopped abruptly as her gaze locked on Sophie. "How did you get in here?"

Sophie stood very still. "Why didn't you return my phone calls?"

"I . . . wasn't feeling well." The room was suffused with a suspicious silence. "Who let you in?"

Sophie walked a few paces closer. "After what John dumped on you last night, I don't doubt you weren't feeling well."

"What do you mean?" Her eyes grew large.

"I know about the bogus Soldiers Grove postmark. I also know you were at Camp Bright Water the same summer Eric Hauley disappeared. What's going on, Kate? What are you a part of?"

Kate's face underwent a distinct change as she drew inward. Her body grew very still.

"I'm not leaving until you tell me the truth. You aren't leaving, either." Sophie let the threat hang in the air.

"I don't know what you're talking about."

"Cut the crap! This concerns my son! If you know something about Hale's death, I want to hear it!"

"But you don't understand."

"No, I don't." Her eyes narrowed in disgust. Even now, Kate wasn't going to come clean. Sophie could feel her resistance.

"I don't know *anything* about his death!"

"Then prove it! Talk to me. I'm not your enemy, Kate. A few days ago I would have said I was one of your best friends."

"You *are* my friend! I just can't . . . I mean . . ." Her body seemed to deflate as she crumpled onto a stool.

Sophie crossed to the back of the room and leaned against the worktable. She knew she was blocking Kate's exit, but she didn't care. She wasn't sure what to expect anymore. Kate looked terrible, as if she hadn't slept in days. Under other circumstances, Sophie might have felt sorry for her. Tonight, she just wanted answers.

"What do you want to know?" asked Kate warily, working to control her face.

"Why don't you start at the beginning?"

She bit her lower lip. Slowly, as if her entire body hurt, she leaned into the light, meeting Sophie's eyes. "Can't you just leave me alone?"

Sophie could see she'd been crying. For some reason, it surprised her. "No, Kate. I can't. What really happened at that arts camp?"

Wrapping her arms around her stomach, Kate glanced again at the mangled drawing. Finally, in a low, flat voice, she said, "You aren't going to let this drop, are you?" It was more a statement than a question.

Sophie shook her head.

"Well, then, I suppose I'll have to trust you."

"Is that so terrible?"

She looked away. Squaring her jaw, she said, "All right, the beginning. I was ten the summer my nightmare started. My name was Katie Nelson, then. My mother divorced my father shortly after I returned from Bright Water that year and we moved to New York. That's why Hale never put it together. He never suspected little Katie Nelson had become Kate Chappeldine. There was a boy at camp. His name was Eric. We were pretty good friends, though he was kind of a loner. For some reason, Hale seemed to have it in for him. At the time, I didn't recognize the verbal abuse as part of Hale's incessant need to denigrate other people's talent, but I've seen it many times since—especially when the talent in question is unusually strong, like Eric's. To tell the truth, I've never understood it. Perhaps Hale was jealous. Or maybe he was thwarted artistically. Whatever the case, I don't care. All I know is, he was a spoiler. Eric couldn't do anything right. A couple of times I heard the other counselors talking about it, but nothing changed.

"On the east side of the camp was a steep cliff overlooking a river. It was off-limits, though I knew Eric went there all the time. At the edge of that cliff was the shell of a house. It had burned down many years before, but part of the structure was still standing. The front wall was intact. And a door—just the frame—overlooked the river. I imagine once it must have led to steps that took you down to a dock. That summer, it was merely an open hole that dropped about two hundred yards to the water.

"One afternoon, I was wandering in the woods. Everyone else was down at the beach for swimming practice, but since I'd cut my big toe on a piece of glass the day before, I was told to keep my foot dry for a few days. I knew I wasn't supposed to go near the river, but I was bored. I also think I may have been a little lost. Anyway, as I got near the burned house, I heard shouting. I walked a bit farther until I could see Hale and Eric inside the structure. Without thinking, I hid behind a tree and watched.

"Hale was yelling that Eric had no business being this far away from camp. Eric responded by saying he was sick of all the rules. After all, this was a summer *arts* program, not a prison. Hale countered by insisting he was a troublemaker. If he couldn't follow simple rules how was he ever going to make it in life? Eric took a swing at him, and in return, Hale shoved him to the ground. After that, the verbal abuse got worse. Hale roared that any pretensions Eric harbored about becoming a dancer were just daydreams. He was pathetic. Graceless. And furthermore, Hale declared that he would see to it Eric was punished severely for breaking camp rules. Dance class would be off-limits for the rest of his stay. Well, by this time, Eric had scrambled to his feet. He took a flying leap at Hale's legs and slammed him to the ground. God, I'd never seen a grownup so furious. Eric was big for his age, but he was no match for a twenty-five-year-old man. Hale picked him up by the scruff of his neck and slapped him hard across the face. Trying to get away, Eric stumbled on a tree root, and fell face first through the open hole."

Sophie's mouth dropped open.

"I just stood there. I couldn't even speak. Hale moved to the edge of the cliff and looked down. He screamed Eric's name over and over, but got no response. When he finally turned around, I could see how scared he was. That's when he spotted me. 'How long have you been standing there?' he yelled. When I said nothing, he rushed over and grabbed me by the shoulders. 'What did you see?' He shook me so hard I thought my head would snap off. All I could get out was that I wanted to know what happened to Eric. 'You didn't see *anything*!' he insisted. He said it over and over. He made me repeat the words after him. 'If you tell anyone about this, the same thing will happen to you!' He brought his face very close to mine and asked if I understood. I nodded. With every fiber of my being, I believed what he said. 'Now, get out of here,' he yelled, shoving me away.

"I ran as fast as I could. Later that same day, at dinner, I could see him watching me. When the police arrived the next morning, I said nothing. When the counselors talked to us about Eric's disappearance, he made sure I was in his group. Two days later I was back home. To my knowledge, the body was never found, or if it was, it was never linked to Eric. Once, before we left the city that fall, I saw Hale standing outside my school yard. He was watching me. I couldn't wait to leave Minneapolis. I never even considered telling my mother. After we got to New York, I tried to forget, but the nightmares wouldn't go away. I saw Eric's face in my dreams for years. I think, when I was still pretty small, I somehow had myself convinced that Eric's death was my fault. As I got older, I realized what Hale had done—not only to Eric, but to me. That's why I came back to Minneapolis two years ago. I knew Hale had made quite a name for himself here. And I'd been part owner of a gallery in New York City and wanted to try my hand elsewhere. But most of all, I wanted to make Hale pay. I wanted revenge." She paused and looked hard at Sophie. "Are you sure you want to hear the rest of this?"

Sophie nodded. She needed to know.

"All right. Several months after I'd opened the gallery, my cousin, who lives in Bloomington, brought in four or five drawings her eight-year-old daughter had done. She wanted to get them matted and framed for their family room. Her daughter had been given a bunch of pastels for Christmas and had really done some nice work. So I matted them. Before I could get them framed, Hale stopped by. He'd already informed me that he was always given special privileges by the other gallery owners in town. He liked to be taken into the back rooms and shown anything new or interesting. The day he came by, my niece's drawings were propped against the easel. He walked straight up to them and began praising their freshness. Their charm. Well, what could I do? I just let him talk. When he asked for the name of the artist, I told him I'd have to check. He said if I ever got any more work by the same person, to call him. He'd come see it right away. And that's how it all started.

"I played with the idea for weeks before I came up with a plan. I was going to humiliate him. I wanted him to go on record somewhere about the pastels and then I was going to tell the truth and show the world what a phony he really was. I don't mean to suggest my niece has no talent, but she *is* eight years old. You get the point. So, I asked her to do more of them. I hung a few of my favorites here and there in the gallery. When Hale came in, I made up this story about a reclusive artist, Ezmer Hawks—named from Eric's initials—who lived in northern Minnesota. Hale was even more excited than he'd been before. After he'd written some comments about Hawks in the paper, I knew I had him. All I had to do was reveal the identity of the artist and he'd be the laughingstock of his profession. Yet, by the time I had him right where I wanted him, I realized it wasn't enough. I wanted more. I wanted to see him sweat. I wanted him to feel pain, to experience real fear. But what really made me reconsider my plan of attack was the realization that, in the end, I wasn't convinced my little joke would last long enough to do him any true damage. That's when I got the idea to bring back Eric."

"Bring him back?" repeated Sophie.

"Sure. Why not? One afternoon, I showed my niece some photographs and I asked if she would draw some specific images. Over the next few weeks she did twenty or thirty. I took the best, had a rubber postmark made, and faked the mailings as if they had come directly from Soldiers Grove. Hale came in to look at the new drawings as soon as they arrived. Each time I doled out two or three more. Inch by inch, I was drawing him into my web. I also used the postmark for a letter I sent him—from Ezmer. You were there the day he got it. By then, he was terrified. He didn't know *what* was going on. I think he may actually have believed Eric was still alive, come back to take his revenge. Since I had no proof of what Hale had done so many years ago, just a child's memory—and our legal system, I should point out, places no credence in *that*—I didn't want to just scare the shit out of him; I wanted to make him confess!"

"But, some might say it was an accident," replied Sophie.

"The fall may have been, but what precipitated it wasn't," said Kate. "Besides, Hale was the adult! He should have seen the danger. And he should never have been harassing Eric in the first place! As for what he did to me—even though it was motivated by fear—it was vicious and unconscionable."

Sophie had to agree. "Go on."

"The night of John Jacobi's opening, I made a phone call to Hale's home. I'd gotten my cousin's five-year-old son to recite a nursery rhyme into a tape recorder. You may know it. 'For every evil under the sun, there is a remedy or there is none.' "

"Of course," said Sophie under her breath. It was all beginning to make sense.

"I found it in a book I was reading to the kids one evening before bed. I thought it was perfect. When I called Hale's house, I waited until the phone was answered and then I played the tape through. I did it several times. I have no idea what specific effect it had on him, but I know he was growing more anxious by the day. I thought it would be only a matter of time before he cracked. But then I got impatient. The night of the party I was so angered by what he'd done to Ben Kiran, I decided to force his hand. I left a note in a catalogue I knew he would pick up. I will confess to a certain thrill when I saw him read it." She stopped, forcing herself to look Sophie square in the eyes. "I'll never know now what he was going to do because . . . someone got to him first. You must understand. I didn't want him to die, I wanted him to *live* with what he'd done. I wanted the world to know! You've got to believe me, Sophie. You knew what kind of man he was! But—" She hesitated. "After his death, I got frightened. I knew if I told the police what I'd done, I was sure to be arrested. I had motive, opportunity—everything. Except I didn't do it!"

Sophie just stared at her. She wasn't sure what to think. "That's quite a story."

"It's not a *story*. It's the truth!"

She wanted to believe her. She knew her reticence must hurt. "I believe what you said about Hale and what happened at the camp. And I can see you've gone to some elaborate means to get back at him. But if you didn't kill him, who did?"

Kate clenched and unclenched her fists. "How should I know? He must have had other enemies."

Sophie could hear the desolation in her voice, but she wasn't going to be sidetracked. She still had questions. "What about the attempts that were made on Ivy's life?"

"What about them? Why would I want to hurt Ivy?"

"She was at the camp that same summer."

"So?"

"Are you telling me she knew nothing about what Hale had done?"

Kate shrugged. "I have no way of knowing."

"But surely you must realize those phone calls had some effect on her as well? Didn't you care?"

Kate looked away. "I didn't think of that. I never meant to hurt Ivy. She was one of Hale's victims, too."

Sophie shivered. What a way to view a man's life—or your own. "The night he died, did you follow him to the gate house?"

"No!"

"But you threatened him in the note. What were you going to do if he didn't call the police? And how would you even know what he'd done if you didn't personally confront him?"

"I hadn't thought that far." Her teeth gnawed anxiously at her lower lip. "Stop pressing me!"

Sophie could tell Kate was at an emotional pitch. She was glad for Rudy's silent presence. "All right, but listen to me for a minute. You've got an important decision to make. John's planning to go to the police with what he knows first thing in the morning."

Her head jerked up. "What?"

"And I must tell you, if he wasn't going, I would be."

She backed off the stool and covered her ears with her hands. "Why can't you trust me?" she pleaded, accidentally bumping into the easel and knocking it to the floor.

"Kate, listen! If John goes to the police with his information, it will look pretty bad. But if *you* get there first, if you have a chance to explain everything from your point of view, I think your chances are much better."

Kate picked up another of the pastel drawings and crushed it angrily in her hands. "One way or another that man has polluted everything he's every touched."

"Maybe," said Sophie, keeping her voice very calm. She knew Kate was still stalling. "But what's it going to be?"

Kate flung the paper to the floor. "All right, damn it! I'll call them."

"Good." Sophie relaxed a bit. "When you're done, I'll drive you down to the station."

"What? You expect me to call them *now*?"

"Why not?"

Kate stared at her.

"Look, you want me to believe you. Everything inside me wants that, too. But I've still got Rudy to consider."

"I know!"

"So what's it going to be? Rudy and I will be glad to stay with you if you want."

"What do you mean, *Rudy*?" The light was beginning to dawn. "So that's how you got in here."

"Afraid so," he said, stepping into the doorway.

Kate looked hard at him and then back at Sophie. "I can drive myself, thank you."

"Are you sure you're not too upset?"

"Just say what you're thinking! You're not sure I'll go if you don't take me there yourself."

The truth was, Sophie wasn't about to let Kate out of her sight until she was sure a full account had been made.

Kate placed an indignant hand on her hip. "Okay. We'll do it your way."

"Our car's out back," said Rudy.

Kate glared at him.

"For what it's worth, you're doing the right thing," offered Sophie. "Maybe it's best to let some of the anger go now. Make a clean breast of it."

"Who died and made you a fucking Zen master?" Angrily she reached up and took hold of the cord attached to the light fixture. "I realize you've been trying to find out who Hale's murderer was just to establish your son's innocence. But consider this: if you think there's any possibility I'm telling the truth—any possibility *at all*—and if our friendship means anything to you, then you still can't stop looking."

It sounded like emotional blackmail. But Kate was desperate. And maybe she had a point. "I promise. I'll do my best. I won't stop."

Kate gave the cord a yank. She moved toward Sophie in the darkness and brushed past her, muttering, "I guess it's my turn to be skeptical. I don't believe *you*."

# 38

The phone awakened Louie the next morning. He was lying across his bed, blankets and sheets in a sweaty snarl around his waist. It had been a bad night. "Hello," he rasped into the receiver. He grabbed for the glass of water on the nightstand and found it empty.

"You sound terrible," came Ivy's voice.

"Yeah," he said, rubbing a hand over his whiskered face. "That about covers it."

"Are you all right? I thought you told me you were getting better."

He groaned. "Ivy, I just have the flu. My throat is sore." That was an understatement. It felt as if he'd been swallowing gravel.

"What you need is some chicken soup."

He felt his stomach lurch at the idea. "I'd rather have a brandy." It was the only thing that numbed the pain, mental and physical.

"Louie?"

"What?"

"You're drinking too much. You're not used to alcohol. You don't know what it can do."

A sermon was the last thing he needed. "Well, I'm worried about you, too." He swung his feet out of bed and glanced around for his robe.

"Why?"

"Because I'm having a terrible time figuring out how to break that will."

"I told you to drop it. Max has several lawyers working on it."

"And that's another thing." He reached under the bed for his slippers, but stopped as the pain in his stomach grew acute.

"What do you mean?"

He put a hand over the receiver to cover his gasp, waiting for the spasm to pass. "I mean," he barked, realizing his voice wasn't completely under his control, "that your relationship with that asshole surgeon has *me* concerned."

Silence.

"Ivy?" Something was wrong. Normally she leapt to Max's defense with sabers drawn.

"I'm here." A pause. "You know what? I think you may be right. When you're feeling better, I'd like to talk to you about . . . something."

"Talk now—or forever hold your peace."

"Don't joke like that!"

He reached for the Maalox. "Come on, Ivy. What's wrong? You can tell me."

"It's nothing. It can wait."

"Is Max hurting you in some way?"

She started to sob. "Oh, Louie. My life is such a mess."

"Then, tell me about it. We've never kept secrets. Maybe I can help." He propped several pillows against the headboard and leaned back.

She sniffed but said nothing.

"You're shutting me out."

"And you're sick. You should rest."

God, why didn't she stop harping on that? He *realized* he was sick. Only he knew *how* sick. "I had a visitor yesterday." He decided to try another approach.

"Really? Who?"

"Sophie Greenway."

"What did she want?"

"She's worried about you, too."

"Oh."

"See, I'm not the only one." He took a swig of antacid.

"You know, Louie, I respect her a great deal."

"Really? Why?"

"She's a Nineties' woman. Confident. Smart. She has everything under control."

"Do tell."

"No, really."

"That's a stereotype, Ivy. It has no meaning in real life—only in magazine ads."

"You're missing my point."

"Am I? Well, whatever the case, she seemed terribly concerned about those attempts on your life. I told her I felt certain Hale was behind them."

"Did you?"

"She also said she felt like you were afraid of Max."

More silence.

"Is it true?" In the background he could hear a doorbell ring.

"Louie . . . I've got to run."

"You're changing the subject." He felt his stomach heave.

"No, I'm not afraid of Max. That's probably him now. He was going to stop by before he went to the hospital."

"Tell him I need a new stomach." He eased out of bed.

"What?"

"I'll talk to you later. I love you, Ivy. You know that, don't you?"

"Don't be a ninny. Call if you need anything."

"Right. Give my best to Dr. Jekyll. Or is it Mr. Hyde? 'Bye." He dropped the phone back on the hook and stumbled into the bathroom.

# 39

Bram burst through the kitchen door carrying a box of fresh croissants. "These were the last raspberry cream cheese they had," he announced, setting them on the counter with an air of triumph. He turned to look at Sophie. "Ah. I can see we're heavily into our mole persona this morning." The shades were still pulled, the kitchen dark and gloomy. He switched on the overhead light and then walked over and waved the box under her nose. "Hmm. This is serious. Not even a twitch." He sat down next to her and pretended to take her pulse. "That's funny. I don't feel any reassuring thumps."

"That's because I'm thin and wan and in desperate need of sustenance." She grabbed a croissant out of the box and took a bite.

"Better," he said, still holding her wrist as he checked his watch. "You didn't sleep a wink last night, did you?"

"I had too much to think about."

"What time did you finally get in?"

"Around two."

Ethel lumbered into the room and sat down directly in front of Bram, sniffing the air. Her gaze came to rest on the croissant in Sophie's hand.

"You know," he said, scratching the dog's ears, "this mutt looks more like a cartoon than a real animal. With those short legs and that large head—"

Sophie put a finger to her lips. "Shh. She's sensitive about her height. I understand completely."

Bram and Ethel both stared as Sophie finished her roll.

"The police are still holding Kate," said Sophie, licking her fingers.

"How do you know?"

"I just called and talked with Detective Cross."

"But they haven't officially arrested her yet?"

"Not yet."

"Do you think she's guilty?" He got up to pour himself a cup of coffee.

Ethel moved over next to Sophie and eased onto the floor, her head resting on Sophie's right foot.

"No, though I wish I were more certain." Even so, she wasn't about to forget her promise. She would not stop her search for the real killer. "I just keep thinking about the night Hale died."

"What about it?" He selected his own croissant and sat down.

Sensing another potential food opportunity, Ethel twitched but remained prone.

"I know I'm missing something—I can just feel it. After Rudy came and got me at the party that night, we immediately ran up to Hale's office. In my mind, I can see his body lying on the floor. His desk was empty, except for an ashtray. He must have been smoking because there was a cigar in it. He'd been using the computer, too, because Rudy said the monitor was warm when he found him."

"But it had been turned off?"

She nodded.

"That's odd."

"What do you mean?"

"Well, think about it. Why would a man who was terrified for his life be staring at a computer screen? He'd just received a threatening note from Ezmer Hawks, right?"

"You mean Kate."

"Whatever."

Sophie bit into another croissant. Raspberry jam oozed from the corners. "You have a point. I wonder if the police subpoenaed any of Hale's computer files?" As she considered the question, she heard a soft knock on the back door.

"It's the health food police!" shrieked Bram, stuffing the last bit of croissant into his mouth. "Quick. You hide the box and I'll start brewing some herbal tea."

Ignoring him, she got up, tucking her shirt inside her jeans.

"Wait! I'll get some sprouts out of the refrigerator and scatter them around the breakfast table. That'll put 'em off the scent."

"Did anyone ever tell you you're nuts?"

"Generally, during my yearly salary review, the subject is *broached*."

She rolled her eyes, opening the door.

Ethel let out an obligatory growl. It was a mere formality. Movement was the farthest thing from her mind.

"Hi," said Ben, giving her a tentative smile. "Is this too early to come calling? I know it's Saturday."

He was the last person she expected to see. "No, of course not. Come in." She glanced at Bram out of the corner of her eye and noticed several thin, green tendrils dangling from his closed mouth. "We were just finishing breakfast."

Ben's eyes fell to the box of croissants.

"Caught red-handed," said Bram, holding his hand to his head like a gun and pulling the trigger. He slumped backward over the chair.

Sophie waved Ben to a seat and then resumed hers. "What can we do for you?"

"Well," he said, unzipping his suede jacket, "actually, I think I have some information you might be interested in. You're a pretty good friend of Chuck Squire's, aren't you?"

"I wouldn't say we were friends," said Sophie. "He was managing editor at the magazine before I took over."

"Well, you know he was recently appointed CEO of Hale's company, IAI."

"I did hear that. By the way, are you going to be shooting their new spring catalogue?"

"Not exactly. Chuckles wouldn't approve the contract."

"I'm sorry."

"Yeah. To be honest, getting that job was a matter of financial survival. I did pick up a couple of other shoots, but nothing to compare with that one. I'm just keeping my fingers crossed. Anyway, in the negotiating process, I found out something interesting. It seems Hale falsified his tax records for 1994."

"Charles told you that?"

"Well, no. See, it seems Hale was selling artwork he never reported as income. He also has several Swiss bank accounts. I don't know what's in them, but I have the numbers. At first I thought Chuckie was part of it, but now I'm not so sure. I think I jumped to a wrong conclusion somewhere along the line. I confronted him with it the other day, and he just blew me off. Said his hands were clean. That's when I got to thinking."

"How *did* you find this information?" asked Bram, scraping the sprouts into a neat pile on the table and then blowing them away.

"It's a long story."

"I don't doubt it."

"Suffice it to say, I'm pretty sure Chuck was gathering evidence on Hale's financial activities for a specific reason. That evidence is what I stumbled across."

"And the reason?" asked Sophie.

"What else? Blackmail."

Bram whistled. "Did Hale know about it?"

"I'm almost positive," said Ben, looking more than pleased with himself.

"How do you know?" asked Bram.

"I called his lawyer's office yesterday morning. I wanted to know the last time Hale had updated his will. It's a matter of public record now. They couldn't put me off."

"And?" said Sophie.

"It was two weeks before his death. In the new document, he designated Mrs. Betty Malmquist as his new heir, but he made Charles Squire the acting CEO of IAI for one year after his death—at a very hefty salary, I might add."

"You think Charles forced him to do it?" asked Sophie.

"Not the heir part. I think Hale did that all on his own. But appointing Chuck president, yeah, I think there was some pressure. Though, I have no proof other than the disk I filched from Hale's office." He put a hand over his mouth. "Oops."

Sophie raised an eyebrow.

"Anyway, I guess I'm wondering if our friend Charles might not have had something to do with Hale's murder. He had ample motive, and I don't doubt opportunity."

Sophie wondered if the police knew any of this. Surely they would've investigated everyone who benefited from Hale's death. The will had to be a big part of it.

Ben pulled some papers from his pocket. "Here are copies of what I have. I dropped these off at the IRS office in downtown St. Paul a couple of days ago, but you know how slowly bureaucracies move. This morning I mailed a set to the police. I wanted to remain anonymous—for obvious reasons." He gave a sheepish smile.

"Very interesting," said Sophie. "As I think about it,

I may just pay a short visit to Charles this afternoon. You never know what might turn up."

"No, you never do," observed Ben, rising from the table. "With a mastermind like Chuck, anything's possible." He winked. "Well, I better get going. Let me know if you find out anything, Sophie. I'm very interested." He stepped quickly to the door. "See you good people around." He grinned, disappearing into a gust of March wind.

# 40

The grand strains of Beethoven's *Emperor* Concerto assaulted Sophie as she climbed the steps to the gate house. Before ringing the bell, she peeked through the glass. Charles was lying on the bare wood floor in the center of the room, his arms outstretched. From this rather odd position, he appeared to be directing the music. His eyes were tightly shut, a wand held in one hand. What a strange man, she thought to herself as she pushed the button.

Instantly he leapt to his feet. He scrambled to the back wall and opened a small cabinet.

Sophie could hear the music being turned down. A second later the door opened.

"Oh," he said, his rapturous expression drooping, "it's you." Somewhere along the way, he'd managed to lose the wand.

"Practicing for a new career?" she asked.

He tightened his lips. "Perhaps. What do you want?"

"To talk to you."

"I'm busy."

"I can see that." She brushed past him into the gallery. She'd never had much respect for Charles. She found that, over the past year, she'd come to treat him more and more like his father did. She should probably try to be nicer, but some things were just too hard. "I understand you were blackmailing Hale."

His Adam's apple almost burst out of his neck as he tried to swallow his surprise. "I beg your pardon?"

"Yes, you probably should." She made herself comfortable in one of the two wing chairs near the front. She nodded to the other.

Charles perched. "You have no right to come in here making accusations like that."

"I know Hale was selling art he never reported to the IRS. If I can find out something like that, so can you. In fact, I'm sure you *did*."

Charles raised his chin, his nose wiggling like a dog sensing the ominous approach of the mailman. "You have no proof."

"No, but I think the police will find it more than interesting that Hale changed his will a mere two weeks before his death."

"So?"

"He appointed you acting president of IAI should anything happen to him."

"I was the logical choice."

"Why? Because you've been working here less than two months? Because nobody else on the board of directors has any expertise in the field? Or maybe it's because you're such a swell fella."

He gave her a disgusted sniff. "What do you want?"

She decided to take a chance. "The night Hale died, you were here in the gate house, weren't you?"

"What if I was?" He played with the leather buttons on his sweater. "Hale was being an ass. He'd made a promise to Ben Kiran to let him shoot the new catalogue, and then he hired someone else. Ben made his displeasure quite clear to me that evening and asked me to pass it on to Hale. Since I couldn't find him anywhere, I thought I'd try the office."

"And you found him sitting behind the desk."

"No. Actually, he wasn't here. I waited for a few minutes and then turned on the computer. I didn't feel much like partying after my little scene with Ben, so I decided to get some work done. That's when Hale stomped in." He grew silent.

"What happened?" she prodded.

"Well . . . I started to tell him what Ben had said. I explained that he'd discovered some information about his illegal activities. I assumed Hale would be pretty upset, but he just ordered me out of his chair and sat down. He looked strange. He got out his gun and set it on the desk, and then he lit a cigar. I waited for a minute and then suggested we fire the other photographer and rehire Ben. But . . . it was as if he wasn't even hearing me. He told me to get out. When I didn't move fast enough, he pointed the gun at me and—and threatened my life! Well, I know when I'm not wanted. I made my escape with great haste."

"You didn't see anyone outside?"

"No one."

"Hale didn't say anything about why he wanted you to leave—why he took out the gun?"

He shook his head. "Nothing."

Sophie wasn't sure how much to believe. "Have you talked to the police about any of this?"

"Yes . . . some of it. The day after the tragedy occurred. But"—he paused, taking a handkerchief out of his pocket and wiping his forehead—"I didn't fill in all the details, if you know what I mean."

"We couldn't have that."

"No," he said, pursing his lips. "We couldn't."

"You know, Charles, you had an awfully good motive for Hale's murder."

"Funny, that beefy police detective said the same

thing. Yet, if it's so great, why haven't I heard from them since?"

Good question, thought Sophie. "Perhaps they're gathering their case."

"Perhaps." His hand shook slightly as he stuffed the handkerchief back into his pocket.

"Well," said Sophie, patting his knee, "if you need character witnesses, don't forget me."

He gave her a sick smile. "Thank you."

"Don't mention it. And don't get up. I'll show myself out."

"You're too kind."

"I know. See you in court."

# 41

As Sophie made her way outside to her car, she noticed Ivy waving at her from the bay of the mansion's dining room window. Sophie waved back. When Ivy pointed to the front door, continuing to wave, Sophie realized she was being summoned inside. She moved quickly around the side of the house.

Ivy was waiting for her when she got to the front door. "Good morning," she said, her expression troubled. "I hoped you might have a few minutes to talk."

"Sure," replied Sophie, stepping into the foyer. Ivy looked positively wired this morning, her eyes jumping from one object to the next as she led the way to the kitchen. Sophie wondered if she was on something—compliments of Max.

"Would you like a cup of tea?" asked Ivy. "I just made a pot."

"That sounds great."

"I noticed you come out of the gate house. Were you visiting Charles?" She kept her voice carefully neutral.

"I was." Sophie thought it was best to keep her reasons for the visit to herself. "I had to talk to him about some back issues of the magazine."

"Oh, right. He was the editor of *Squires Magazine* for a while."

As Sophie got comfortable at the kitchen table she noticed a German chocolate cake on the far end of one counter. She wondered if it was going to be served tonight at Max and Ivy's dinner for Betty Malmquist. Sophie wasn't entirely convinced the dinner was a good idea.

Ivy finished preparing the tray with cream, sugar, cups and saucers, and a plate of cookies. Carefully lifting the teapot onto it, she approached the table, following Sophie's gaze to the cake. "It sort of screams cholesterol at you, doesn't it? It's Max's favorite. I've planned a German dinner tonight. I've had the sauerbraten marinating since yesterday afternoon."

"You know, I'm curious." Sophie waited while Ivy poured.

"About what?"

"Why did you really invite Betty here tonight?"

Ivy sat down, covering her discomfort with a thoughtful frown. "Mainly curiosity, I guess. I haven't talked to her in years, not since she stopped walking her dog past the house. I was astonished to find Hale had kept up the . . . relationship." She shook her head in a kind of perplexed reverie as she stirred cream into her tea.

"But Max mentioned yesterday you were going to try to convince her to go to the police with what she found in the bottom of that sack. The rifle shells, Lasix, and bottle of arsenic."

Once again, her expression became uneasy. "Yes, well that, too."

Clearly she wasn't comfortable with the subject. Sophie decided to try the direct approach. "What did you want to talk about?" she asked, taking a sip from her cup. The tea was good. Most probably Indian.

"Oh. There was something, yes." Rising from her chair, Ivy moved to the sink. She seemed to have too much nervous energy to remain seated. Keeping her back to the table, she said, "I don't know how to begin this, Sophie, but . . . I've done something . . . stupid. I need to talk about it—to ask for an opinion." She looked out the window, squeezing her eyes shut. "I can't keep it inside any longer. I thought about going to confession at St. Jude's this morning, but I haven't been to church in so many years, it has no meaning for me anymore." She hesitated, turning around. "Maybe you can give me some advice. You know everyone involved. To be honest, you're one of the few people left I can trust."

Sophie was flattered. She was also amazed at her good luck. Here they were, alone in the house—no Max calling the shots. Maybe she'd finally find out what Ivy was so nervous about yesterday. "Advice?"

"First, you have to understand"—she fidgeted with the wisps of hair that had fallen out of her bun—"I've been terribly unhappy in my marriage for a very long time. I'm not the kind of woman who deals well with being alone. That's why, a little more than a year ago, I became involved with . . . another man."

"You mean Max," said Sophie.

Ivy looked surprised. "Is it that obvious?"

"Sorry." She shrugged.

Ivy returned to the table. "I've never had a relationship like it before. At first it was wonderful. I was head over heels in love. But now . . ." She paused, her voice dropping to a more confidential tone. "How can I put this without sounding paranoid? I'm beginning to worry about . . . the intensity of his feelings. Max has become obsessed with me. He's horribly jealous. He doesn't even want me talking to Louie—and you know how long *we've* been friends."

Sophie had guessed it was something like that. Max did seem to be heavily into control.

"It's difficult to admit, but I'm almost frightened of him."

"You think he'd hurt you?"

"Well, no." She said it too quickly. "Not in my more sane moments."

Sophie could sense her ambivalence. "You know, when we met yesterday, I had the impression he was blaming you for something."

Her eyes fell to her lap. "He is. You have to understand how this all started. It began as a joke. Just a silly game. Sometimes Max and I would sit around in the evenings and fantasize about what it would be like to have all of Hale's money. Usually Max was drinking. We'd talk about what we'd buy—where we'd live. Max knows about a tiny island close to Jamaica. He talked about buying it, living there together, building a house."

"But as a surgeon, he must do pretty well for himself."

She shook her head. "He's never been able to hang on to a dime. He spends money as fast as he makes it. Now that he's approaching retirement age, his financial future is beginning to worry him."

Another obsession? wondered Sophie.

"That's when he got this idea." Ivy leaned into the table, lowering her head. "I'm so ashamed."

Sophie gave her some time, knowing the conversation was a hard one. "What idea?" she asked finally.

"Max wanted to fake several attempts on my life and frame Hale for them." She searched Sophie's face for signs of reproach. "I know what we did was wrong. And I don't mean to suggest that he twisted my arm in some way. I wanted Hale out of my life as much as he did. I wanted my share of the money, too, which Hale completely controlled. My God, I'd put the man through school! Supported him for years while he was making a name for himself. I even wrote that column for him."

"The one in the newspaper?"

She nodded. "And for all that, I got nothing. Nothing but a worthless MRS. in front of my name. If he'd gone to jail, I would have taken over IAI!"

Sophie was almost speechless. "You really hated him that much?"

"More," said Ivy.

"And if he died, you would control IAI forever."

"No!" She nearly knocked the cream pitcher off the table. "That was never part of it! As much as I hated him, I would never have done anything like that!"

"What about Max? Perhaps he didn't have your scruples." Such as they were.

With great vehemence, Ivy shook her head. "He didn't murder Hale. I'm sure of it."

Even with all the histrionics, Sophie could sense her uncertainty. "He wasn't at the party that night. Did he say where he was?"

"At home," answered Ivy. "Alone."

"You believe him?"

She rubbed the back of her neck. "I know what you're thinking, but it's . . . impossible."

Sophie wasn't so sure. "How did that box get into the sack Hale gave Betty?"

"I put it there. Max and I were going to make one more fake attempt on my life."

"The arsenic?"

She nodded. "When it was over, we would have sent an anonymous note to the police saying Hale was responsible. If they searched the house, they'd find proof."

Sophie couldn't believe her ears. Were they really

both that naïve? "Don't you think the police might have found that a bit too convenient?"

"What do you mean?"

"It looks like a setup."

"It does?" She cocked her head. "I never— Max was sure it would work."

Sophie had to work hard to control the disgust in her voice. Not only were they naïve, they were stupid. "How were you going to use the arsenic?"

Ivy raised a jerky hand to her forehead. "That's what I'm so worried about!" She jumped up again and began to pace in front of the refrigerator. "Max bought a bag of pretzels and sprinkled some of the powder over the contents. Then he stuck it in one of the kitchen cupboards. Hale hates pretzels. He would never have touched them. Since I love them, we thought it would be a perfect way to stage a poisoning. Max told me we all have tiny amounts of arsenic in our bodies. If I ate a *few*, it would elevate my level some, but there would be no lasting effect. But the night of the party, the bag disappeared!" She began to wring her hands. "Maybe one of the caterers used it. They weren't supposed to, but I know they were running short of food toward the end of the evening. Maybe they searched through the cupboards. If they did—and they served them—Max said we still had nothing to worry about. A handful might give someone a bad stomachache, but that's about it."

"But you're not so sure?"

She continued to pace. "What if the caterers took the sack with them? How can I call and demand they return a measly bag of pretzels! I can't exactly tell them the truth. Bags of junk food rarely have sentimental value. What am I supposed to do? Accuse them of stealing? Break into their offices in the middle of the night and ransack the place?" She slumped against the counter.

"I don't know," answered Sophie.

"And how can I live with the idea that some innocent person might get hurt? Max just tells me to forget it. All he's thinking about right now is the evidence Hale inadvertently gave Betty. He was furious when he found out that's where I'd hidden the box. I wish he could see it from my perspective. I thought it was a perfect hiding place. How was I supposed to know Hale was saving those presents for her? He often gave gifts to business associates. He kept a stash in our bedroom closet."

Sophie sat back and shook her head. Ivy already had a motive for Hale's murder. This stupid, careless scheme just made it worse. What if he'd found out and decided to turn them in? How could they stop him? And even more important, Ivy probably didn't know Hale had changed his will, since he'd done it a mere two weeks before his death. If she was willing to put him in jail to get his money, was it a big leap to think she might kill? And wasn't Max in the same boat? "I think you need to speak with a lawyer."

Ivy gasped.

"When all this comes out, you'll need to know what your rights are."

"*When!* Why would it come out?"

Sophie resisted the urge to roll her eyes. Ivy might be a smart woman when it came to art and the academic world, but in real life, she didn't have a clue. "Listen to me, Ivy. You wanted my advice? Here it is. You need legal counsel. At the very least, you must admit Max could have been responsible for Hale's murder. If that *does* turn out to be the case, your only protection would be to talk to the police about it now. The sooner the better. Do you have a lawyer?"

Ivy's eyes swept the room. "Sure—Louie. But he's never practiced criminal law. And anyway, how can I lay this on him? His wife just died!"

"Then find someone else. But get a legal opinion."

"I can't do that," said Ivy, her voice taking on an almost hysterical edge. "Max would—" Her eyes grew round and frightened. "I can't."

"It's up to you."

Ivy grabbed Sophie's hand. "You mustn't tell anyone about this. What I told you was in the strictest confidence. Promise me!"

In her mind's eye, Sophie flashed to Kate sitting in a holding cell. "I can't do that."

"Why?"

"Listen, Ivy, you're a friend of Kate Chappeldine's."

"Don't change the subject!"

"I'm not. The police think she may have murdered Hale."

"Really?" Her eyes blinked rapidly. Hopefully.

Sophie was sickened by the response. "I don't believe she did it."

"Come on! The police must have their reasons."

"They do. But without knowing about what you and Max were up to, they don't have all the facts."

"No!" she shrieked, her voice becoming desperate. "It's not true. And besides, what was it you said yesterday? Something about a threatening note from Ezmer Hawks? Maybe he's responsible! I don't see how he could know . . ." Her voice trailed off.

"About Eric Hauley?"

Her head snapped up. "What did you say?"

"I know the whole story, Ivy. I assume you do, too."

She just stared.

"You were protecting Hale all these years. Why?"

Her expression was full of amazement. "How did you find out?"

"Another long story."

She shook her head, a sneer pulling at the corners of her mouth. "You always were a snoop."

"I beg your pardon?"

"Even in kindergarten, you were into everyone else's business."

"I was not!"

"I heard your nickname in high school was 'The Nose.' "

"You're making that up!"

"Am I?"

Sophie was livid. "Whatever you may think of me, I have a good reason for trying to get to the bottom of Hale's murder."

"Your son."

"Exactly."

"You think he's innocent."

"Without a doubt."

"Well, so was Hale. What happened to Eric was an accident. Hale came to me that same afternoon. He was beside himself with grief. The problem was, it could have ruined his life!"

"And yours as well."

Ivy narrowed her eyes. "I couldn't let that happen."

"I'm sure you couldn't. But why are you still protecting him?"

Her eyes searched the room for an answer. "I don't know. A reflex, I suppose."

"After all that's happened, you're still concerned about his innocence. Maybe you can understand why my conscience won't let me condemn an innocent person. I have to tell the police what I know about you and Max."

"No!"

Carefully Sophie stood, backing toward the exit. "I think I need to be going, Ivy. Bram is expecting me."

"You can't do this!"

"Please. You've got to calm down."

"I am calm! Perfectly calm. And lucid. Just like the night Hale told me he wanted a divorce! He had the audacity to suggest he was going to divorce *me*!"

"I didn't know." Sophie was in the hallway now, inching toward the front foyer. "I really have to be going. Thanks for the tea." She glanced over her shoulder and saw she was almost to the front door. All she wanted to do was get the hell out.

"You don't believe I'm innocent, do you?" demanded Ivy, flying at her out of the kitchen. She swooped in front of her and laid a heavy hand over the doorknob.

"If you tell me you're innocent, then you're innocent."

"It's Max!" she snapped. "I don't know how to get away from him. He wants to own me, just like Hale. Why do I always pick the same kind of man? What's wrong with me?"

"I don't know," said Sophie.

Ivy stared at her, all color draining from her face. After what felt like an eternity, she turned away, muttering, "Get out. This was a mistake." Without another word, she rushed up the stairs. A second later, a door slammed, the sound echoing like a gunshot in the silent mansion.

# 42

"Are you sure you did the right thing by talking to Cross this afternoon?" asked Bram. He was propped up in bed, eating the last bite of a cherry Popsicle. It was nearly midnight.

"I did what I had to do," answered Sophie, shutting her book. "If the information about Ivy and Max can help Kate, then so be it. Detective Cross seemed more than interested. And I called Betty Malmquist as soon as I got home, too. She would have walked into a hornet's nest if she'd gone to Ivy's house tonight. I had to warn her away."

"Good thinking," he said, dropping the Popsicle stick on a plate. He quickly unwrapped another. "And Charles, a blackmailer. To think he had it in him. Did you mention that to Cross as well?"

"Since I have no proof, I was a bit more reticent. But he's pretty quick. He got the message."

Bram waved the Popsicle back and forth in front of him, thinking. "One last question?"

"What?" She leaned over and bit off the tip.

"Who murdered Hale?"

"I'm still working on that."

"To no avail?"

Wearily she nodded, shutting off the light.

"Hey! How's a fella supposed to eat a Popsicle in the dark?"

"You're usually quite proficient in the dark, darling. I'm sure you'll manage."

Sophie slept fitfully. Every half hour she looked at the clock on the nightstand and changed positions. She kept coming back to the murder scene. *What was she missing?* There were the two chairs in the front of the desk, one pulled up close. Undoubtedly Hale had had a visitor. But who? Rudy had seen a woman go into the back door of the mansion. Was it Ivy—or Kate? Neither had worn a red or pink dress. Come to think of it, the only red dress she remembered seeing was worn by Rhea Kiran. But why would she be outside? Sophie could still see the cigar in the ashtray—the tip crushed, the cigar itself broken in half. An empty glass rested next to it. Crumbs were scattered on the desktop. What had Hale and this visitor been talking about? Up until the final moments, had it been a friendly conversation?

Sophie changed positions, rolling over on her right side. Thankfully Bram could sleep through anything.

She thought again of the people she'd talked to during the past week. Kate and John. Ivy and Max. Louie. Charles. Even Ben. One thing she knew for sure. Someone was lying. But why was Hale murdered that particular night? And what was the motive? Money? Revenge?

Poor Ivy. She was trapped all over again in a relationship she didn't really want, with a man who not only ignored her feelings, but one whose jealousy frightened her. She would never rest easily until she knew where that bag of pretzels had gone. She needed a good friend right about now, but Louie was part of her problem. Max saw him as a threat. Sophie had tried to call Louie earlier in the evening, but all she'd gotten was his answering machine. In her mind's eye, she pictured him sitting on his couch surrounded by NO SMOKING signs, a drink in one hand, a bag of— Her eyes popped open. *A bag of pretzels on the coffee table!* "Oh, my God!" she said out loud, siting bolt upright in bed. He'd been at the party that night. He'd obviously had access to the kitchen. She felt a sinking feeling inside her stomach as she realized he *was* sick. He'd called it the flu, but what had that book on poisons said? The symptoms of arsenic poisoning were gastric in nature, often misdiagnosed as gastroenteritis. And wasn't there something about vomiting?

She poked Bram in the ribs. "Get up."

He groaned. "Call my secretary. Make an appointment."

She poked him again. "I've got to make a phone call. I think I know where that bag of pretzels went."

"What?" he mumbled, rubbing the sleep out of his eyes.

"It's Louie! Somehow or other, he managed to get hold of it. He's already sick. I hope we're not too late."

Bram sat up as Sophie turned on the light.

After punching in the number, she held her breath as

the call went through. "It's ringing," she whispered. After almost a minute, she let her breath out slowly. "He's not answering."

"Maybe you should call 911. The paramedics can get there a lot faster than we can."

"What if I'm wrong? What if he really does have the flu?"

"Then I apologize in advance for employing a cliché: Better safe than sorry."

"Good point." She jumped out of bed and pulled on her jeans. "You phone them. I'm going downstairs to use the other line in your office. I want to call Ivy."

"Okay, but—"

"And then get dressed. We're driving over." As she pulled on a sweater, the murder scene flashed once again inside her mind. Her hand flew to her mouth as she realized what she'd missed.

"What is it?" asked Bram.

"No time. I'll explain it to you in the car. Call 911 and meet me downstairs right away."

Sophie saw the flashing red lights as soon as they turned onto Louie's street. As they came closer, she saw that one of the first-floor windows had been smashed to allow the paramedics to enter.

Bram swung the car into the drive. "I'm blocking the ambulance here," he said. "I'll have to find another place to park. I'll meet you inside in a few minutes."

"Great," she said as she leapt out. She couldn't lose another minute. She raced in through the open front door and dashed to the rear of the building. She remembered enough of the layout to know that's where the bedrooms were.

A tall man in a brown uniform stopped her before she got very far. "Wait just a minute, lady. Where do you think you're going?"

"My husband called about the owner of the house.

Louie Sigerson. Is he all right? Did you make it in time?" She made a move toward the bedroom where she could see several others had gathered.

The man grabbed her arm. "Sorry. You can't go in there."

"But—"

"No buts. The man is dead."

Sophie could feel a lump rise into her throat. "Oh, God," she gasped. She turned her face away. The poor man. If she'd just put it together sooner! He was the only one who knew for sure what had happened that night, and now that he was gone, they might never know the truth. "How—how did he die?"

"We don't know that yet. I'm waiting for my supervisor."

She nodded, covering her mouth with her hand. The smell in the house was rank.

"Was he a friend?" asked the paramedic, a bit more sympathetically.

"Yes. He was."

"Looks like he was pretty sick before he died."

She didn't have to ask for details. "He'd been sick for several days."

"Does he have any family you could notify?"

"I only know about his wife. And she died very recently."

He withdrew his hand from her arm. "I'm sorry. But you still can't go in there."

She glanced into the study. "Would you mind if I waited in there?" She pointed. "I promise, I won't touch anything."

The man hesitated. "Well, I shouldn't . . . but seeing as how he was your friend . . . I guess it wouldn't hurt."

"Thanks." She waited for him to return to the bedroom and then, very quietly, she entered the study. The room was a mess. On the floor next to the couch was the bag of pretzels. Stepping closer, she saw that there were three left. She shivered. Well, at least the police would have proof how he died. As she turned to the desk, she noticed that the painting above the bookcase was missing. That was odd. She wondered what he'd done with it. She examined the books he'd been reading before his death. Law books mostly. And a *People* magazine. A piece of paper was lying next to his typewriter. Switching on the desk lamp, she bent closer and read:

To Whom It May Concern: March 5

I, Louie Sigerson, being of sound mind if not sound body, wish to make a statement concerning the death of Hale Micklenberg. I am afraid my health will not permit me to make this statement in person. On the night of Mr. Micklenberg's death, I delivered a message to him from his wife, Ivy. His response was, to me, so hateful, that the longer I thought about it, the more angry I became. I had been drinking rather heavily that evening. I am not blaming the champagne for any of my actions, but I *am* unused to alcohol. As I came through the kitchen, I grabbed a sack of pretzels from the cupboard, a bottle of Scotch from the counter, and made my way out to the gate house. The front door was ajar. I noticed Charles Squire's car speeding out of the drive and assumed he must have just come from talking to Hale.

As I climbed the stairs, Hale appeared at the top. He was holding a gun and swearing. When he saw the bottle of Scotch, he seemed to reconsider. He ordered me up, saying, "You might as well wait with me." I had no idea what he was waiting for, but as I meant to talk to him about the way he treated me, as well as his wife, I accepted his invitation.

As I sat down, I noticed that Hale seemed terribly nervous. I poured the Scotch. To be honest, I gave myself more than I gave him, because like now, I was a little drunk. Just as an aside, I find that alcohol doesn't do as much for emotional pain as I'd originally thought. A pity. Nevertheless, Hale and I drank for a few minutes in silence. I asked him, finally, why he had the gun. He answered that he needed it for protection. I suggested that if he were a bit nicer to those around him, he might not need it at all.

He exploded! He told me I was a pathetic excuse for a man. A totally useless human being. I'm afraid to say it struck a nerve inside me. I've called myself those same names—and worse—for more years than I dare count. But what he didn't know was that in the past two days, I'd changed. He was talking to a new man—one who wasn't going to take that kind of crap anymore. A man with real grit. At least, that's how I saw myself that night.

After he was done with me, he started in on Ivy. He said he was going to divorce her. To ruin her name and leave her without a penny. He was sure there were still people around who cared about things like adultery. And Ivy was an adulteress! As I drank and listened, I became more and more agitated. I couldn't let this happen. Ivy was too dear to me! I had to do something to protect her, to save her from Hale. The room started to spin. I stared at the gun. Just the sight of it made me feel powerful. I can't explain it. I don't know if I was more intoxicated by my newfound sense of self, or the Scotch, but as I looked down, I saw the gun was in my hand. I touched it. Felt its coldness. Its weight.

Hale ignored me. He'd begun talking about someone named Ezmer Hawks. And about a boy named Eric. At one point, I think I even saw tears in his eyes, but by then I wasn't listening very carefully. My attention was on his face. On the famous sneer. The large pores in his bulbous nose. The sweat on his forehead.

The repulsive way he chewed the end of his cigar. I don't even remember pointing the gun at him, but I do remember firing. He fell to the floor. I believe he died instantly. I sat for a moment simply to enjoy the silence.

Then I got up. I knew I didn't have time to wipe my prints off everything I'd touched. I'd been in his office many times before, so I wasn't worried about the general fingerprints. Just the ones on the Scotch bottle, the cup, the gun, and the pretzel bag. I wiped off the bottle and took everything else with me. When I got back to the main house, I hid the gun in the flower box outside the window and then I lay down on my borrowed bed and fell asleep. Next thing I knew, the police were knocking at the door. After searching the room briefly, they left. No one ever suspected what I'd done.

I have had some remorse since the incident, but not as much as one would suspect. Perhaps, in the end, I have become evil. Whatever the case, I do not want an innocent person to suffer for what I did. I waited, hoping I would never need to make this confession, but, it looks as though I may not make it through another night. Doctors know nothing. I place my soul in the hands of fate, cruel or kind, I no longer care which. The gun you will find downstairs in the furnace room. It is still loaded.

I have only two regrets. First, that I botched every thing so badly for Ivy. My action was impulsive. I didn't consider the consequences, and for that, I am truly sorry. Second, I deeply regret that I did so little to help my wife during her long illness. If I'd only had the courage, I would have ended her life as well. God have pity on me. Sarah and Ivy, forgive me. I've failed you both.

As I sit here, I can still hear that boy's voice on the phone. Since the night I heard the rhyme, it has never left my mind. "For every evil under the sun, there is a remedy or there is none. If there be one, seek till you find it. If there be none, never mind it."

My life *and* my death may indeed be a remedy for evil, Hale's and my own. That, I am afraid, is for others to ponder.

The letter was unsigned.

Sophie stood up straight and glanced over her shoulder as she heard Bram talking to the same paramedic who'd stopped her earlier. She gave herself a moment and then walked out into the hall. "I think you'll want to call the police," she said, her voice barely audible.

"We already have," said the paramedic. "It seems your friend in there was poisoned."

# 43

Rudy scratched Ethel as he watched Bram build a fire in the fireplace.

From the kitchen, Sophie shouted, "Do you fellows want coffee with your sandwiches, or milk?"

"Coffee," hollered Bram, lighting a match to the newspaper and waiting for it to catch.

"A Coke," shouted Rudy.

"Don't be difficult." She appeared a moment later carrying a tray. Setting it down carefully on the coffee table, she fell into a chair, warming her hands as the kindling ignited. "Another month and it'll be too warm for a fire."

Bram picked up his mug and sat down on the floor in front of her, resting his back against her knees. "Right. Then it's time to test out the new mosquito netting. And the electric bug fryer. These seasons in Minnesota really keep you hopping."

Rudy sipped his Coke. "So, come on, Mom, give. You never told me how you finally figured out who the murderer was."

Sophie shrugged. "I didn't really know for sure, but I had a pretty strong clue." She rested her hands on Bram's shoulders and gazed into the fire. "It was that ashtray on Hale's desk. There was a cigar in it—one of Hale's. It wasn't merely crushed, it was cracked apart. I should have noticed that sooner. I don't know if you remember the way Hale treated his stogies, but he always said they were too good to throw away. He smoked them to the last inch. He never would have treated one like that."

"But why Louie?" asked Rudy.

"Because he *hated* smoking. His wife had just died of emphysema, so you can see why his emotions were so close to the surface. If you'd ever been to his house, you would have understood. He had NO SMOKING signs everywhere."

"And in a fit of anger, he crushed out Hale's cigar, breaking it into two pieces."

"Exactly. Not proof positive, but something I shouldn't have missed. Where a normal person might not even think to put it out, or if they did, they'd just crush the tip and leave it at that, Louie wanted to obliterate the vile thing."

Bram took a sip of coffee. "My wife, the genius."

"Not really." She lowered her eyes. "I was too late to save his life."

"You did everything you could, Mom," insisted Rudy. "More than anyone could expect."

She shook her head.

"Well, I think you're pretty amazing."

"You do?" She looked at her son, turning from the fire.

"You bet. So does Kate. By the way, I talked to her this afternoon when I was over at the gallery. She wanted me to give you a message. She said she hopes you'll give her another chance to explain things. Maybe over breakfast sometime next week."

Sophie's eyes rose to the small etching Kate had given her—the one of the house. She'd set it lovingly on the mantel in a special place of honor. Kate was probably right. They did need to sort things out. "I'll give her a call."

Rudy nodded his approval.

"That woman owes *you* an apology, too," said Bram, offering Rudy the plate of chicken sandwiches.

He took one. "She already did. Even gave me a raise."

"Well, that's a start in the right direction."

"Not to change the subject," said Sophie, taking a sip of coffee, "but there is one small mystery I still don't fathom."

"What's that?" asked Bram.

"Louie had a painting above his bookcase. It was a de Kooning. Worth a ton of money. When I was in his study last night, it was gone. I hardly think he spent much time in the last few days rearranging his house."

"Point well-taken." Bram picked up the poker and gave the fire a good stoke. "I wonder where he got it in the first place? Rare artwork wasn't exactly his style."

"I think I remember Ivy giving it to him for his birthday many years ago."

"Quite a gift."

"He was a very special friend."

"I feel sorry for Ivy," said Rudy, finishing the first half of his sandwich and starting on the second. "Talk about a victim of circumstance. Kate said the police took both her and Max into custody today. They're being charged with manslaughter."

Sophie shivered.

"Who were the victims?" mused Bram. "And who the victimizers? In some ways, they all participated in their own demise."

"Hoist on their own petard," agreed Sophie, her eyes mesmerized by the glowing fire. "I don't know how Ivy's ever going to forgive herself. She may have loathed Hale, but she loved Louie. You know, I've been thinking about Hale all day. After talking to Betty Malmquist, I think I understand him better."

"It's important to understand the role of The Asshole in modern society," said Bram, his voice turning professorial.

"I'm serious," said Sophie. "You know how people like to say that critics are frustrated artists. People with no talent of their own."

Bram nodded.

"That certainly wasn't true of Hale. He had a great deal of talent. Witness the artwork filling Betty's walls. As a matter of fact, she called me this morning. It seems a gallery was out to look at his paintings a few days ago. They offered to include them in a forthcoming show."

Bram shook his head. "God, how ironic."

"The thing is," continued Sophie, "Hale told Betty once that he'd never lacked confidence, what he lacked was courage."

"Odd comment," said Bram.

"I agree. But now I think I know what he meant. It's terribly difficult to create—to be a painter, or a writer, or a composer. You put your work out there and hope some will find value in it. It's a lot like standing naked in front of a crowd and not knowing whether people are going to laugh, or throw you a towel. That effort is an act of courage. If someone's never done it, they don't understand. Hale was terribly competitive. Whatever he did, he wanted to be on top—king of the hill. He wasn't sure his work was brilliant, even though he knew it was good. And that's where he failed to show courage. What Hale lacked was the fundamental courage just to be good, not great. Not the best. Not number one. But *just good*. And without that, he would never know where he really stood. In a very true sense, it undermined his entire creative life."

"Fascinating," said Rudy. He sipped his soda thoughtfully. "I hope that never happens to me."

"It won't," said Sophie, turning and squeezing his knee. "With a voice like Richard Burton and a face like—"

"If you say Elizabeth Taylor, you're dead."

She grinned. "No, I was thinking more along the lines of Christian Slater."

"Okay. That'll do."

"You certainly have a good shot."

"And if nothing else, I can always go to New York with my talent and become a waiter. Not necessarily a great waiter, but definitely a *good* one."

She just let her eyes wash over him. He was so beautiful. Her son was finally home. Where he belonged.

"Well," said Bram, picking up a sandwich, "if you believe that nursery rhyme, maybe everything that's happened in the past couple of weeks was fate's remedy."

"I don't believe in fate," said Sophie.

"Neither do I," said Rudy.

Sophie cocked her head. "What do you mean? If you don't believe in predestination, how can you belive in prophecy?"

"Oh, no!" shrieked Bram, covering his ears with his hands. "Not another religious discussion."

"Get used to them." Sophie smiled, then rose and walked into the kitchen. She shouted over her shoulder, "Once we've settled all that, we're starting on Minnesota politics."

# 44

On Monday morning, Ben rushed to the door, a towel wrapped around his waist. He'd just gotten out of the shower. Rhea was in the bedroom getting ready for her class at the dance studio.

"Morning," said a Federal Express driver as Ben opened the door. "Got a package here for Ben and Rhea Kiran."

"I'm Ben."

"Okay. Sign this." He held the clipboard steady. When Ben was finished, he handed him the parcel and said, "Have a nice day."

"You, too." Ben took the package and shook it next to his ear.

"Who was that?" asked Rhea, breezing out of the bedroom and ducking immediately into the kitchen. "Breakfast should be ready in ten minutes—that is, unless you want to reconsider and settle for toaster waffles."

He turned up his nose. "I'd rather eat sawdust."

"No, you wouldn't."

She was right. He wouldn't. He stepped into the kitchen and watched her at work next to the sink. She was chopping peppers and onions. God, but he loved her. He never wanted her to go away again. But what could he offer other than a bunch of unpaid bills and worthless dreams? "It was Federal Express."

"What was?"

"The guy at the door."

"Oh." She turned. "Something important?"

He could see the look of worry on her face. "I don't know." He opened one of the drawers and removed a sharp knife, making short work of the wrapping. "It's . . . a painting." He turned it around, so Rhea could see, giving her a puzzled shrug.

"Is there a note?"

"I don't know." He rummaged through the paper. "Yes. It's a letter."

"Well, open it up." She moved closer.

"It's from . . . Louie Sigerson." He gave her a bewildered look. "Who the hell is Louie Sigerson?"

"You know. That guy we met at the Micklenberg party. He's a lawyer. A friend of Ivy's."

"The drunk?"

"He's not a drunk, Ben. He was just sad that evening. His wife had just died."

"Oh. Sorry. I didn't know." He returned his attention to the paper, reading out loud:

Dear Rhea and Ben.

Here is a small gift. It's a painting I've never really liked. I hope it will bring you more joy than it ever has me. I have it on good authority that it's worth money, though I have no idea how much. Sell it or keep it, whatever you like, but put it to good use. I know you will. By the way, Rhea, I tried talking to Charles Squire about that little matter of rehiring Ben for the shoot. I'm sorry to say, I struck out. I guess I'm hoping this gift will make up for my failure. I don't like feeling useless. This way, maybe I've helped you after all. I wish you both a wonderful life.

With all good thoughts,

Louie

Ben looked up. "When did you talk to him?"

"Early last week."

"You asked him to call Chuck Squire?"

"I thought maybe he could help."

Ben shook his head in amazement.

"You're not mad?"

"Of course not. At this point, I'd take help from anyone." He gave her a kiss on the cheek and then returned his gaze to the letter. "Can you beat that?"

Rhea lifted the painting off the table, examining it with growing interest. "Ben?"

"Uhm?" He was reading through the note again.

"Look at the signature on this."

"What's it say?"

"De Kooning."

"Is that good?"

She took hold of his arm to steady herself. "Very good."

"How good?"

"I'm not sure, but I think we've just been handed a fortune."

He took the painting and stared at it. "Why would a man we hardly know do something like this?"

"I don't know. We've got to call him right away and thank him."

Ben set the painting on the table and then held her shoulders. "All right. But first, I have a question."

"What?"

"You have to answer honestly."

"I'm always honest."

He narrowed one eye. "All right. Do you love me?"

She gazed up into his handsome face. "You know I do."

"Then whatever this picture means, for better or for worse, we're together. A team."

"Yes, Ben. We're together."

He crushed her in his arms. "All that's left is to make it official."

"What are you saying?"

"I refuse to live in sin any longer."

"I beg your pardon?"

"It's time to go find a ring." He gave her a sheepish grin. *"Again."*

"Do you think we should?"

"Why not?"

"I don't mind living in sin."

He thought for a moment. "You afraid to make a commitment?"

She backed up a step, yanking off his towel. "Do I look like a woman afraid of commitment?"

"No, actually you don't."

"Then it's settled."

Very gently, he touched her cheek. "You won't regret it."

"I know," she said, leaning against his bare chest. "This time, no matter what it takes, we're going to get it right."

Ellen Hart's other novels include her first Sophie Greenway mystery, *This Little Piggy Went to Murder*, and the Jane Lawless mysteries: *Hallowed Murder, Vital Lies, Stage Fright*, and *A Killing Cure*. She lives in Minneapolis.

# CHAPPELDINE GALLERY WAS PACKED TO DEATH....

The stylish new drawing show in Minneapolis pulled in all the important movers and shakers. Except one. Powerful critic Hale Micklenberg and his wife remained home, chatting with police about the bullet that had shot through their living room window. As Micklenberg had promised the show a bad review, he wasn't missed at all. Nor was he mourned when another bullet killed him.

Food critic Sophie Greenway was troubled to learn that her own son could be involved in the murder. But so could a host of others, including the "unhappy" widow, who was tired of keeping a scandalous secret at her own expense.

Guided by rumor, a bizarre phone message, and Micklenberg's obsession with an obscure artist, Sophie canvassed for a killer. Among the cheats, adulterers, and sleaze balls lurking beneath the civilized skins of her friends and colleagues, she finds what she's looking for. And it's quite a deadly surprise....

Cover printed in USA